VERNELL CHAPMAN

The Fountain: Secrets of Seulmonde

Book 1

ISBN- 10: 1481866125
ISBN-13: 978-1481866125

∞

For Deanna — I wish you'd had someone to show you the love
you always showed to me.
And for Lee — I hope you made it to heaven.

Acknowledgements

I am honored to acknowledge the people who have been most supportive of me in the completion of this work of fiction.

My husband Kirk has encouraged me in this endeavor and many others. He has never doubted my ability to achieve any goal and he has been my biggest cheerleader. I am forever grateful to him.

My friends have been very supportive of me as well. They help me to keep my head in the clouds when I want to, they help me to keep my feet on the ground when I need to and they help me to stay connected to my spirituality.

Carrie, Karen and Kimmie, I love you all.

Preface

In the late 17th century, Captain James Misson led a band of pirates to establish a free colony on the island of Madagascar. Captain Misson was on leave from the French warship Victoire when he visited Rome. It was there that he lost his faith; disgusted by the decadence of the Papal Court.

Using the warship Victoire and her two hundred man crew, Misson began waging war against states and lawmakers, attacking their ships, sparing prisoners, and freeing slaves. They called themselves *Liberi*, renouncing their titles of English, French, Dutch or African. While most settlers continued speaking their native languages, English became the most widely used language in the settlement.

And as the number of Liberi increased, the colony became over crowded. The settlers moved inland to find a more suitable location. During that search, a unique fountain was discovered. The colonists would have their destinies transformed. Their primary focus became the protection of the fountain and maintaining their secret society. Shortly thereafter, the colony was renamed Seulmonde.

THE FOUNTAIN: SECRETS OF SEULMONDE

Chapter 1

Tonight would be the night. I would finally put an end to my so-called relationship with Garland Malloy. We worked for the same bank, and dating between employees was not exactly the norm. Garland seemed to capitalize on that fact because in the seven months that we dated, he never even tried to work past the secret nature of our relationship. The arrangement worked for him, but it wasn't working for me.

My hands started to shake as I drove closer to his penthouse apartment. I must admit that I never felt really comfortable there. It was as if my gut was trying to tell me something all along. I drove up to the Concord Building and slowed down as I passed. I continued down the street as I normally did to find a parking space outside. I never parked in the basement of his building because someone might see me crossing the main lobby. We were always afraid of that. Well, he was always afraid of that. I pulled into a space about two blocks north of his building and checked my reflection in the rear view mirror. I don't really know why, but I sat there for a few minutes thinking about how we met.

My branch manager, Lillian McLean, was off on maternity leave and I was attending the Annual Banker's Ball in her place. Each year, the branch managers, bank officers and industry leaders attended the coveted event. That was where I saw him first, or should I say where he saw me. I thought it was a sign of good things to come - and that was what I told myself practically every day.

I was so excited to be going to the ball that I went to extreme lengths to prepare. I enlisted the aid of my only girlfriend, Gia Carides. We spent countless afternoons planning a complete look. Make up, hair and accessories became the only topic of our conversations for weeks. I had finally settled on a dress, which Gia insisted was the most important detail. She was convinced that my attendance at the ball was somehow linked to my future success at the bank. I agreed with her and I tried to indulge her enthusiasm. I knew how much I needed her help. I was admittedly fashion and make-up challenged and pretty much challenged by anything glam. I couldn't have made it through the preparations without her.

The next few weeks went by in a blur. I would periodically check in with Gia to make sure I was on my diet plan. Or rather, she was checking in with me. My idea of a balanced meal was a tuna sandwich and a Twinkie. I did drink plenty of water, but apparently, that still wasn't good enough for Gia.

When the big night arrived, Gia came up from her apartment to help me with my hair and make-up. She added a soft powder to my face that made my skin glow. Then she applied a shiny gloss to my lips and dark eye liner and shadow for a smoky eye effect. My grey eyes never looked more alluring. Gia added loose curls to my auburn hair giving it volume and movement. With my hair and make-up completed, I slid into my peach, one shoulder gown and looked at myself in the mirror.

"You're beautiful." Gia said as she stood behind me.
"Thanks to you, I might actually pull this off," I replied excitedly.
"You're gonna knock 'em dead tonight. And what are you supposed to do if you see any cute Italian guys?"
"I'll take his picture and get his number for you, I know. See you later."
"I hope not too soon." She was laughing as she closed the door.

I smiled to myself as I grabbed my clutch and headed out the door. While driving to the ball, I felt my stomach slowly churning. I felt good about the way I looked, but my mind was still racing. I'd never attended a function like this before. I was well out of my comfort zone.

As I made the final turn onto Columbia Parkway, my mind began to clear. I had to catch my breath when I caught a glimpse of the nighttime flare surrounding the Hilton Marquis; I was mesmerized.

As I slowed down and veered towards the hotel, I saw the parking attendants waving me down. I slowly pulled in front of the valet booth as my Civic hatchback came to a screeching halt. I launched from my car, handed the attendant a single key and headed for the entrance.

I walked through the crowded entry of the fabulous structure. It was one of the newest additions to Columbia's downtown scene and everyone was excited to have a look inside. I made my way to the front desk in the lobby. Everything inside was as beautiful as I knew it would be. The lobby itself was the most exquisitely decorated atrium imaginable. The front desk was made with a beautiful wood grain and a granite top. It had two high stools in front that could easily be maneuvered in front of, and behind the desk. The lighting seemed to be coming from everywhere. It took me a while to realize that the light fixtures were set into the wall on both the right and left of the desk. It created a soft light effect that made you feel that the front desk attendants were friends and not mechanized robots set up to make you feel like you didn't belong.

Everywhere you looked there were flowers. Stargazers, dahlias and tulips were strategically placed throughout the lobby. The colors were just short of overwhelming. The dahlias, with their lavender flowers and white tips created an unmatched spectacle. Every vase in the lobby had enormous, multi-colored tulips at the centers.

Not only was the hotel visually stunning but so was everyone who worked there. They were either platinum blonde or brunette and nothing in between. Their outfits were all well fitted and freshly pressed. Their smiles were blinding. They must have a great dental plan.

"Hello Miss, Welcome to the Hilton Marquis, how may I assist you?" asked Kelly, the front desk attendant.

"Um…uh yes," I stammered. "I'm attending the Banker's Ball in the main ballroom."

"Oh yes, Miss. Right this way," Kelly said as she led me to an escalator to the left of the hotel lobby.

The large elevator doors opened quickly and smoothly and I stepped inside. I turned around to brace myself against the back of the elevator and the last thing I saw before the doors whizzed shut was Kelly's blinding smile. I hit the large 'B' on the shiny key pad and I instantly felt myself lifting. A few seconds later the elevator stopped and the doors breezed open. I cautiously stepped out to find two attractive, young men in well fitted suits on either side of me. I smiled at the attendant to my right and he offered me his arm. I guess they were there to make unattended women feel less awkward. It definitely worked for me.

I tried to gather some confidence so I roped my arm through his as he flashed me a brilliant smile. I put on a smile of my own and started towards the crowd. The attendant asked me my name and then he veered us delicately to the left where a counter stood holding table assignments for all of the guests. After finding out where I was sitting, we eyed out the location and made our way across the floor.

My temporary escort pulled out my chair and I sat down. I thanked him and he bowed slightly. I couldn't help but smile. Right away I noticed that everyone was dressed to the nines. They were making polite conversation and drinking what I'm sure was the finest champagne and mixed drinks. I tried to convince myself to relax.

Of course, I didn't know anyone there. It's not like branch managers from other bank locations stopped by for tea and cake. But I made a promise to Gia that I was going to mingle and talk to people. Everyone's seating card had their home branch written on it. I noticed that the woman across from me worked at a branch not far from mine. I decided to introduce myself to her. She actually looked relieved.

"I'm Veronica Adler from Branch 221," I said calmly.

"Nice to meet you. I'm Lisa Taylor from Branch 223," she said with a smile. "I'm glad they finally replaced Lillian. No one expected her to return after she delivered."
"Well, she hasn't actually resigned yet. I'm filling in for her. Officially, I'm still the Assistant Manager there."

"Oh, well please tell her I said hello then." She looked a little embarrassed.

"I certainly will." I needed to turn the conversation around somehow. "You came to our branch for the grand re-opening, right?"

We ended up talking about banking for the next hour, which was great for me. That was a subject I was comfortable with. Before long, everyone at the table joined in and it actually felt like a party. I turned to ask Jamie from Branch 225 about her dress, when I felt someone staring at me. I looked a little farther over my shoulder at a guy seated two tables over. He appeared to be very amused. I looked away quickly and tried to act like I was already engaged in heated conversation with what's-her-name to my right.

I waited about thirty seconds and decided to look over and see if I was still holding his attention. I glanced over quickly, but he had left his chair. I was a little disappointed that he was gone because unfortunately that exchange was the most exciting thing I'd done tonight. I took a deep breath and decided I would really shake things up by having a drink. I was getting up from my chair when I realized someone was standing in front of me.

He was tall with blue eyes and light brown hair. I tried not to stare at him, but he was so attractive. What I noticed most about him was how good he smelled. There was just no way that he was single.

"Would you like a glass of champagne?" he asked.

I tried to think on my feet without stuttering. "Do you work here? I wasn't aware that we could order drinks from our seat," I said with a smile.

He laughed but quickly added, "I guess you could say that. But more than anything, I was trying to be sociable. That is why we're here this evening. So what do you say?"

"That's very kind of you," I said. "But before you offer me a drink, you might want to introduce yourself." I breathed the words so calmly, I even surprised myself.

He seemed very pleased by my comment and he gifted me with a wide grin. "I'm Garland Malloy and you are?"

"I'm Ronnie, I mean Veronica Adler." I extended my hand to him and he shook it gently.

"It's a pleasure to meet you Ronnie. Shall we go to the bar together?"

We spent the rest of the night talking at a table tucked away in the corner. Gia would have been so upset, but at least I wasn't sitting alone. I was taken with him instantly. Little did I know that this would be the only time we would be in public together.

Chapter 2

"Well, here goes everything," I told myself as I shut the car door and started down the sidewalk. I wasn't that good in heels, but I was getting better. It didn't take long for me to get to the side door of his building. I was glad because I might have lost my nerve. I went over to his elevator and entered the four digit code. Once inside, my heart started beating faster. But I knew I had to do this. I wasn't going to chicken out now.

I started thinking about my dad and how I had been lying to him these past months. He would ask me sometimes if I had someone special in my life. I would always skirt around the question or make up some kind of joke. I know that he wasn't trying to pry. He was just concerned about my happiness. It was getting harder and harder to be so dishonest with my dad who loved me more than anyone in the world. He deserved the truth. And so did my friends. But no one knew that I was dating Garland and now no one ever would.

The elevator made its usual humming sound as it glided easily up to the eighteenth and final floor. The doors opened and I stepped off. I immediately smelled the aroma of my favorite crab soup and garlic potatoes. The food alone was almost enough to make me lose sight of my task for the evening. Garland strode into the entry way followed by a violinist who gave me a quick bow. He was playing Bellini's Casta Diva. I had to work hard to hide my astonishment.

"Hello darling, you look lovely." Garland whispered to me.
"Thank you. I wasn't expecting all of this. What's the occasion?"
"I just felt like listening to some real music for a change. Follow me."
"I really need to talk to you Garland." I gave myself a silent pep talk.

I placed my purse on the hall table and followed him towards the dining room. I glanced into the large family room as I neared the end of the hall. It was decorated in deep hues of brown and grey as was most of the apartment. I always wondered what one man needed with twelve rooms. When I walked into the dining room, I got a full view of the spread he'd prepared for us.

The violinist entered the room and took a position in the far corner from where we were standing. I quickly took my seat in an attempt to compose myself. As lovely as the evening could have been, I knew that it would change nothing. Our secret relationship would still be a secret and that isn't what I wanted. Our trip to Greece would be another reminder that our relationship was just a façade. We would go on a dream vacation and come back exactly as we had left. And that scenario just wouldn't do.

"This isn't easy for me to say, but I can't see you anymore." The violinist was definitely a professional because he only showed the slightest change in his playing with my unexpected announcement. Garland completely lost the playful look in his eyes and exchanged it for one of shock.

"What are you talking about? You can't be serious." He said it softly as he sat down in the chair next to me.

My voice didn't seem to want to work so I looked him in the eyes and nodded my head.

"Why would you do this now? What about Greece?" He started raising his voice as the realization of what I'd said washed over him. I started to think that maybe I'd made a mistake. Did he care about me more than I realized? Before I could continue to question my actions however, he leapt from his chair, startling the violinist from his playing. We both watched Garland saunter out of room like only he could. I just sat there trying to think of what to do next.

A few moments later he returned, handed the violinist a check and escorted him to the elevator. He didn't even look my way when he came back and sat down. He had a glass of bourbon in his hand, which he started drinking rather hastily. I took this new choice of beverage as my cue to leave. I began to rise from my chair when I felt his hand on my left forearm. "Please don't," I said. "It's time for me to leave."

He released my arm, but stood up to block my escape. "You are making a big mistake," he muttered. "What are you trying to accomplish? No one at the bank can know about us. Why can't you just accept that and be happy with what we have?"

I looked at him with the most determined stare I could muster. "I want a real relationship," I said. "I don't want to play this game anymore."

I excused myself, moved slowly around him and made my way out of the room. I glanced back once, but he hadn't moved. Once out of the dining room, I reached the hall table where I had placed my favorite clutch, and walked over and stood in front of the elevator.

As I waited for it to arrive, Garland walked quietly up to me and touched my hand. I couldn't look at him for fear that I might change my mind.

He took hold of my chin and turned my face to his. He gave me the softest kiss on my lips and then he walked away. A few moments later the elevator arrived. I took one last look around and stepped in.

I couldn't wait to reach the lobby. When the elevator doors opened, I walked briskly out the front door. I didn't care who might have seen me. Once outside, I felt a huge weight lift off my shoulders. But there was also a sense of loss. While I wasn't in love with him, I did care for him. I slowed my pace as I started walking towards my car. This would be my last time parked on this street. I jumped in the car, started it and took off driving. I didn't even let the engine warm up which was a dangerous proposition for my old car.

I decided to keep driving north past Victory Park before heading home. So many times I'd imagined Garland and I walking in that park. I imagined the stares of onlookers as they watched us showing our affection for one another out in public. But it never happened. It would never happen. And I would just have to accept it. That thirty minute drive home would be one of the longest thirty minutes of my life.

When I arrived home, I still had the memory of Garland's kiss on my lips. Even though I'd ended things, I found it hard to stop thinking about him. Would he pursue me? Would he ask me to come back to him? I couldn't be sure. The only thing I was sure of was that I needed more than he was willing to give. I needed to focus on that, but not tonight. Getting some sleep would take priority now.

I brushed my teeth, put on my nightgown and laid down across the foot of my bed. When I closed my eyes, I began to hear a familiar thumping noise. Gia was having a party. The music was pretty loud and full of bass. She had a party most weekends. It was a welcome event before I started dating Garland. I always had some place to go on a Saturday night. Unfortunately, it became harder to hide Garland when Gia and I were hanging out a lot. The more I saw of him, the less I saw of Gia. We still spent time together, but it wasn't the same. The worst part was that I couldn't tell her why. I couldn't gossip to my only girlfriend about the guy I was dating.

I realized that sleep wasn't an option. I decided to go into the living room and take an inventory of my life. Why did I let this thing with Garland go on for so long? I'd had other guys ask me out. It's not like I'm desperate. I'm a one-guy kind of girl and I thought that our amity would blossom into something more.

It started out like any other friendship. He invited me over to his place for a drink, and I was flattered by the invitation. We had good conversation and the chemistry seemed to be there. Whenever I mentioned going to a particular place, he always shot it down. After a while, I stopped asking. It just took me too long to get a clue.

So here I sit on my living room sofa listening to Gia's party. I could feel the pang of loneliness creeping over me that only a fresh breakup can bring. I was almost tempted to change out of my bathrobe, head downstairs and try to blend in with the party goers.

As I sat there contemplating the possibilities, I heard a knock at my front door. Maybe Gia heard me come in early and was coming to invite me down. I waited a few seconds before I approached the door. I didn't want to appear desperate. When I looked out the peephole, I saw a scrawny kid holding a bike wheel.

"Who is it?" I scream. The music is so loud.
"It's Justin, I'm with Metro Messaging," he screams back. "I have a message for you from Mr. Malloy."
I actually felt my heart skip a beat. "What is it?" I asked him.
"I can't read the message ma'am. Can you open the door and I can give it to you? I'd leave it here, but I need you to sign for it." He sounded slightly irritated.

I opened the door without answering. I tried to give him a half smile. He returned the favor. I signed for the letter and he handed it to me. He took a deep breath as he looked in the direction of the crowd at the bottom of the stairs. It was getting pretty rowdy and Justin looked more nervous as the seconds ticked by.

"They're not so bad; just looking to have a good time," I said. He turned to me and gave me a genuine smile this time. He held his bike tire in front of him and slowly descended the stairs. I didn't realize we had bike messengers in Columbia. I thought that was a New York thing. But leave it to Garland to do something so out-of-the-ordinary. If I gave him points for anything, it was definitely for originality.

Standing there in the doorway, the letter began to burn in my hand. I went inside and shut the door. I decided to return to the sofa since that was my most comfortable place. I was about to rip the letter package open when there was another knock at the door.

"What is this grand central station?" I spoke out loud to myself. "Who is it?" I yelled through the door.

"It's me, Nick." Gia's favorite cousin was yelling back to me.

"Oh Nick." I opened the door and motioned for him to come in. "Hi, how are you?"

"I'm fine. I was actually just checking on you. My cousin Paulie saw someone at your door and he told Gia. She sent me up here to make sure you were okay."

"Oh, thank you, I'm perfectly fine. The guy was a messenger, a bike messenger. He had a message for me." I don't know why I was rambling. Maybe I was worried Nick might ask questions I didn't want to answer.

"A messenger? At this hour? It must have been a pretty important message," he said with a hint of humor in his voice.

"I made a last minute change to my trip. I had to get new forms and stuff." I tried to sound convincing.

By the look on his face he seemed to buy my story. I was glad because I knew he wouldn't leave until he was sure I was all right. I thanked him for coming up and he gave me a quick hug. He walked out of the apartment door and I locked the door behind him.

I walked back to my sofa and ripped the letter open. It was a type-written letter from Garland. He must have typed it on his computer and sent the letter request by e-mail. I can't imagine how else he would have delivered the letter to me so quickly when I was just at his place an hour ago. I took a deep breath and started to read.

Dearest Ronnie,

When you left my apartment tonight, I was so angry. But I realize that you were just being honest with me. I should be honest with you too. I'm not ready for a serious relationship right now. I liked the way we were. But I understand that you need something more. No matter what our differences are, I know what this trip means to you. I'd still like for you to go without me. I'll send you the information next week. I really hope you'll let me do this for you. And maybe you could think of me a little differently one day.

Yours, Garland

When I finished reading the letter for the second time, my face was damp. I'd started to cry and I hadn't realized it. I did the only thing that I could think of at that moment. I went into the bedroom and picked up my phone. I hit the number '5' on speed dial. On the third ring he answered. I wasn't surprised that he was still awake.

"Hello," Garland said.
"I accept your offer." I said.
"Glad to hear it. I thought that you might not." He paused for a moment before speaking again. "Well, Goodnight Ronnie."
"Goodnight."

I hung up the phone and lay across the bed. Even the loud music couldn't keep me awake now. Within minutes, I drifted off to sleep.

THE FOUNTAIN: SECRETS OF SEULMONDE

Chapter 3

I knew that going to work on Monday would be tough. Even though no one knew about me and Garland, I still felt awful. As I drove to work, I considered going back home several times. But what would I say is the matter? I had no reason not to go in; well no reason that I could say. I would just have to put on the performance of a lifetime.

I arrived at the branch making good time. I opened the main door and turned off the alarm. Just like normal, the other staff came in behind me setting up their stations. I usually made small talk with Marsha because she was newest in her position. She started out working in customer service but had been promoted to loan officer. I liked the fact that Centennial Bank hired from within. If Lillian didn't return to work after her maternity leave was over, there was a strong chance that I'd be the new branch manager. That thought gave me little joy this morning however, as I made my way to the kitchen to get a cup of tea.

When I came back to my office, Marsha was sitting across from my desk waiting for me. I quickly sat down and tried to look nonchalant. It didn't work.

"Hello Ronnie, wow, you look like crap," Marsha blurted.
"Gee, thanks Marsha. Now tell me how you really feel."
"I'm sorry, it's just that you always look so put together. But today, well, you don't."

I suddenly felt that tingle in my nose that comes when I'm about to cry. I shrugged it off. I had to hold it together at least until lunchtime.

Then I could hide in my office with the door shut.

"Marsha, I thank you for your concern but I'm fine. Now if you'll excuse me, I have a lot of work to do."

I tried to sound steady and in control as I turned my attention to my computer. She rose slowly to leave giving me one final glance.

"Well, if you need me or you want to talk, I'll be on the main floor."

"Thank you Marsha, but that won't be necessary. Once I get my desk cleared a bit, I'll be able to relax." I lied.

Much to my delight, the morning seemed to pass quickly. I was getting a lot done and I was feeling better about leaving for my trip. I was still sad about the Garland situation, but because I kept to myself, I didn't have to deal with the worried stares from Marsha or anyone else who might look my way. Before my small bit of relief could continue however, Marsha popped her head into my office and gently knocked on the open door.

"How's it going boss lady?" She said trying to make me smile.

"I'm still fine." I didn't look up when I spoke.

"Ok, I'm going to lunch. Be back in thirty minutes if you need me."

"Ok. Sounds good. I'll see you later."

"Are you really ok?"

"Fine." That was all I could get out. I breathed a sigh of relief as I heard her walk down the hall.

I was not ok. I needed about a week under a rock. That's what I wanted to say. I liked Marsha, but I didn't know her that well. And like everyone else in my life, I couldn't admit to her what was wrong with me. This was just another side effect of engaging in a secret relationship. I stood up, walked over and shut the door, and turned out the light. I couldn't hold it in any longer. As hard as I'd fought them, the tears just wouldn't stay away.

As I sat there wondering what I could have done differently, the steady ringing of my desk phone pulled me from my thoughts. I checked the caller ID and cringed as I realized it was my father. I should have expected his call since I failed to keep our standing Sunday appointment. I spent all of yesterday eating Swedish fish and purging my apartment of anything that reminded me of Garland. I had completely forgotten to call my father. Besides, if I had, he would have known that something was wrong from the sound of my voice.

"Hi Lee, how are you?" I asked using my best business voice.
"Hello Ronnie, I'm quite well," he said. "I'm just concerned about you. I thought I'd be getting a call from you yesterday."
"I'm fine. I was just out with friends and lost track of the time. I didn't want to call you late in the evening when I returned."
"Well, as long as you're alright." His tone said that he didn't believe me. I wasn't good at making up stories especially when I was talking to Lee.

My father preferred that I call him by his name. He said that a lot of people rely on titles because they're not confident in who they are. He definitely has a special way of looking at the world. Even though I'd forgotten to call him yesterday, I felt better soon after we started talking. He was an excellent conversationalist. We could be talking about weather balloons and I still learned something.

"So has Lillian decided on whether or not to return to work?" He asked.
"No, not yet. And to be honest, I'd really rather deal with it when I get back."
"Well, I don't want to be an alarmist, but it seems rather odd that she's been away so long."
"I must admit that speaking with our Regional Manager last week was a little uncomfortable. I can't believe they didn't realize that Lillian

has been out for almost eight months."

"Well, I'm sure it'll all work out just fine. As soon as you get back, they'll make you the new branch manager."

"Thanks for saying that. I really appreciate it."

"Well, I mean it. You know I wouldn't say it otherwise."

"I know. Well, I'd better get back to work. I have a feeling it's going to be a long week."

He hesitated before speaking again. "I just wanted to say that I really am very proud of you."

"Thank you Lee." I felt a large lump growing in my throat. Lee wasn't one for the dramatics so I tried to pull it together quickly. "Well, Good-bye Ronnie."

"Good-bye."

I hung up the phone and walked over to the window in the far corner of my office. I looked over to the large maple tree that I labeled as my favorite. It reminded me of when I was a child and it always helped me to relax. After standing there for about five minutes, I realized that my lunch break was over. I headed out the door towards the main teller area. I wanted to show Marsha and the rest of the staff that I was all right.

The rest of the day went on pretty much as usual. I helped a few customers with their personal loan applications and a few who had special issues at the teller window. I realized in the three years that I worked for Centennial Bank that I really enjoyed it. Our customers really seemed to enjoy the services we provided and we were growing. It wouldn't be long before we would need another loan officer and another teller to work evenings and weekends. The branch was doing well. I only wished I could say the same about my personal life.

The next day at work was still hard but it had its interesting moments. I talked to Marsha in the morning and tried to make it seem like everything was all right. She didn't mention my mood yesterday and I was glad. Tuesdays were usually the slowest day of the week and this one was no exception. I was listening to voicemail messages when Marsha popped her head in my door.

"Excuse me Ronnie. There's a guy here from Metro Messaging. He says he needs to give you a package in person."
"Oh yes. I'll be out in just a minute."

I needed to compose myself before I went out into the lobby. I rose from my chair and started walking towards the door. My hands started to shake a little so I just held them down at my sides. I walked out into the hall and Marsha fell into step beside me. I rounded the corner and walked into the lobby to see my favorite bike messenger. He was standing by the main entrance holding his bike tire and a small package. As soon as he saw me he gave me a quick smile and I saw what appeared to be a look of relief as well.

"It's Justin, right?" I said trying to seem relaxed.
"Yes ma'am. That's right. I tried to drop this off yesterday, but I made it here too late." He extended the package out to me and I grabbed it with both hands. Then he pulled out a signature pad from his jacket pocket with his free hand.
"I just need you to sign for it."
"No problem. Thanks a lot."
"You have yourself a great day now." He smiled again and made his way out the front door.

From the corner of my eye, I could see Marsha staring at me. I stood there for a minute trying to think of what I could say to her that would prevent her from asking a bunch of questions. Bike messenger deliveries were not a normal occurrence so I wasn't surprised when she finally spoke.

"That was so weird," she said without breathing. "I didn't even know there were bike messengers in Columbia."

"Yeah, I thought the same thing up until a few days ago."

"So what is it?"

"I don't know. It's probably some official bank business." I tried to sound bored so that she would become disinterested. It didn't quite work.

"Maybe it's an official request for you to take over as branch manager."

"I doubt that. I'm sure Mr. Simms would just call me or come here in person to discuss a leadership change."

"Yeah, you're probably right. But wouldn't that be exciting?"

"I suppose so. Well Marsha, I'm going to get back to work. I have a lot to do before I start my leave on Friday."

"Yes, of course. I'll let you get to it. I have work to do myself. But if there's anything fun in that package, will you call me?"

"Sure, I will."

I tried to walk to my office at a leisurely pace. It wasn't easy. When I made it back, I shut the door and locked it. I quickly pulled my letter opener from my top desk drawer. I ripped the entire seam and pulled out the letter.

Dearest Ronnie,

I hope this letter finds you well. I am sending you this information as I promised I would. Although I'm still processing what has transpired between us, I do realize that this is what you want. And I know that I forced you to the decision you made, so I won't try to change your mind. I really do hope that you will enjoy yourself. Your flight information hasn't changed. But your suite at the resort has been upgraded to a Villa. That way you won't be disturbed and you can have people waiting on you for a change. Don't worry about the expense. It's the least I can do. You are a very special lady. I hope you know that.

Yours, Garland

I just sat there for a minute staring at the letter. Part of me felt sad, but part of me felt strangely liberated. It's not as if I hadn't been contemplating ending things for a few weeks now. For every positive aspect in our relationship, there was also a negative one. I always thought that any relationship worth having should have more happy times than sad ones.

I continued removing the contents of the package. I pulled out the airline tickets, some resort brochures and a cell phone. It didn't look like a normal cell phone though. It was slightly longer with a small antenna on the side. I hit the power button and waited to hear a dial tone. When the keypad illuminated, I noticed that the voicemail light was flashing. I hit the button and then put the phone to my ear.

"Hello Ronnie, I guess by now you are wondering why I've sent you this phone. I wanted to make sure that you had something dependable to use in case your cell phone didn't work. This phone is a satellite phone and it will work anywhere in the world. Please consider it a gift from me to help ensure that you have a safe trip. If you want to reach me for any reason, please don't hesitate to call. Good-bye."

I could hardly believe my ears. This phone must have cost a fortune and I was glad to be taking it along. "If only Garland had"- no, I wasn't going to say it. I needed to look to the future. I would use this trip to clear my head and make a fresh start. I was going to focus on me and me alone. I stuffed all of the items back into the delivery package and put the package in my right desk drawer.

During lunch, I called an employee meeting to talk about everyone's roles while I would be gone. I also discussed the gentleman that would be filling in for me while I was away. It was pretty strange that no one even asked about Lillian. I doubt that anyone expected her to return to work. If she didn't, it would be fine with me. I welcomed the opportunity to become branch manager permanently.

The rest of the week was pretty uneventful. My only real task was getting Mr. Adams up to speed on our branch procedures. I was sure he'd do well. All of the staff was helping him to feel welcome. I hoped that he would let Corporate know how well we were doing.

I received my answer late Friday evening. I must say that it was not what I expected. I was packing up to leave when Mr. Adams knocked on my office door.

"Ms. Adler, may I have a word?" he said.
"Please, come in. Did you have any last minute questions for me?"
"Not exactly. I just wanted to tell you what a fine job I think you've done here. You've had to get by without a branch manager and I know how hard that must have been. I wanted to let you know that I hope to stay on permanently should Lillian resign. I hope that you will give me your support."
"Is that so?" I felt as if I had been punched in the stomach.
"Well, no one expects her to return to work. Anyone else would've been forced to resign after all these months but it doesn't hurt that she's married to the Bank President's eldest son." He spoke softly.

"I-I didn't know that she was married to… Why is her name McLean?" That was the second stomach punch.

"Maybe she doesn't want people to treat her differently because of who she's married to. I do commend her for that."

"Well, I think we should wait for her decision." I belted out impatiently. "I don't want to be rude Mr. Adams, but I do have an early flight in the morning. I must be on my way."

"Oh, of course. I should've come around earlier. Have a safe trip and don't worry about this place. We'll be just fine."

"Yes. I'm sure you will."

I grabbed my purse and practically ran for the door. By the time I reached my car, I could feel the tears on my cheeks.

Not only was I without my boyfriend, but the job that I thought was mine was going to be stolen from me too. I didn't want to think about anything. I drove home as quickly as I could. All I wanted to do was go to sleep and that's exactly what I did.

Chapter 4

When I woke up the next morning, I still had my clothes on. I rolled out of bed and lumbered to the bathroom. My eyes were a little puffy, but other than that I looked fine. I hurried to get ready hoping I wouldn't have time to think about the developments from the last twenty-four hours.

But as soon as I stepped into the shower and let the water wash over me, my mind began to drift. I just couldn't understand how I didn't know who Lillian was married to. He never came into our branch but there were many times that she would go downtown to meet him for lunch. She didn't have any pictures of him in her office, but that never struck me as odd considering none of us at the branch had pictures of our families displayed. Whenever she mentioned her husband though, she referred to him as 'Billy'. How could I possibly know that 'Billy' was actually William G. Malloy, Senior Vice President of our bank?

Garland Malloy was another matter all together. He led me to believe that our relationship being discovered was tantamount to the Iran Contra Affair – and I believed him. I suppose I wanted to believe him. I mean, what reason would he have to lie to me? I'd probably never understand him. All I knew was that he deceived me and there was nothing that I could do but move on with my life.

Then there was Mr. Adams. I had no idea what to do about that situation. If Lillian decided not to come back, would they automatically give the job to him? I hoped that they wouldn't make a decision without me being there. I wanted the job so badly but I had to be realistic. I'd be gone for two months. A lot could happen in that time. But I wasn't going to second guess my decision to go to Greece. I needed this vacation. It had been a dream of mine since I was a little girl.

Before I could drift too far in my thoughts, the water turned cold. I jumped out of the shower and got dressed. Next, I put the last few items in my luggage and called my dad. He reminded me to be careful and to call him when I landed.

After we hung up, I gathered my luggage up to take downstairs. I wanted to wait for my cab outside. I'd almost reached the bottom of the stairs when Gia walked out of her apartment.

"You weren't trying to sneak off without saying goodbye, were you?" She smirked at me.
"Of course I wasn't. I was coming to talk to you while I waited for my cab to get here." I walked down to where Gia was standing.
"Well, I hope so." Her smile replaced her smirk. "It's too bad I'm not going with you. I'd make sure you had all kinds of fun."
"Yeah, you're probably right about that. But on this trip, I just want to relax and unwind."
"Well, there's always next time." She reached out to hold the door for me. Once we were outside, I sat the bags down on the step so that I could give her a hug. "Take care of yourself over there and don't forget to call me when you get settled in. Got it?"
"I got it."

I stepped back to see that she was close to tears. I tried to act like I didn't notice while I fought back tears of my own. Before I started dating Garland Malloy, Gia and I were inseparable. Maybe now that he was out of my life, we could get back to where we once were. The thought of that possibility made me smile.

While we were standing there, I heard the sound of a car approaching and I turned to see the taxi driver pull up and beep the horn. I carried my bags over to the curb and climbed into the back of the cab. It was a fitting scenario that Gia was the one seeing me off. I got excited just from our conversation.

As I pulled away from the curb, I waved goodbye to her with both hands. She was waving back, but then she started making faces and doing a silly dance on the steps of our building. I laughed out loud and shook my head at her. I decided right then that I would make things right with her as soon as I got back. She was a true friend and that was what I needed.

I was more excited as we turned onto Interstate 295. The airport was only a twenty minute drive north. Once I arrived, I made my way through security and then headed to the terminal. I'd never been to the International terminal before. There were currency exchange booths, Rosetta Stone kiosks and the smell of roasting coffee beans from around the world. I felt like I'd already left the States.

Before I got too carried away watching other passengers board flights to Europe, I decided to get breakfast. I stopped at a French style café and ordered scrambled eggs, a croissant and a small orange juice. *C'est delicieux!* After I finished eating, I headed toward the gate to wait for the boarding process to begin. I was flying Olympic Air and I couldn't wait to see the airplane. Once the plane reached the gate, I wasn't disappointed. It was larger than any I'd seen before. I couldn't wait to get on board.

When it was time for me to board the plane, I grabbed my back pack and followed the other first class passengers down the jet way. I reached my seat and was surprised at how different it was from the seat of a regular domestic airplane. The seat looked like a recliner and there was extra storage to the right of the chair. I placed my backpack in the compartment and sat down.

All of the first class seats were taken except for the seat next to me. I suppose Garland didn't bother cancelling his ticket. I was a little self-conscious thinking everyone on board would know why I was sitting alone. I took out a magazine and tried to relax. I was just about to dig into a story about a woman who had a child by each of her brothers when there was a commotion in front of me.

"You are such an ass!" Exclaimed the woman in the seat two rows ahead.
"Will you quiet down? You're making a scene." Her male companion responded in an irritated tone.
"I'm not going to sit here and listen to any more of your stupidity."
"What other choice do you have?" He said and let out a sarcastic laugh.

I was trying to pay attention to my magazine but it wasn't working. The woman got up from her seat and walked toward the galley. She looked like she was about to cry and was trying to compose herself. The last of the passengers were coming on board and I could see the flight crew taking their positions. Just as I was about to focus on my magazine again, the woman from two rows up came over to me and knelt down next to my seat.

"Excuse me. Is anyone sitting in the seat next to you?" She spoke so quietly that I could barely hear her.
"No, it's empty," I replied just as quietly.
"Do you mind if I sit there?"
"No, not at all." I gave her a shaky smile.
"Thank you." She smiled back at me.

She went back to where she was sitting before and picked up her purse and her magazines. Once she sat down, I got a good look at her. She appeared to be about my age with beautifully tan skin and long dark hair that was draped over her shoulder in one long braid. She was beautiful and I immediately wished I'd gone tanning at least once before my trip.

She was dressed casually in straight legged blue jeans, a pink cashmere sweater and Grecian sandals. She must have felt my stare because she looked up from the magazine she was reading.

"I must apologize for my outburst earlier. My brother sometimes brings out the worst in me."
"I hardly noticed." I quickly glanced back at my magazine.
"Well, I'm embarrassed all the same. Oh my, where are my manners? I'm Shelby." She extended her hand to me.
"I'm Ronnie. It's nice to meet you." I reached out and shook her hand.
"Is this your first trip to Greece?" she asked.
"Yes, it is. I've wanted to visit Athens since I was a child."
"That's great. You know, I'm doing the same thing. I'd wanted to visit Atlanta every since they hosted the Summer Olympics. We've just come from a month's stay there."
"Really? I always liked the Summer Games too."
"At one point, my brother hoped to participate in the games."
"Was he a really good athlete?"
"No, but you couldn't tell him that." We both started laughing.

Shelby and I went on talking for hours. We had similar interests including American football and watching old movies. She was completely down to earth. I could tell from talking to her that her family was well off but there wasn't a snobbish bone in her body. The only woman I ever talked to like this was Gia.

After several hours, we were both tired. Shelby was kind enough to show me how to recline my seat which folded down into a bed. I let myself relax and then focused on the music playing overhead. Within minutes, I was asleep.

I woke up as the flight attendant moved about the first class cabin. Dinner service was starting and I waited patiently for a stewardess to get to us. I looked over to my right and saw that Shelby had started to stir.

"Shelby, are you hungry?" I said trying to whisper as other passengers were still asleep.
"Yes, I'm famished." She tried to whisper as well.

After Shelby and I ate dinner, we started reading our magazines. I was engrossed in an article on the perils of wearing high heels when I heard the captain's voice come over the loud speaker.

"We're turning on the 'fasten seat belt' sign. We may be experiencing some rough air up ahead. Flight attendants please take your seats."

"You know I'm not a big fan of flying either but I like to travel. It comes with the territory." Shelby noticed the concerned look on my face.
"Yeah, I don't really mind flying. I'm just ready to be on the ground."

The plane touched down on the runway with an abrupt bounce and I breathed a sigh of relief. I turned to see Shelby smiling at me.

"Hey, do you want to get a cup of coffee or something when we get off the plane?" She asked kindly.
"Sure. I'd like that but what about your brother?"
"He'll be fine on his own. I'm not ready to deal with him yet."

"Alright."

"I know a great place to get coffee across the street from the airport."

"What about our luggage?"

"Oh, that's easy. I have a service I use to hold my luggage. It's much more convenient than carrying your bags around. You can just put your luggage in with mine."

"Ok, thanks."

"Glad that's settled. Now let's get off this plane."

We headed to baggage claim to pick up our luggage. Within minutes of our arrival, Shelby and her brother were engaged in another unpleasant conversation. I moved to the other side of the conveyor to give them some privacy. When I turned around, I saw her brother pull a large suitcase off the conveyor and storm off. I waited a few seconds and then walked back to where Shelby was standing. She didn't look upset this time which was a relief.

I saw my three bags coming around and I grabbed them off quickly. Shelby grabbed the last of her bags and then motioned for one of the airport staff to come over with a cart. He loaded all of our bags on the cart and handed Shelby a blue ticket. Once we started down the corridor near the restrooms, her brother seemed to come out of nowhere.

"Give me your luggage ticket Queenie. Where do you want to meet"? He said with a sarcastic tone. This guy was becoming a pain in my ass and I didn't even know him.

"I'll be at the Sofitel in one hour," she said quickly. "Oh, Ronnie this is my brother Don. Don this is Ronnie."

"Hi," I said weakly.

"Hi, yeah, whatever. Queenie don't be late. We're on a schedule," he said briskly and walked away.

"Hey Shelby… Is he always like that?"

"Yeah, he's a royal pain." She said matter-of-factly.

"Hey, so where is this place you're taking me?" I tried to change the subject.

"It's right across the street. But let's take the long way though. I want to show you some of the shops."

Chapter 5

I could tell that Shelby had been in this airport many times because she knew exactly where everything was. She probably could have walked around blind-folded and still made it to all of the shops. This section of the airport resembled a two story shopping mall. We started on the upper level and she led me to all of the fancy clothing shops and souvenir stores. I picked out small items that I could easily fit into my backpack. I bought a tie for Lee and a red scarf for Gia. I also grabbed postcards for the ladies at the bank.

On the lower level, there was one more store that Shelby wanted to show me. The Mastiha shop sold open roast pumpkin and feta pies. I imagined that we'd spend the next couple hours there. I couldn't have been more wrong.

We were walking on the lower level toward the Mastiha shop when a concussive blast rippled through the corridor behind us. We were thrown forward with such force that I fell to my knees. My eyes were watering badly but I could still see people running in all directions. My hearing was affected too. It just sounded like people screaming in a tunnel. Smoke started filling the air and it was becoming harder to see. Somehow I made out the shape of a lighted doorway ahead so I moved toward it. I called to Shelby and told her to follow me. She'd somehow found my hand and we were moving shakily forward.

Just when I thought we were in the clear, a second blast shook the corridor. The force of this explosion caused me to fly forward landing on my stomach. I turned to look for Shelby and noticed that she had fallen as well. I moved towards her and realized that she wasn't moving. I gently turned her face towards me and that's when I saw the gash above her right eye. I knew that I had to do something. Panicking just wasn't an option. I grabbed her purse and put it in my back pack. I was afraid to move her but I knew we couldn't stay there. I had to get us to the open door up ahead.

There were empty luggage carts along the wall so I grabbed the one closest to us. My plan was to pull Shelby onto the cart and roll her outside. In my current condition, I wouldn't have been able to carry her. I went around behind her and put my arms under hers. I pulled her slowly onto the cart and then pushed the cart forward towards the open door. I've never been more afraid in my life. I had no idea what I'd see when we got outside but anything was better than waiting in the airport to be blown to bits.

Once we were outside, I looked around for a place to rest. Wounded people were everywhere. I started to feel like we were the lucky ones. I moved the cart across the street which wasn't easy. Cars were stopped all along the street. When I finally got the cart to the other side, I started to relax a little.

Most of the damage was contained on the airport side of the street. Just when I started to feel less than terrified, the entire side of the terminal facing the street collapsed in on itself. If Shelby and I had stayed inside by the shops, we would certainly have been crushed to death.

As the realization of everything set in, I suddenly felt like I was going to faint. I fell to my knees and started to shake. I put my hands over my face and tried to calm myself. In the midst of my calming exercise, I heard a cell phone ringing that wasn't mine. It was faint, but it was close. I reached for Shelby's purse and pulled out her phone. It had stopped ringing by then. Luckily, the phone wasn't locked so I was able to dial the number for the missed call.

"Hello, hello." I said frantically into the phone.

"Who is this? Where is Shelby?" said an irate male voice.

"We were in the airport and there was an explosion. Shelby got hurt. She hit her head on something."

"Where are you now? This is her brother. Please tell me exactly where you are."

"We're across the street in front of the Sofitel. But please hurry. I don't know if she's ok." I tried to speak clearly as tears ran down my cheeks.

"I'll be there as fast as I can. Just don't let her out of your sight."

"Ok." I put her cell phone back in her purse and put the purse in my backpack.

I could feel a fresh wave of fear creep over me. I looked down at Shelby to make sure she was still breathing. She was. Her face was a little pale and she had blood running from the wound on her forehead. Her pant leg was torn by her left knee but I was more worried about her head wound. I pulled my backpack off my shoulder and took out the bottled water I kept from the plane. Then I took out some napkins from my purse. I gently turned her head to the right and poured water to clean the wound and get the blood off her face.

Once I'd cleaned the gash on her head, I could see how deep it was. She was definitely going to need a few stitches. Now that the wound was clean, I wanted to cover it. All I had were some napkins and a Wonder Woman band aide. These would just have to do. I folded a piece of napkin and put it against her forehead. I made sure that the piece was small enough that the band aide could make contact with her skin on both sides.

My attention shifted to the area around us. Other airport patrons were staggering around seeking aide or trying to help others. Police cars and fire trucks were navigating the mass of vehicles in the street.

I don't think anyone knew what was going on. Hopefully whatever happened in the airport corridor wouldn't spill out into the street.

"What's going on? Where am I?" Shelby seemed to be talking to herself. She was trying to move a little but I could tell she was in pain.
"Shelby, it's ok. Don't try to move. You've been hurt." I placed my hand on her shoulder.
"Ronnie?" she replied almost as a question.
"Yes, it's me. You're brother is on his way. Just relax."
"Does Don know where we are?"
"Yes. I told him."

"Shelby, where are you?" Don called out as he was making his way towards us.
"She's here. We're over here." I replied.

When he reached us, I could see the look of relief on his face. But it was quickly replaced by something else, urgency.

"We have to get out of here. The authorities are scrambling. Those idiots have no idea what's happened."
"Where can we go? Traffic is at a standstill." I added quietly.

He glanced at me and then replied rather curtly, "Miss, I thank you for helping my sister but it's time for us to go our separate ways."
"She's going with us." Shelby spoke in a voice much stronger than I thought her capable of.
His gaze shifted from me to Shelby. He took a breath before he spoke. "We cannot take her..."
"She is going with us. Ronnie saved my life. I won't leave her here on her own."
"Queenie, you must have hit your head pretty hard if you think she's getting on that plane with us."
"Well, if she isn't going, neither am I. If it wasn't for her, I would be

over there under a pile of rubble. So go ahead and leave me here. I'm sure you'll have no problem explaining everything to Chaunce.

The amused look on his face quickly faded when he realized she was serious.

"Fine, she can come with us. But you'll be the one explaining to Chaunce just what you intend to do with her."
"I'm ready to go now." She sat up on the luggage cart trying to look dignified.

I struggled not to laugh as she sat there with the Wonder Woman band aide on her forehead. I pulled her purse out of my backpack and handed it to her. She pulled it over her shoulder and attempted to stand up not realizing the damage she sustained to her left leg. She was about to topple over when Don caught her by the arm. He picked her up with ease.

"Let's go." He yelled over his shoulder as he started down the crowded pavement. I tried not to look at the people on the ground around us. It looked more like a sidewalk in Beirut than a sidewalk adjacent to the newly remodeled Athens International Airport.

Once we reached the end of the block, there was actually a wide opening for us to make it back across the street to the airport side. I didn't want to go back across but Don was walking at such a quick pace. I was too afraid to get separated so I kept following him. We walked along the pavement until we came to an opening in the gate. The opening led directly to the air field.

I was surprised that Don was able to carry his sister as far as he had without slowing down. I'm sure she wasn't heavy but we walked about half a mile before we reached the airplane.

The plane's engines stirred to life as Don stood impatiently by the door. Within moments, the door was opened from the inside and a middle-aged man came down the stairs. He took Shelby and carried her on the plane.

I had no idea where we were going and at that moment, I really didn't care. I just knew that I didn't want to be here alone. I did have one uncomfortable realization though.

"I don't have my luggage!" I'm sure I sounded pretty frantic.
"You'll just have to borrow some clothes from my sister. There's no way in hell we're going back for your bags."
"I know that." I really didn't need him stating the obvious. I sat down in the first seat behind the cockpit and put on my seatbelt.

Don gave the pilot final instructions and we took off within minutes. I don't know how we got permission to take off in all of the mayhem but I was certainly relieved.

"Well, Miss, we have a little problem," Don said as he hovered over my chair.
"And what might that be?" I tried to sound irritated but I was just too tired.
"I can't let you see where we're going."
"So what do you suggest? Will you cover my face with a blindfold?"
"You know, that's not a bad idea."
"Are you insane? I was joking."
"Well, we'll need to figure something out." He walked to the back of the plane but returned a few minutes later. "Would you like something to drink?"
"Sure, that'd be great."
"Here you go." He handed me a cup of grape juice and sat down not far from me.
"Thank you." I even managed to smile at him.

I'd only just realized how thirsty I was. The grape juice was good and cold. I drank it quickly. Don was staring at me as if he was waiting for something to happen. I turned away from him and stared out the window.

As soon as I finished drinking the juice, I started feeling sleepy. No matter how hard I tried, I couldn't keep my eyes open.

"Let me help you with that." Don took the cup from my hand. It was a good thing he did or I would've probably dropped it.
"Did you put something in my juice?" I have no idea if he ever replied. I'd fallen asleep.

Chapter 6

When I woke up, I had a terrible headache. I had no idea where I was, and I was scared. I slowly stared around the room I was in. In addition to the fact that I could have fit my whole apartment in the room, it was decorated beautifully. The huge bed I lay on was covered in a soft ivory duvet and all of the delicate furnishings were a mixture of taupe and ivory. Even the plush window seat was decorated with a variety of fancy, ivory-colored pillows.

I took a few deep breaths and tried to relax myself. Someone with a house this nice couldn't be a serial killer, right?

I began to hear voices in the hallway so I decided to see who it was. But before I could reach the door, Shelby's brother Don burst into the room. She was trailing behind him and she didn't look happy.

"Answer one question for me, how does a bank teller afford a phone like this?" He was holding my backpack in one hand and Garland's satellite phone in the other.
"What are you doing with my backpack?" I asked sternly.
"Answer the question." He wasn't backing down.
"The phone was a gift from a friend. Now give it to me."

"Don, please give her the bag. I'm taking responsibility for her." Shelby interjected.
"I'll do no such thing. I need to make sure she is who she says she is." Don gave her a stern look.
"I won't ask you again to give me my backpack. Do you think you can just treat people any way you want?"

"Yes, I can." He laughed and threw the backpack on the floor at my feet. "Who gave you the phone?"

"My ex-boyfriend was supposed to come on this trip with me but we broke up. He gave me the phone to make sure I was safe. Anymore questions?"

"Well unless your boyfriend owns that bank you work for, I don't see how he could afford to buy a ten thousand dollar phone for an ex-girlfriend."

"Well aren't you more than just a pretty face." I could tell by the way he looked at me that my sarcasm caught him off guard. Shelby was trying hard to hide her amusement. "He's the bank President's son. He wanted to keep our relationship a secret. We dated about eight months but I got tired of it; end of story."

"So you can keep a secret, too. You'll fit in nicely here." He laughed out loud.

Shelby's amused look turned to one of concern. She hobbled over to him and held out her hand for the phone. He gave it to her and then left the room. I'd almost forgotten about her injured left knee until I saw her limping. I wanted to ask her how she was feeling but I was too upset about the exchange with her brother.

"Shelby, I thank you for your hospitality but if you can direct me to the airport, I'll be on my way. I don't want to be any trouble."

"Ronnie, I apologize about Don. As you've already guessed, he enjoys being a pain in the ass. You really helped me in Greece. At least let me show you my appreciation. Just give me a couple days until Chaunce gets back and if you still want to leave, I'll get you back to Athens. I promise." She handed me the satellite phone and gave me a reassuring smile.

"Who is Chaunce?" I asked quietly.

"He takes care of us." She hesitated for a few moments. "He's like a big brother; a nice one in fact."

"Ok. I'll stay a while if it's not too much trouble and if Chaunce agrees." I said.

"Great. It's no trouble at all." Shelby smiled and clapped her hands together.

"I hope I don't regret this." I smiled back at her.

I didn't have the heart to say no to her. We really did hit it off well. My only alternative was going back to Athens alone. After the destruction at the airport, I wasn't really comfortable with that. I still had no idea what caused the explosions.

"I know you must have so many questions." Shelby said with a nervous smile on her face.

"Yes, I do. For starters, where are we? I remember being on the plane and then I woke up here in this room."

"You're in my home and Don did give you something to make you sleep. It's better that way. It's a long flight from Athens."

"A long flight to where?" I asked cautiously.

"We're on the island of Madagascar. But don't worry; I'll explain more later. Are you hungry?"

"Actually, I'm starving." I immediately pictured a dancing lemur but it didn't seem like a good time to make a joke.

"Great. Let's go get something downstairs." I followed Shelby from the room as she continued talking. "Oh and your bags are here too. Don was able to get our bags before the explosions started."

"That's great. I guess that means I should thank him." Yeah, like that was going to happen. "Does Don know what caused the explosions at the airport?"

"No, he was too busy getting us out of there. He hasn't had time to look into it."

We walked into the hall and headed to the left towards the stairwell. The stairs formed a large semi-circle and ended in a large foyer.

There was a huge chandelier in the center of the high ceiling that must have been made of a thousand tiny crystals. And there were beautiful paintings that lined the wall of the stairwell.

The first painting was of Shelby and the one next to it was of Don. Even though it was just a painting, I was bothered by Don's obnoxious gaze. The third painting was of another man. He was very handsome but the most striking thing about him was his eyes. I made a mental note to ask Shelby about the paintings later. Right now, all I could think about was food.

To the right of the foyer was a large dining room. Inside the room, there were fifteen high back chairs lining the cherry wood table. I wondered how many people lived in the house.

We walked through the dining room and into a large kitchen. I quickly realized that everything about this house was larger than life. As I stared around the room at the beautiful wood cabinets and stainless steel appliances, I noticed a small woman sitting in a chair in the far corner.

She looked at us and smiled. "Can I get you something to eat?"
"Yes Kalani. We'll have some of your wonderful chicken salad." Shelby spoke very kindly to the woman. "We'll just wait in the dining room."
"Of course dear." She smiled at Shelby and me, and then set about preparing our meal.

"Ronnie, come. Let's wait here." We walked into the dining room and sat at the large table.
"Is it lunch time? I have no idea what time it is." I was feeling weird. I guess the time difference was getting to me.
"It's Monday afternoon. We arrived here this morning."
"Shelby, I have a question. What made you decide to bring me here?"

"You remember how bad things were in Athens, right? Well, I've brought you somewhere that's completely safe." She let out a nervous laugh. "It's called Seulmonde. It's not on any map though."

"And why, pray tell, is that?"

"Because we prefer it that way. The natural resources near this valley are extremely rare and equally as valuable."

"Ok. Well, I still don't understand why this place isn't on any map."

"Because no one knows about it."

"My head is starting to hurt." I didn't want to think too hard about what she was telling me. "Is this one of those weird settlements where every man has five wives?"

"Of course not. Marriage is a bond between two people. You probably watch too much television." She laughed and shook her head.

Kalani walked in with our lunch and we both ate quickly. This limited our ability to carry on a real conversation. I finished eating and just leaned back in my chair.

"Ronnie, come on. I'd like to show you something." Shelby got up from her chair and motioned for me to follow her into the foyer. "Let's go outside and get some fresh air."

She opened the pair of entry doors and let me walk out ahead of her. I wasn't prepared for what I saw. The lawn was beautifully manicured and the entire grounds were surrounded by a large stone fence. I couldn't resist the urge to walk down the stone path and stare out at the lush, green grass.

When I reached the front gate and I saw two more houses similar to Shelby's about a half mile away in either direction. They were situated around a large open field. The entire area was unlike anything I'd ever seen before.

When I looked directly ahead, I could see many more houses off in the distance. But the most interesting things I saw were the trees. The trunks were quite large at the bottom with a weird pink bloom at the very tops.

"So we're on an island?" I was trying to keep the mood light even though I was feeling overwhelmed.

"Yes. It's a very large island off the coast of Africa." She said reassuringly.

"This place is so beautiful. I just don't understand how you've been able to keep it a secret."

"We have our methods for keeping people away. Seulmonde was founded by a small group of sailors several hundred years ago. Our desire to live separately is one of our most basic tenets."

"And that's exactly why you shouldn't be here, outlander." Don spoke with his usual sardonic tone as he approached us.

"If my presence here bothers you so much then why don't you just stay away from me?" I didn't care about being rude with Don anymore.

"I think that's a wonderful idea." Shelby added quickly.

"I decide who goes where around here Queenie; don't you forget that."

"Not yet you don't."

I felt like I was witnessing one piece of a much larger puzzle. Shelby and Don seemed to be at odds a lot and I didn't want to be one more reason why. I walked outside the gate and headed for the open field.

All around me there was beauty. I'd always wanted to visit Greece but that was because I didn't know places like this existed. I sat down on the grass and put my arms over my knees. The air was light and fresh. I could smell the flowers in the trees and it pleased me. I'd never in my life felt more serene than at that moment.

I don't know how long I was sitting there when Shelby came and joined me. She sat down beside me but she didn't say anything. She looked like she was close to tears. I felt bad for her and I wanted to cheer her up.

"Is it always like this?" I decided to lean back a little so that I could include more of the sky in my view.

"No. It gets better. The sunny days are warm and clear and the rain that comes tastes sweet."

"That sounds amazing."

"There's more to see. Would you like to go for a walk?" Her mood was already improving.

"Yes, I'd like that."

We started walking and I immediately noticed that she wasn't limping anymore. That surprised me. Perhaps she'd taken some kind of pain medicine. I didn't want to make a big deal about it anyway.

We were planning to walk around the house but I soon realized that would be no small feat. There wasn't a distinct walking trail so we just fanned out around the stone fence. We walked at a leisurely pace stopping occasionally to look at flowers.

We had a lot to talk about. I found out that Shelby had another brother who didn't spend a lot of time at the house. I could tell that she wasn't that comfortable talking about him so I changed the subject. I told her about Gia and the ladies at the bank. I even told her more about Garland. It felt like a sort of cleansing. And while I was clearing my head, I had to ask her about Don.

"Ok, why does he call you Queenie? That would drive me crazy."

"He's been calling me that since we were kids. I could never get him to stop." She let out a nervous laugh.

"He doesn't like me, does he?"

"It's not you. He's just caught up in who he thinks he is."

"Yeah, I know the type. My ex thinks he's going to be the next President or something."

"You know, you didn't have to tell Don about your break up with Garland. It's not his business."

"It's fine. I can't be ashamed anymore that I wasted my time in a dead end relationship."

"But you cared about him, right?"

"Yes. I thought he cared about me, too. I lied to my father, my friends, everyone. I was such a fool."

"Ronnie, you cared for him. That makes him the fool." She smiled at me.

We finally made it back to the front gate. We walked inside the house and Shelby escorted me back to the room I would be using so that I could freshen up and relax.

I showered and put on fresh clothes. Then I crawled into my window seat to watch the daylight fade into night.

I'd probably spent twenty minutes staring out my bedroom window when Shelby announced it was time for dinner. Meal times were adhered to pretty strictly here which I found interesting.

When I got downstairs, Shelby and Don were already at the table. I couldn't help but notice that Don was staring at me and I braced myself for the impending onslaught of his childish critiques.

"Well, you certainly clean up nice, doesn't she Queenie?" He announced with a wide grin.

"I think you look beautiful Ronnie." She smiled at me and then gave Don a scornful glance.

"Thank you Shelby. You're very kind."

Kalani brought our dinner in and then disappeared back into the kitchen. I thought this might be a good time to make polite conversation.

"Shelby, I was wondering. Why doesn't your other brother join us for dinner?" I regretted asking her the question almost immediately.

"He has a lot to do this time of year." She smiled lightly.

We finished eating in silence. The only sound was our forks against our plates. I noticed Don staring at me so I tried to ignore him. I was pretty relieved when Shelby broke the silence.

"Hey Ronnie, let me take you for a tour of the house. You haven't seen everything yet."

I was dead tired but I agreed. We started the tour downstairs and now I understood why it took us so long to walk around the house. Every room was considerable in size with high ceilings and exquisite furnishings. I was so tempted to ask her which African diamond mines they owned, but for once I was able to keep my mouth shut. By the time we made our way upstairs, I was on sensory overload. I just couldn't look at another leather chaise or antique clock.

When she mentioned that we were going to peep in her brothers' rooms though, I perked right up. I didn't have any siblings so this was all new territory for me. We walked around the corner from where my room was located and caught sight of Don with a pretty brunette girl. They didn't see Shelby and me, as they were just arriving themselves. Shelby grabbed my arm and pulled me back behind the wall.

"Sorry. I didn't want him to see us." She motioned for me to come forward and then she leaned her head around just enough to see his doorway.

I bent down on one knee and peeped around the corner as well. I just caught sight of him kissing the girl lightly on her forehead. She smiled at him and then he led her into the bedroom. Shelby moved back from the hall and started walking in the direction of our bedrooms. Her face was expressionless. Perhaps she'd witnessed that scene with her brother too many times to be affected by it.

"Shelby, are you alright?"
"I'm fine. It's just been a long day. Do you mind if we finish the tour tomorrow?"
"Sure. I'm tired too."
"Ok. Goodnight."
"Goodnight."

I was so happy to finally be in my room. I took off my shoes and just let my body fall to the bed.

Chapter 7

I slowly opened my eyes the next morning feeling only a little rested. It would probably take another day or two for me to feel like myself again. I decided that carrying out my morning ritual would help me too. I brushed my teeth and enjoyed a nice, hot shower. I got dressed and unpacked my clothes. I didn't know how long I would be staying here but unpacking seemed like a good idea.

While brushing my hair, I made a conscious decision to avoid Don as much as possible. I enjoyed being here with Shelby and I wanted to focus on that. My Grecian vacation was a bust and now I was on hidden safari. At least it wasn't boring. I was immersed in my thoughts when I heard a knock at the bedroom door.

"Who is it?" I asked cautiously.
"It's me, Shelby. May I come in?"
"Of course, come on in." I was relieved to hear it was her.
"So, how did you sleep?"
"I slept like a log. What about you?"
"I slept very well, thanks."
"So when's breakfast?" I said with a nervous giggle.
"Breakfast is right now." Shelby smiled and nodded towards the door. "I have some good news, too."

While we were eating breakfast, Shelby informed me that we were invited to accompany her friend Luca and his family to the *Place de la Ville*.

"Oh yes. It's like the town square. That sounds like fun."
"And he also wants to thank you for saving me. In his eyes you're a

hero. So be prepared." She gave me a weary smile.

"Shelby, before we meet up with your friends, can I ask you something?"

"Sure. What is it?"

"How did we get here? I mean, there doesn't appear to be any roads or an airfield anywhere nearby." I said quietly.

"Well, my little brother is kind of a genius. We don't have vehicles inside the valley but he built a transport that takes us to the edge of the settlement. That's how we travel to the airport." Shelby replied.

"And that's enough with the questions." Don spoke as he walked into the dining room. "You might be a spy for all we know."

"Don you're always putting your foot in your mouth. So why don't you do us a favor and leave it there permanently." Shelby shot back at him.

"Let me get this straight. You're suggesting that I travelled to Greece, destroyed Athens Airport and befriended your sister just so I could gain access to this valley?"

"Stranger things have happened." Don muttered.

"I've heard enough of this." Shelby got up from the table and headed towards the entry way. "Ronnie let's go."

I got up and followed her out of the dining room. When I reached the front doors, I felt a little nervous. I guess I was worried if I'd make a good impression. We walked down the front path and out the gate. I was once again in awe of the beautiful landscape. Shelby motioned for us to continue out to the field to wait for Luca. She looked as nervous as I was.

Out of the corner of my eye, I saw Don walking outside the gate by the house. I couldn't help but wonder where he was going. Maybe he found another girl to sexually harass. I was laughing to myself when Shelby grabbed my hand and squeezed it tightly.

"They're coming." She said excitedly. "Let's walk to meet them."

"Ok. But can you loosen your grip a little. I need to get some blood to those fingers." I laughed as she quickly let go.

As we walked toward Luca's house, I noticed three people walking towards us. When we reached them, I knew right away which one was Luca. His eyes were locked on Shelby almost immediately.

"Hello Shelby." Luca reached out to touch the bandage on Shelby's head and then quickly moved his hand away. "And this must be Ronnie."
"Yes, this is Ronnie." She was giving him a weird look but then smiled.
"Luca, I've heard so many wonderful things about you." I reached my hand out to shake his.

He smiled at me and then leaned in to kiss my left cheek and then my right. I was caught off guard but I tried to respond in kind. Shelby was amused at my reaction.

"Ronnie, I'd like you to meet my brother Rocco and my sister Claudia." They smiled as he mentioned their names.

"It's very nice to meet you, Ronnie." Rocco said as he kissed each side of my face. Claudia hugged me for a moment and then stepped back.
"It's so nice to meet you both." I replied.
"Well, now that introductions have been made, why don't we get going?" Shelby spoke in a modest tone.

We started toward the town square. Shelby explained that there were no vehicles so people walked everywhere. It was a pleasant enough walk to the square. It reminded me of a college campus but with little cottages scattered about instead of dormitories.
The square had a town hall of sorts, a religious center, a school, a

medical center and a recreation hub. I probably would have felt more comfortable if I didn't have such a large audience.

"Why are they staring at me?" I tried to say it quietly enough that only Shelby could hear.
"We don't get many visitors here." Luca responded in answer to my question. "They're curious about you."
"As we all are." Claudia said over her shoulder.
"I'm no one special." I said matter-of-factly.
"Ah, but you're wrong." Luca said kindly. "Your bravery is why Shelby is still with us. You saved Shelby's life and therefore you saved mine." His tone changed to a more serious one. He stared at Shelby intently.

I could tell that she was affected by his words as she returned his steady gaze. I started feeling awkward walking next to them. I walked ahead to join in conversation with Claudia. She and Rocco were contemplating what to get for lunch. We decided to head for the recreation hub. Half of the first floor was a restaurant that catered to a variety of palates.

"So what should we have?" Rocco asked to no one in particular.
"I think a bottle of wine is in order." Luca said excitedly. "Shelby's agreed to have dinner with me."
"Wine sounds good." I said excitedly. "I'll have some."

Claudia suggested that I order for us. I was relieved that the eatery was able to make an American style pizza. It was a healthier version but it was pizza all the same. We were talking and eating and having a great time. I almost forgot where I was. People were still staring but I just pretended not to notice. I was enjoying myself so much that when it came time to make a toast, I volunteered.

"To new friends and good times," I said with a smile.
"To my new friend." Shelby said to me.
"To Ronnie." Luca said enthusiastically.
"To Ronnie." Everyone chimed in together.

My cheeks turned red and the smile on my face would not be moved.
I tried to hide behind my pizza as the conversation at our table
ramped up again. When we were all done eating, we headed over to
the school. Rocco was interested in taking an art class. The instructor
was an older gentleman named Pierre and he made the course sound
very appealing.

We were leaving through the front door of the school, when a young
woman approached us. She was followed by six children that
appeared to be between the ages of ten and twelve. They looked like
normal kids but I noticed that one of them was injured.

"Mira, what happened to Caleb?" Shelby asked warily.
"Well, he and Bronson wandered off from the group. They were
playing near the thickets when he fell. He's lucky to only have a few
scrapes."
"How were you able to find them?" Luca asked calmly.
"I didn't. Shenzy found them and brought them back to me."
"My brother was here?" Shelby asked excitedly.

I started looking around expecting to see him. My curiosity was going
into overdrive.

"Shenzy was here but he left when the boys rejoined our group. That
was about a half hour ago."
"Of course, he was probably on a patrol." Shelby said quietly.

I could tell that she was disappointed to have missed Shenzy and
Luca noticed too. He touched her hand and smiled at her.

"Mira, why don't you take Caleb to the medical center? My father isn't there but someone else can take a look at him." Luca touched the boy on the head before turning to us. "Let's head home."

We were pretty quiet on the walk back to Shelby's house. Even though I was wearing comfortable shoes, my feet were sore. I wasn't used to walking for hours on end. But I couldn't deny how much fun I had. We reached Luca's house first so we said goodbye to Claudia and Rocco. Luca asked if he could walk Shelby and I back to her house.

"I don't mind. Ronnie, do you?" Shelby replied in a questioning tone.
"Of course not," I said with a smile.

As we continued walking, I started feeling like a third wheel again. I was glad that we reached the field pretty quickly. I walked up ahead to give them some time alone.

"Hey Ronnie, I'll be in a little later."
"Ok." I gave her a wide grin. "It was nice to meet you Luca."
"It was wonderful to meet you Ronnie," he replied.

I turned and walked toward the house feeling pretty good about myself. That all changed when I got inside and realized I'd be alone with Don. He would only have me to pick on.

I decided not to give Don a chance to get on my nerves. I hurried up the stairs and went to my room. I needed to call Lee and Gia anyway. I didn't know what they'd heard about the explosions in Greece and I wanted to let them know that I was alright. I called my dad first which was a good thing.
It was really good to hear his voice and he definitely had a lot to say. He started with questions about the Athens airport explosions. No one knew what caused them. I tried to reassure him that I was

unharmed and I promised to call him regularly. He did seem surprised that I wasn't in a rush to come home but I hoped that was proof for him that I was alright.

After I hung up with him though, I felt a little homesick. But I was determined to use this time to enjoy myself and clear my head. I decided to call Gia and get that out of the way too. She answered the phone with normal Gia flare.

"I don't know what the hell's going on but you better come clean right now." Gia started in without as much as a hello.

"Hi Gia, how are you?" I replied sarcastically.

"Well for starters, I had to find out quite by accident that you're involved with some guy from school."

"What are you talking about?"

"Some guy named Jim came by here last night asking me if I'd heard from you. He said that you two were friends from college." She finally took a breath and waited for me to reply.

"Yeah, we're friends; we were friends. But we're not now."

"How come you never mentioned him? And where the hell are you? I've heard so many stories on the news about explosions and stuff. I tried to reach you at your hotel but they said you never checked in."

"Gia, I'm staying with a friend and everything's fine. Don't worry about me. When I get home, we'll sit down and I'll tell you all about Jim."

"When are you coming home? The airport pictures I've seen look pretty bad."

"Gia, I came on this trip to figure some things out and that's exactly what I'm going to do."

"Ok, well whatever. I can't believe you wait until now to grow a pair. Just call me every now and again and let me know that you're safe."

"I will. I appreciate you looking out for me. And if you need to reach me, just call this number."

"Well, it hasn't worked for Jim but I'll give it a shot."

"What do you mean?"

"Check your messages Ronnie. I'll be in touch."

When I hung up with Gia, I just sat there staring at the phone. I hadn't thought about the fact that someone might call me. I certainly didn't expect GM or Jim which was his code name, to call me. I was almost afraid to listen to the messages but I decided to anyway. I hit the voicemail button and put the phone to my ear.

"Ronnie, please call me and let me know that you're alright. I've been so worried. I feel like you're in harm's way because of me. I insisted you take this trip alone. Just call me please."

That was Garland's first message. I just couldn't listen to anymore. I didn't care what he thought and I certainly wasn't going to call and put his mind at ease. I just sat there for a minute staring at the phone.

I felt like crying but I wouldn't let myself waste another tear on Garland Malloy. I went into the bathroom and washed my face. I just took off my clothes and lay across the bed.

Chapter 8

I was up before the sun which didn't surprise me. I'd gotten the sleep I needed last night and then some. I got up and walked over to the window seat. I was still adjusting to my new surroundings but sitting there in the window somehow comforted me.

Just as I was about to ponder the significance of my new comfort zone, I caught sight of the rising sun. It was glorious. I sat there in the window seat until the sunlight completely filled the room. I probably would have stayed there longer if not for my empty stomach.

I took my time getting dressed hoping that everyone would be awake soon. Skipping meals was not a normal practice of mine and certainly not something that I would recommend.

I made my way downstairs and headed for the kitchen. When I got there, Kalani was in her comfy chair in the corner. But there was a new addition to the room. A man who appeared to be about thirty years old was leaning against the kitchen island drinking a cup of tea. His hair and eyes were dark and he reminded me a lot of Shenzy's painting.

"You must be Ronnie." He put down his cup and came over to shake my hand. "I've heard so much about you. I'm Chaunce."
"Yes. It's so nice to finally meet you." I said with a weak smile. I was impressed by his stature. He was attractive and younger than I expected. "I hope that my being here isn't a problem."
"Of course not my dear. We are eternally grateful to you. I understand that you'd planned a summer vacation away from home.

We'd be honored if you would remain here with us." He seemed very sincere.

"I'd like that. I've enjoyed being here with Shelby."

"She's pleased you're here as well. We don't have many visitors."

"Well that fits. I've never been anywhere." I said with a nervous laugh.

"Well, make yourself at home."

"Chaunce, you're back!" Shelby burst into the kitchen and wrapped her arms around his waist.

"Oui, ma Cheri." He hugged her close to him and kissed the top of her head.

Chaunce led Shelby into the dining room and I followed them. He sat down at the head of the table and didn't let go of Shelby's hand until Kalani placed his tea cup on the table. Shelby started talking about our trip to the square yesterday and I followed along with the discussion remarking how beautiful everything was there.

We started eating our breakfast but Shelby and Chaunce continued their conversation. He was very attentive to her and I soon realized why she adored him. And looking at his face, the feeling was mutual.

Just as we were finishing our breakfast, Don sauntered into the dining room and sat down across from Shelby and I.

"Good morning Sheldon, so nice of you to join us. Where are your manners when we have a house guest?" Chaunce was smiling but I could see the irritation on his face.

"Please accept my sincerest apologies. I had rather a long day and didn't get a full night's rest." He cut his eyes to Shelby. "You know how that can be, don't you Queenie?"

Shelby ignored Don's childish jibe. "Chaunce, I'd like to have a dinner party tonight." Shelby seemed pretty excited. "I wanted to invite the Caraccioli family."

"Is that so?" Chaunce seemed pleased by the suggestion. "That sounds like a fine idea. Perhaps we can start to repair the relationship between our families."

The look of guilt on Don's face gave me the impression that he had something to do with why there was tension.
"Maybe we could invite the Tew family as well. They might want to meet Shelby's new friend." Don's sarcastic smile returned.
"Then why don't you go and invite them." Chaunce replied. "You might as well start working on your diplomacy even if in small measure."
"As you wish." Don replied. He crammed some food in his mouth and quickly left the room.
"Shelby, why don't you invite Luca's family? Tonight we'll have a fine dinner party; like we used to."
"I'll go right now." She kissed him on the cheek and headed towards the door. "Ronnie, I'll see you later." She called back to me.

"Chaunce, is there anything I can do to help?" I asked.
"Actually there is. Behind the house, there's a trail that leads to a large cluster of baobab trees. Can you go and collect four pieces of fruit from the largest tree? Kalani will give you something to carry them in."
"Sure, I'll get going." I was glad to have an excuse to go exploring.

I walked outside carrying the fruit bag and a fresh case of nervous jitters. I had no idea where I was going or how long it would take to get there. My first task would be to find the trail Chaunce spoke about.
I started out from the back of the house and walked straight ahead until I saw a paved surface jet out from the edge of the grass. The

path would lead me to the trees so I felt some relief in finding it. After walking for about twenty minutes though, I realized that the trees were not as close as I thought. When I looked behind me, I couldn't even tell how far I'd come and my feet were a little sore.

It took another twenty minutes for me to reach my destination. The trees here were like the ones near Shelby's house but they were much larger. The smell of the pink flowers was much stronger too. I felt like a small child immersed in the enormous tree trunks. I came upon a tree that was by far the largest. It had fruit hanging on it that were too numerous to count. I picked one off and put it carefully in my bag. I was about to reach for another one when I heard a distinct sound.

It was the sound of water and it was coming from behind me. I walked through the remaining trees and right before me was a lake. But it was no ordinary lake. The water seemed to be glowing with iridescent light. It was the most beautiful emerald color I'd ever seen. I just stood there for a few moments watching the movement of the water.

The area was totally secluded. It was as if the lake had a natural border surrounding it. I glanced to the far side of the lake where a thick wall of rock stood towering over thirty feet in the air. To the right of the cliff, was a large trail of rocks that cascaded down into the water. And all around the remaining edges stood the giant baobab trees.

I was standing there holding my fruit bag, when I suddenly felt the urge to get into the water. It looked so inviting. Before I could second guess myself, I sat my fruit bag down and took off my shoes and socks. I pulled off my track pants and tank top and walked slowly into the water. I expected it to be cold but it was like nothing I'd ever experienced. My skin felt as if it were surrounded by a thousand tiny effervescent crystals. It tingled and tickled my skin as I moved further into its depths.

When I was waist high in the water, I started to swim. I went out about half way across the lake and then started floating on my back. I could have stayed there enjoying the gentle movement of the water for hours. But before long, I started thinking about the baobab fruit and why Chaunce sent me out here. I rolled onto my stomach and started swimming back towards the shore. I wasn't ready to leave though. I sat down at the water's edge and let my feet hang in the water. My entire body felt exhilarated. The soreness in my feet slowly faded away.

"What do you think you're doing?" A young man's voice spoke behind me.
"I-I was getting some fruit." I stood up just in time to have my cheeks go up in flames. The embarrassment set in quickly as I realized that I was barely dressed. I put one hand over my chest and the other across my underwear. "What are you doing out here?" I tried to sound accusatory.
"I'm supposed to be here and you are not. How did you find this place?" His tone was hard.
"Chaunce sent me. I'm Ronnie," I said almost in a whisper.
"I am Shenzy."

I didn't need him to tell me his name. I recognized him from his painting; a painting that did not fully convey the piercing nature of his eyes. When he looked at me, it was as if he was staring right through me. He appeared to be about my age but there was something about him that radiated confidence and knowledge. I tried to look away from him but I couldn't.

His dark hair was tousled like he'd just run his fingers through it. He wasn't wearing a shirt and his camouflage pants, which were cut off at the knee, hung a little low on his waist. His body was lean but muscular. He probably swam every day. His feet were bare and there was a thin band around his left ankle.

When he noticed that I was staring at him, he turned away from me and went to pick up my clothes.

"Put these on. It's time for you to leave." He handed me my clothes. Then he turned his back to me while I put them on.
"I don't know if I can find my way back." I spoke slowly still feeling the effects of the water. I put on my shoes and socks as quickly as I could. Then I picked up my fruit bag and put it over my shoulder.

"I'll show you the way," he said.
"I need to get more fruit."
He looked at me quizzically. "How many?"
"I need three more."

He reached his hand out to me and I handed him the fruit bag. I followed behind him as he walked towards the baobab trees. I needed these precious moments to compose myself. I wasn't sure what affected me more; him or the lake. When we reached the largest tree, he filled the bag with fruit and then threw it over his shoulder. He glanced back at me and then started walking down the path towards the house. I followed him without speaking. We'd been walking for several minutes when he finally broke the silence.

"Thank you." He said the words so quickly that I almost didn't hear him. "Thank you for saving my sister."
"You're welcome." I said quietly.
"Why did you do it? You couldn't have known who she was."
"We were shopping together. I don't know. Everything happened so fast." I shook my head as the memory of that day at the airport sprung back into my mind.

"Were you frightened?"

"Yes, I was terrified. I've never been more afraid in my life."

"And still you helped her." He said it but not really as a question.

"She's my friend."

"Everyone should have a friend like that."

I didn't know how to respond. We walked the rest of the way in silence. I wanted to ask him about the lake but there just wasn't enough time. When we reached the end of the path, he abruptly stopped. He pulled the bag from his shoulder and handed it to me.

"This is as far as I go," Shenzy announced as he started walking back toward the lake.

"Thank you for getting me back. Will you come to dinner tonight?"

"I don't think so." He spoke over his shoulder but kept walking.

"But it would be an insult to me if you didn't." I lied. "Where I come from, that's how you say thank you."

He stopped walking for a moment but he didn't turn around. "I'll try," he said softly and then continued down the path.

I walked the rest of the way to the house. When I came around to the front gate, Chaunce was coming out of the house. He looked at my wet hair but said nothing. He just smiled. I smiled back and kept going inside. I brought the bag of fruit into the kitchen and handed it to Kalani. She didn't seem to care that I was wet either.

"Thank you for the fruit Ronnie. I'll use them for dessert tonight." Kalani smiled at me and started pulling the fruit from the bag.

"You're welcome. I'll see you later."

"Alright dear."

I left the kitchen and headed upstairs. I couldn't wait to get changed. Before I could make it inside the bedroom door, I heard Shelby calling my name.

68

"Ronnie, is that you?" She called from her bedroom.

"Yes. I'll be right there. I just need to get cleaned up."

"Ok, come down when you get done."

"Alright."

I felt a rush of relief as I shut the bedroom door. I removed my wet clothes and put them in the bathroom to dry. I was about to get into the shower, when I caught my reflection in the mirror. I looked completely refreshed. I couldn't resist the urge to touch my cheek.

As I stood there watching my reflection, I remembered that Shelby wanted to talk to me. I took a shower and got dressed quickly. When I walked into her room, she was sitting on her chaise staring out of the window.

"Hey Shelby, what's up?"

"Ronnie, I'd like to talk to you about tonight." She sounded nervous.

"Is it about the dinner? How many people are coming anyway?"

"Well, let's just say most of the founding families will be here." She stared out the window again.

"Is that a bad thing?" I wasn't sure what to say to her.

"Not really. It's just that... I think Luca's going to ask me to marry him tonight." She blurted out the last part.

"Wow... That's good news, right?"

"I don't know. But it's not like I haven't had time to consider it. Luca has been hinting at marriage for a really long time."

"So what's wrong with that? He seems like a very nice man and he's obviously in love with you."

"I know. But what if I can't handle it? What if I'm like my mother?"

"I don't understand. What was wrong with your mother?"

"I'm sorry. I shouldn't have said that." She looked really uncomfortable and it was obvious she wasn't going to say anything else on the subject. "Why don't we go get some lunch?"

When we got down to the dining room, Chaunce and Don were

sitting at the table. Shelby and I sat down and started talking about what we were going to wear for the dinner party. She joked that she had a dress to match the bandage on her head. I laughed but Don just rolled his eyes and shook his head.

Once we all started eating, the table got quiet. I noticed that Don was staring at me which always made me uncomfortable. I tried to ignore him but that only seemed to increase his interest.

"So Ronnie, how has your day been so far?" Don chided.
"It's been good," I quickly replied.
"I sent her on an errand. I trust that went well Ronnie?" Chaunce had a look of amusement on his face.
"Yes. It was fine." I don't know why I was embarrassed.
"Wonderful. All of the arrangements have been made for tonight. The Tew family and the Caraccioli family are joining us for dinner and cocktails. I expect that we'll all be on our best behavior." Chaunce looked directly at Don when he said the last part.
"I don't know if this is the right time to say it but I wanted to thank you all for your hospitality." I glanced at Chaunce and then at Shelby.
"You're very welcome Ronnie. If it wasn't for you, we might be having a very different occasion." Chaunce said quite sincerely. Shelby smiled at me and Don just nodded.

When Shelby and I got back to her room, she was really obsessing over what she would wear tonight. I knew that she was worried about Luca proposing and I understood how she felt. Well, I tried to imagine how she felt.

Then I remembered that I needed to go find my own outfit. As I walked back to my room, I started thinking about how lucky Shelby

was to have Luca. It was obvious that he adored her. That's all any woman could ask for in a man. I know that's what I wanted.

When I got back to my room, I started looking through my closet. I had a few options but I wanted to make sure my dress sent the right message. I wanted to wear a dress that wasn't too sexy but didn't label me as a candidate for the convent either. I settled on a knee length black dress that had a close fit but with moderate cleavage. You can't go wrong with the little black dress.

Now that my attire for tonight was decided, I had a little time to spare. I decided to see if Kalani needed any help in the kitchen. To be honest, I could use the distraction.

"You're very sweet my dear. I thank you for helping me." Kalani gave me a wide grin.
"Just tell me where everything goes," I replied brightly.

Kalani showed me how to arrange the china and silverware. She also had some serving dishes that needed to be arranged in the center of the table. We were almost finished when I heard the front doors open and close.

"Now you're coming to the aide of Kalani. Is there no end to your charity work and good deeds?" Shenzy spoke behind me.
"I'm just trying to help out." I turned around to see his piercing gaze. I immediately felt flushed. Why did he affect me this way?
"I see." He raised one eyebrow and headed for the stairs.
"Are you staying for dinner?" I asked nervously.
"I said I would try." He continued walking up the stairs.

Chapter 9

I was ready when Shelby knocked on the bedroom door. I was wearing my black mini dress and my hair was pinned back on one side and brushed straight down my back.

"Come on in." I tried to sound enthusiastic.
"Well, are you ready to go downstairs? I have a big surprise for you."
She looped her arm through mine and steered me towards the open door.
"Yeah, I have a surprise for you too." I said cautiously.

We walked out of the bedroom and over to the stairwell. I glanced over the railing and saw that the guests were down in the foyer exchanging pleasantries. A strange thought suddenly crossed my mind. There didn't appear to be anyone in the group older than Chaunce.

They were all young. Then I thought back to our trip to the square. There were only a couple of people who looked a little older than me. I couldn't believe what my mind was putting together.

"Ronnie, let's go downstairs." Shelby's voice pulled me from my thoughts as did her outfit. She was wearing a yellow silk shift dress with black peep toe pumps. She looked amazing.
"Ok. I'm ready." I was so not ready.

We went downstairs and Chaunce appeared from the study on the other side of the entry way. When he emerged from the room, Shenzy was right behind him. I was so happy that he came for dinner. Shelby grabbed my hand and squeezed it so tightly that I had to stifle a scream. Only then did I notice Luca walk out of the study behind Shenzy. Shelby had to be thinking what I was thinking. Luca had talked to her family about proposing to her tonight.

"Hello everyone, I'm so glad you could all be here this evening." Chaunce glanced around at everyone as he spoke. "Now that the ladies of the house have joined us, we can adjourn to the dining room."

I tried to wait until everyone was seated before I went in. Shelby seemed to have the same idea. When we entered the room, Shelby sat in the chair to the right of Chaunce. Luca was seated next to her and then there was another empty chair. I sat down and realized that Rocco was seated to my right.

Everyone else was seated and started making small talk. I was even starting to relax. That is until I noticed Shenzy watching me. It wasn't like when Don stared. With Shenzy it was different; I wanted him to stare at me. I wanted him to like me.

I smiled at him and he nodded his head to me. Then he turned to Chaunce who was asking him a question. I realized that I was the only person at the table who didn't look comfortable. Even Shelby had relaxed. I suppose it was because I would be meeting so many new people tonight.

Chaunce must have noticed my expression because he gave me a reassuring smile. Then he picked up his water goblet and tapped his knife to its base.

"Ladies and gentleman, May I have your attention? I just wanted to thank you all for coming on such short notice. I'd also like to introduce you all to Ronnie. She's a very special guest in our home.

Ronnie, you've already met Luca, Rocco and Claudia Caraccioli, but I'd also like you to meet Ariana, Nicholas, Kylie, Fenton and Ruth Tew." He went around the table and everyone nodded as he spoke their names.

"It's so nice to meet you all," I said nervously.
"Ronnie, I also want to introduce you to my brother Shenzy. He just returned today." Shelby said with a smile.
"We've already met." Shenzy said matter-of-factly. When he spoke it surprised everyone including me.

Before any more awkward seconds could pass, Chaunce called for Kalani to start serving the meal. Don looked at me suspiciously from the other end of the table but I did my best to ignore him. I was getting better at blocking him out.

I looked up to see Shenzy staring at me again. I got up the nerve to return his stare. I wanted to see which one of us would give up first. I think I surprised him because after a few seconds he turned away. I saw the beginnings of a smile at the corner of his lips. It was only there for a second and then it was gone. I wondered what it sounded like when he laughed, and if I'd ever hear it. I decided then and there that I would spend the rest of my time in this valley waiting to see him smile.

"Did you hear me?" Rocco asked somewhat impatiently.
"I'm sorry, did you say something?"
"I said are you enjoying your visit so far?"
"Oh, yes. I am. It's very pretty here and everyone is so nice."
"Well it's easy to be nice when you're blessed the way we are."
Rocco smiled as he spoke.
"I agree. This place is unbelievable. I wish I could take a piece of it back home with me."

"Well, I can show you more of Seulmonde if you'd like."

"That's a very kind offer." I smiled lightly. I'll keep that in mind.

Kalani had outdone herself tonight. She prepared a lobster bisque soup, grilled salmon with roasted asparagus and baby red potatoes. I'd probably taken four bites too many but everything tasted so good.

Shelby was enjoying herself as she engaged in polite conversation with several people around the table. Chaunce had been joining in as well but I noticed his focus abruptly move to the other end of the table. There was a bottle of champagne in front of Don's plate and it was obvious that he'd drunk most of its contents.

Kalani started clearing away the plates as several conversations ensued around the table. Claudia was telling me how she enjoyed Paris fashion week and she was surprised when I told her that I'd never been. Shelby overheard us and chimed in saying that she liked the clothes but the models were too skinny. She said I wasn't missing much. I made a mental note to thank her for that comment later.

"Excuse me everyone, now that we've finished our wonderful meal, please follow me into the study." Chaunce stood up and motioned for us all to follow him.

I'd only been in the study once before and it was a brief visit. The room was large with bookshelves lining the walls. The chairs were made of smooth brown leather that looked like it would never crease. The one sofa chair in the room was tan suede and it complemented all of the other furniture in the room.

Everyone was strolling in at a leisurely pace. I sat on the sofa and Shelby and Luca joined me. The last person to enter the room was Don. He was carrying the bottle of champagne and looking less in control by the minute. It made me very uncomfortable but I would be the last person to comment on his stupor.

"So Ronnie, tell us more about your home. What's your family like?" Don spoke with slurred speech but I could still understand his question.

I wasn't sure if I should answer but I realized that everyone had stopped talking to hear what I'd say. "Well, I was raised by my dad. I don't have any brothers or sisters so it was just the two of us." I paused to gather my thoughts when I was interrupted.

"Where's your mother?" Claudia asked.

"Um, she's gone." I had a hard time saying it out loud especially with everyone watching.

"What happened to her? Did she run off with the mailman?" Don said with a sarcastic laugh.

"No, she's dead."

"Ronnie, I'm sorry." Claudia said.

"It's fine. She died a long time ago." I tried to smile.

"So, your dad never remarried?" Claudia asked.

"No, he said he could never love another woman after my mother." I actually did manage a smile then.

"How did they meet, if you don't mind my asking?" Ruth asked cautiously.

"Well, they met in high school. My mom had moved to town right after her sixteenth birthday. My father was drawn to her instantly. They had a few classes together and after a few weeks he asked her out on a date. She said no of course so he decided that he'd just try to be friends with her. They started studying together and they even worked at the same burger joint. It was the weirdest thing. After a few months, she asked him out."

I glanced at Shelby and she was smiling at me. I was still holding everyone else's attention so I kept talking.

"They were together pretty much after that. They finished high school and went to the same college. She studied economics and he studied engineering. They got married six months after graduation. They worked in their respective fields but they still made time for their true passions; travel and each other. They didn't start a family right away. They just wanted to enjoy each other."

"So after almost fifteen years of marriage, they decided to have a child. They tried for almost a year to get pregnant. There were a few setbacks but eventually it happened; I was conceived. They were very excited."

"But halfway through the pregnancy, my mother was diagnosed with preeclampsia. Her blood pressure skyrocketed and she was showing signs of a rare heart condition. The doctors warned her of the risks but she didn't care. She wanted to give my father a child of his own."

"As the months went on, my mother's health continued to deteriorate. My father was devastated. He desperately wanted a child but he was losing the only woman he'd ever loved. When I was born, she held me for three hours before she slipped away. My father told me that she never regretted the decision to have me. I just wish I'd gotten the chance to know her."

I stopped talking and realized that my face was damp. I let out an awkward laugh. When I glanced around the room, I saw that most everyone else was crying too. Chaunce abruptly left the room and Shenzy followed behind him.

"I'm sorry. I didn't mean to upset everyone." I looked at Shelby and she put her head down before speaking.
"Ronnie, please don't feel badly. I'm honored that you shared your story with us."
"We all are." Luca said as he reached out to touch my hand.

No one else said anything. I wasn't sure if talking about my parents was a good idea. I didn't want to ruin the dinner party.

For Don, though it was business as usual. Nothing could disturb his good time. I noticed that he was in the corner talking to Ariana. I also saw Claudia acting like she didn't notice the two of them. Maybe that's what Chaunce was talking about when he mentioned an effort to repair the family relationships. Claudia and Don must have dated before.

Chaunce returned to the study after a few minutes but Shenzy wasn't with him. I admit I was disappointed. I tried to make small talk but I ran out of things to say. I was glad when Ruth announced that she was getting sleepy from the champagne. The Tew's seemed like a nice family but they were a little subdued.

Chaunce, who was always a gracious host, walked them out to the front doors. When Ariana stayed behind I wasn't surprised. She made up some excuse about using the bathroom. Don volunteered to show her the way.

Rocco and Claudia were next to leave. As Claudia walked towards the study door, she seemed to be looking for Don. He'd already slipped out of the room behind Ariana. Luca stayed behind with Shelby; they were still talking in the study when I left. I was on my way upstairs to turn in when Chaunce caught up to me.

"Ronnie my dear, I must apologize for leaving the room earlier. When you were talking about your parents it reminded me of someone and I was touched."

"You don't have to apologize. I don't usually talk that much and I never tell that story. My father still doesn't talk about my mother. I think it's too painful for him."

"Your father is a very lucky man. Not everyone finds their soul mate.

It's just unfortunate that he didn't get to spend more time with her."

"Thank you. Well, I'm going to get some sleep. I really enjoyed dinner."

"As did I." He walked back down the steps and into the study.

I'd almost reached the doorway to my bedroom when I heard laughter coming from the other hallway. I crept down past Shelby's room and peeped around the corner. I saw Don at his bedroom door with Ariana. He was talking in her ear and she was laughing at everything he said. I'm sure he wasn't that funny.

After a few minutes the laughing stopped but I could still hear their voices. Don must have finally convinced her to go into his bedroom. She nodded her head in agreement and put her arms around his waist. He kissed her on the forehead and pulled her into his room. I realized I must look pretty pathetic spying on him this way. I headed back towards my room to get some sleep.

Just as I reached my bedroom door, Shelby came around the corner from the stairs. She didn't look happy.

"Shelby, are you ok? You look upset."

"Well, I'm not upset. I'm just tired." She was obviously upset.

"Ok. If you want to talk, just let me know."

"I don't want to talk. I'm just confused." She wrapped her arms around herself. "He didn't ask me to marry him tonight. He didn't even bring it up."

"Maybe he's waiting for the right time."

"I suppose."

Relationship problems were not my specialty. So as usual, I changed the subject. "Hey Shelby, have you seen Shenzy?"

"He left right after dinner."

"He's not staying here tonight?" I was crushed.

"No, he never stays here anymore. Why do you ask?" She seemed only partially concerned.

"I just wanted to see if he was alright. He left so suddenly." I stretched the truth just a little.

"That's Shenzy. You know, I was actually surprised he even came tonight."

"That is something."

"Well, I'm going to bed. Goodnight Ronnie."

"Goodnight."

I thought I would fall asleep quickly but I didn't. I couldn't stop thinking about Shenzy. I wished I'd been able to see him before he left. After laying in the dark for about an hour, I made a monumental decision. I was going to go look for him tomorrow. I had no idea what I would say to him but I wouldn't let that stop me.

THE FOUNTAIN: SECRETS OF SEULMONDE

Chapter 10

I wasn't sure what time it was when I woke up but I was ready to start my mission. I got dressed in comfortable clothes. I knew I'd be doing a lot of walking today. I put on jean shorts, a cotton t-shirt and my track shoes. When I got downstairs, there was no one around. I grabbed an apple from the fridge and headed out the door.

I had a feeling of excitement within me as I started down the path. I didn't know for sure if I would see him but I figured this was the best place to start. I realized my pace was a little quicker too. The walk to the lake didn't take as long as it did the first time.

When I walked through the baobab trees, I caught sight of the lake. The water was shimmering as the sunlight hit it. I decided to sit down for a minute and just enjoy the view. Once I got home, I wouldn't see anything like this. I was so caught up in the moment that I didn't hear him approach.

"So what brings you out here today? Do you need more fruit?" Shenzy spoke behind me.
"Are you the fruit police?" I stood up to face him and tried to keep my voice even.
"Actually, I am. What are you doing here?" I thought I heard a hint of humor in his voice.
"I was looking for you."
"Looking for me, why?"
"You left last night without saying goodbye." I realized it was still difficult to look in his eyes.
"I fulfilled my debt to you and then I left."
"Well, there's nothing wrong with a friendly goodbye, see you

around, that sort of thing."

"A friendly goodbye; so we're friends now?"

"I'd like us to be friends." I looked away from him as I spoke.

"I don't have any friends. Come on, let's go." He turned his back to me and started walking towards the trees.

"Where are we going?" I asked plainly.

"I'm going to show you the way back to the house or can you make it on your own?" He spoke to me over his shoulder.

"I'm not ready to leave. Does it bother you that much that I'm here?"

He stopped walking. He seemed to be thinking about what I'd just said. "Suit yourself. But don't go into the water. It's not safe for you." He turned to give me a sharp look.

"Fine, you won't even know that I'm here."

"I doubt that." He turned around and started walking around the edge of the lake.

"Why isn't the water safe for me? It didn't bother me before." I added quickly.

"Because it's not."

He kept walking until I'd lost sight of him behind the steep cliff that bordered the lake on the far side. I decided to try and relax a bit. I sat there taking in everything around me; the blue sky, the enormous trees and the glistening water.

I started watching the water as it trickled over the rocks. I wondered where it was coming from. Just then, my eyes were drawn to the top of the cliff opposite me. Shenzy was standing on top of it looking down. I thought he might be looking at me too but I couldn't be sure. After a few seconds, he walked back from the edge and I couldn't see him anymore.

I know I promised to stay put, but I was just too curious about the lake. I figured this was as good a time as any to talk to him about it. I stood up and started walking around the lake in the same direction Shenzy had walked. It was so beautiful and I hadn't seen it from this angle before. I kept walking until the stone face of the cliff was right in front of me. Now I could see how Shenzy reached the top. The cliff was covered with jagged edges that could easily be used for climbing.

I was glad that I'd worn my track shoes. I started climbing making sure I had a good foot hold with each step. But I used my hands to sort out where I would put my feet. Once I got a good rhythm going, the climb went pretty well. It took me about ten minutes to make it to the top. When I got there, I saw that Shenzy was sitting with his legs folded and his eyes closed. He was meditating. Even without opening his eyes, he knew that I was approaching.

"You're like a small child. Aren't you supposed to be sitting at the water's edge and behaving yourself?" He spoke without opening his eyes.

"Yes, but I'm curious about the lake. What is it that makes the water so special?"

"You ask a lot of questions for someone who shouldn't even be here." His eyes were still closed.

"And this is where you're supposed to be?"

"Yes."

"Well, I thought I'd just keep you company." I sat down next to him.

"What if I don't want you here?" He opened his eyes to look at me.

"Then I'll leave. But I don't think you want me to. No one wants to be by themselves all of the time." I didn't look at him. I was too afraid he would disagree with me.

"What do you know about being alone?" He said the words softly almost like a whisper.

"I know a lot about being alone. I didn't have many girlfriends growing up. Do you have a girlfriend?" I felt so bold at that moment.

"No. I don't." He looked up at the sky.

"Why not?"

"Why bother? It would just be a waste of time."

"What does that mean?"

"It means that you ask too many questions and it's time for you to leave." He said the words without anger.

"Alright. I'll leave. Will you walk me back?"

"If you promise not to ask any more questions, then I will."

"Deal," I said and reached out my hand so that he could shake it.

"Deal." He gently shook my hand.

He started down the cliff side scaling the distance with ease. Unfortunately, my journey down was not as trouble free. I tried to make sure that each step was a good one which was a little difficult in reverse. I looked down and saw that he was right under me. That did make me feel a little better. I just hoped that if I lost my footing, he would be there to catch me.

And wouldn't you know it, about halfway down my shoelace got caught under my left shoe. I tried to reestablish my footing but I lost my grip and fell back off the rock face. Thankfully, Shenzy caught me. He stood there for a few moments cradling me in his arms. He was warm and his shirtless body seemed to be getting warmer. Or maybe that was me. I finally found my voice.

"You can put me down now." I said slowly.

"Yes, of course. Are you alright?"

"I'm fine."

He put me down on my feet slowly and then started walking towards the path. I reluctantly followed him. I didn't want to go but I promised I would. As I followed behind him, I couldn't help staring at his body.

His back was nicely toned and his pants were hanging in their normal position on his hips. The hair at the nape of his neck was making a cute curl pattern that also curled around the back of his ears. I couldn't understand why the women here didn't chase him the way they chased Don.

He must have felt my gaze because he suddenly turned in my direction. He had a curious look on his face.

"What?" I'm sure I looked guilty.

"Why are you looking at me that way?"

"What do you mean? I wasn't looking at you like anything."

"Are you sure?"

"Aren't we in the no questions phase of the journey?" I asked jokingly.

"You're right." He almost smiled.

We walked on for a while. I couldn't seem to get the smile off my face. I was sure he noticed but he didn't say anything.

"Alright, how about one question each and I promise nothing too personal?" I didn't know if he would go for it but I had to try.

"Ok. But technically you just asked me a question. You go first," he said playfully.

"Why don't you ever smile? I'm sure you have a nice smile."

"I don't know. I guess I don't have a lot to smile about. Now I have a question for you. Why did you come here today?"

"I answered that already. But if you want to waste your question, that's fine with me. I wanted to see you again and I like being out here. It's peaceful."

"You wouldn't like it so much after a while." He spoke under his breath.

"How can you say that? It's so beautiful here and the water is so…"

"What? What were you going to say?"

"No more questions. Sorry." I laughed.

He smiled a little which was nice. We kept walking until we reached the end of the path.

"This is as far as I go."

"Can I have a hug goodbye?" I asked quietly.

"Was that a question?"

"No. That wasn't a question. I'm going to hug you, right now." I moved towards him slowly.

He looked unsure of what to do. I put my arms around his neck and he bent over slightly. He put his arms around my waist very gently and I took in the scent of him. He smelled like sun tan lotion, honey and heat. I didn't want to let go.

"Ronnie, I have to go." He spoke softly in my ear.

"Yes, I know." I pulled my arms from around his neck. "Will I see you again?"

"You know where I am." He replied flatly.

He stared at me for a few moments and then started back down the path. I watched him walk away. As soon as he was out of sight, I heard the first low growl coming from my stomach. I continued on to the house hoping that I hadn't missed lunch. When I walked in the front door, I headed straight for the kitchen.

Kalani was kind enough to set aside a sandwich for me. I carried it into the dining room and sat down. I was too busy eating to notice when Don came in and stood behind me.

"We were looking for you. Where have you been?" He spoke with his usual sarcastic tone.

"I went sightseeing."

"It's not safe for you to wonder off. There are real dangers out there. You might think you're at some resort but you're not."

"Don, I thank you for your concern but I can manage."

"You can manage what? You have no idea what you're doing here." He became increasingly irritated as our exchange continued.

"Well, it's a good thing I won't be here that long." I got up and left the room.

I could hear Don yelling something after I'd left but I just ignored him. When I got up to my room, I shut the door behind me and lay across the bed. I didn't want to let Don's constant aggravation upset me.

I lay on the bed staring out the window. I watched the clouds in the sky and I thought about home. I wondered if I'd made the best decision in staying here. But I knew that if I was home, I'd spend my vacation thinking about my failed relationship. As I lay there weighing out my options, there was knock at the bedroom door.

"Who is it?" I asked cautiously.
"It's Shelby. May I come in?"
"Of course." I sat up on the bed.
"Ronnie, I just wanted to make sure you were alright."
"Why? What's happened?"
"Don was going on about how you'd been out roaming around the valley."
"That's not completely accurate." I said defensively. "I only went to the lake."

I told her about my plan to go and talk to Shenzy. She didn't seem too surprised; more amused than anything. But I did leave out a few details.

I didn't tell her that Shenzy made me forget about the Garland situation completely and that I was really attracted to him. Somehow I didn't think I needed to.
"You smell like him; Shenzy I mean." Shelby smiled at me.
"He hugged me before he left but only because I asked him to."
"He can be really charming, even when he's not trying to be."

I felt like Shelby might question me further about my visit to the lake so I decided to change the subject.

"Shelby, have you talked to Luca today?"

"No. I haven't. Chaunce and I were out this morning and I couldn't decide if I should go and see him. I keep feeling like he'll get tired of waiting for me to get it together."

"I don't believe that. Why don't you ask him out on a date?"

"Do you really think I should?"

"Yes, you should. He'll be flattered."

Yeah, I was giving out relationship advice. That was laughable. But Shelby needed to talk to someone and I wanted to be there for her.

I suggested that she take Luca on a picnic by the lake. It was such a beautiful place. If I were going on a date, that's where I would go. She was a little hesitant at first but after a while she warmed up to the idea.

She was actually excited when she left the house. I was sure he would say yes to her. I hadn't had much luck in the man department but I knew Shelby had nothing to worry about. Luca loved her and everyone knew it.

I lay back down on the bed feeling pretty good about myself. But after my busy morning, I found it hard to keep my eyes open. One minute I was staring at the sky and the next minute I was fast asleep.

I don't know how long I was out, but I was awakened by the sound of someone calling my name.

"Ronnie, are you awake?" Shelby was calling to me from outside the bedroom door.

"Come in Shelby. I'm not sleeping." I spoke half into the air and half into my pillow.

"Ronnie, you're a genius. Luca loved the idea and he was so flattered that I asked him to go out."

"That's great Shelby. I figured as much."

"There is one little wrinkle that I wasn't counting on though."

"Yeah, what's that?"

"He asked if Rocco could go along and he asked about you too."

"Me and Rocco? How romantic will it be with the two of us there?" With this newest development, I was fully awake.

"I think it was Rocco's idea."

Apparently, Rocco thinks I'm interesting. I thought he was nice but he wasn't the guy I wanted to go on a picnic with. What's worse, I didn't want Shenzy to see us together and get the wrong idea. Unfortunately, I couldn't tell Shelby what my concerns were without saying too much. I was stuck.

Of course I agreed to go with her. It was the least I could do. She thanked me about a hundred times and then immediately went into planning mode. She wanted to make sure the picnic was perfect and I didn't blame her.

I got up and followed Shelly downstairs to dinner. I knew I needed to eat quickly since I agreed to go over the picnic details with her after we ate. It seemed like a good idea at the time. I just didn't realize we'd get sidetracked into another discussion.

When we finished eating, we followed Chaunce into his study. He started talking about some of his investments which I was eager to hear about. I wondered how they supported themselves in the manner in which they lived.

But after a while, Shelby seemed to grow tired of hearing about mutual funds and direct investments. I knew that her mind was focused on the picnic she'd planned for tomorrow. Chaunce realized it too because he brought the money discussion to a close and excused himself for the night.

"I couldn't wait for him to finish talking," Shelby said with a sigh.
"I thought it was interesting. You know Shelby; I actually work for a bank."
"I know. But I want to get to the important stuff."
"Yeah, I figured you'd say that. The picnic is tomorrow. What do we still need to figure out?"
"What food should we take tomorrow? And what should I wear?"
"Ok. Let's take one issue at a time. We should start with the food."

We spent the next couple hours talking about the picnic arrangements. Shelby wasn't going to be happy until every facet of the lunch was planned. As much as I enjoyed the preparations, I was glad when we were finally done. It was getting late and I could feel myself getting sleepy again.

Shelby and I left the study and headed upstairs. As soon as I got to my room, I laid across the bed. I didn't even put on my pajamas.

Chapter 11

One of my first thoughts this morning was about the picnic with Shelby and Luca. I started thinking that I was needlessly worried. Shelby wanted me there and I wanted to be a supportive friend. If going on this picnic would help her, then I would do it, and I would be happy about it.

I got up and got dressed quickly not wanting to waste the morning. As much as I tried to avoid the bathroom mirror, I couldn't resist the urge to stare at my reflection. I could tell that I looked better but I really didn't know what to make of it. My skin was smoother, healthier looking.

Shelby knocked on my bedroom door and I invited her to come in. She plopped down on the bed as I spent a few self-indulged moments in the mirror.

"Shelby, do I look different to you?"
"No, you look fine. Why?" She looked a little concerned at my question.
"You're going to think I'm crazy but…Oh forget it. Let's go get some breakfast." I decided to just keep my mouth shut. Shelby might start to doubt my sanity and that wasn't a pleasant thought.

While we were eating breakfast, Chaunce mentioned that he was going to the *Place de la Ville* and he invited Shelby and I to go along. I was excited about meeting more of the people here and I still had a lot of questions about the island. I'd been here for almost a week and I still didn't fully understand why they lived separately from normal society. I'm sure there were places like this in different parts of the world but I'd never dreamed that I would visit one of them.

Don provided me with his usual stare. I decided to focus on what Chaunce was saying instead of letting him get to me. Apparently, Chaunce was delivering some important documents that related to Seulmonde. I couldn't resist the urge to throw in a question or two.

"So Chaunce, I'm guessing you're like a politician of sorts?" I asked quietly.

"I suppose you could say that. But we don't indulge in the partisan politics that you're probably familiar with. However, we do understand the need for societal structure. If there's a matter that we're confronted with that doesn't fall under one of our current edicts, I'll provide a resolution for the two parties involved."

"What happens if someone doesn't agree with your ruling?"

"That's a very interesting question but no one ever has," Chaunce said with a smile.

"You see, this is what's wrong with outlanders; always questioning authority." Don belted out.

"That's not what I was trying to do. I find the culture here interesting and I was just curious." I'm sure I sounded defensive.

"It's alright Ronnie. This is just a sore subject for Sheldon." Chaunce gave Don a weary glance.

"Everything is a sore subject for him," Shelby said under her breath.

"Oh and now you're a pillar of society because you have an actual friend for the first time in your life. Give me a break." Don responded with his usual sarcasm.

"Let's try to be civil, shall we? Let's not forget that we have a guest in our home." Chaunce responded without looking at anyone in particular.

"Well, since we're talking about our happy house guest, do you know that she's been sneaking off to see Shenzy? She has some kind of infatuation with him."

"Sheldon Alduron Misson, that is quite enough. Ronnie is our guest here and you will at least pretend to have some social graces." Chaunce raised his voice which surprised me.

"I need to excuse myself. I'll wait in my room until we're ready to leave."

I raced up the stairs as quickly as I could. I've never been more embarrassed than at that moment. I couldn't face anyone and I didn't want to hear any remnant of the conversation that started after I left.

When I got to my room, I shut the door and just lay on the bed staring up at the ceiling. I must seem so pathetic. Don was right. Shenzy probably thought I was weird to come to the lake looking for him. He was just too nice to tell me to my face. I was replaying the scene from downstairs in my mind when there was a knock at the door.

"Shelby, is that you?" I said in the direction of the door.
"It's Chaunce. May I come in?"
"Yes, please." I sat up quickly. He came into the room but stayed close to the open door.
"I must apologize for Don's behavior. There's no excuse for it."
"I suppose it must be hard having me here like this. Don doesn't seem comfortable with it."
"That very well may be. But it's not Don's decision." Chaunce said with a smile.
"Ok." I smiled back.
"Well, we're leaving shortly. Shelby is insisting we stay on schedule. She mentioned something about this afternoon." He smiled again before leaving the room.

Talking to Chaunce actually made me feel better. It reminded me of when I talked to my father. Then I remembered that I forgot to call

Lee yesterday. It was too early to call him now so I would have to wait until around dinner time; that is if I survived lunch.

I wasn't sure that I could face Shenzy now that everyone knew how I felt. Before I could continue my thought process, Shelby popped her head into the doorway.

"Are you ready to go?" Shelby asked excitedly.
"I think so." I got up from the bed and followed her out the door.

When we got downstairs, Chaunce was waiting for us in the foyer. Don was nowhere to be found. Maybe he went off to boil bunnies or something.

"Alright girls. Let's go." Chaunce held the front door open for us.

We headed out the gate and towards the open field. It was a beautiful day for a morning walk. I don't think I remember the sky being this beautiful back home or maybe there were just too many buildings for me to notice. It didn't seem to take that long for us to get to the town square either. I had on comfortable shoes and I was enjoying the scenery.

We arrived at the town hall building. It looked like a fancy set of offices with a statue of a pirate in front of it. I moved closer to read the inscription at the foot of the statue. The inscription read as follows:

James Misson
Founder of Seulmonde
1651 - Death

The statue appeared to be made of bronze but I couldn't be sure. Chaunce and Shelby were headed into the building, so I walked quickly to catch up with them. Chaunce walked into the first office to the left of the front doors while Shelby and I waited in the huge atrium. There was a large glass window between the atrium and the office Chaunce was in.

The young woman sitting behind the desk greeted him with a smile and handed him an envelope. He pulled the contents from it and reviewed the pages. She handed him a pen and he signed the bottom page. Then he slid the contents back into the envelope and handed it to her.

They started talking about something but I couldn't hear their voices. Shelby had already walked away from the glass. She apparently had no interest in what Chaunce was doing.

"Are you thinking about the picnic?" I asked her, already sure of the answer.
"Yes. I keep thinking over all of the details. And there's something else." Shelby said cautiously.
"What? What is it?"
"After what happened in Greece, I've really been thinking hard about my life. I've thought hard about Luca."
"He seems like such a great guy and he's devoted to you. But I understand that you want to make sure you feel the same way. There's nothing wrong with that."
"But I know how I feel. I guess I was just scared and I figured we didn't need to rush. But that's not what you do to someone you care about, especially when you know how they feel about you."
"And when I told you about Garland, it reminded you of yourself." I said it but not as a question.
"Yes, it did." She answered me but without looking my way.
"Shelby, its fine. Garland and I were totally different than you and Luca. I don't think he ever cared about me. I was just someone to hang out with." It hurt to admit the truth. Shelby must have seen the

pain in my face because she put her arm over my shoulder.

"If you care about him, I think you should tell him."

"That's why I'm so nervous. Because that's exactly what I'm planning to do."

"Well, I think that's a great idea."

We just sat there quietly for a few minutes watching the people as they entered and exited the building. I was actually starting to feel excited about the picnic. I didn't get my guy but Shelby would get hers. And it gave me real hope that there would be someone for me one day. Just then, Chaunce came out of the office and started walking toward us.

"Ready to head back to the house?" Chaunce asked with a smile.

"Yes. We're having lunch with Luca and Rocco." Shelby said enthusiastically.

"Is that so? Well, we better get going. We wouldn't want to keep them waiting."

As we made our way out into the square, I realized that many more people were walking about than when we first arrived. Some of them were watching us, only this time, they weren't staring at me. They were staring at Chaunce. He was smiling at them and waving hello. I'd never know anyone famous, so I guess this might count in that area. But the ironic part was that outside of this valley, no one knew that he existed.

The walk back to the house went quickly but it was still very pleasant. I would take occasional glances at Shelby and I could tell she was lost in her thoughts. I decided not to disturb her. Chaunce apparently didn't get the memo.

"You've started spending time with Luca again."

"Yes. We're good friends and we have been for a very long time."

"Friends are good to have, I suppose."

"Yes, they are."

I could tell that Shelby wasn't comfortable with the conversation. And Chaunce must have finally picked up on it because he didn't say anything else. Once the house was in view, Shelby started to relax again. We crossed the field and headed through the gate. When we walked in the front door, I could smell the food Kalani was preparing for our picnic. Chaunce thanked us for accompanying him to the town square and headed towards the study.

Shelby grabbed my arm and started running for the stairs. I had no choice but to match her pace or I would have been dragged like a rag doll. She didn't change her momentum until she was staring into her bathroom mirror.

"What shall I do with my hair?" Shelby asked me with a smile on her face.

"You're asking the wrong person." I smiled back at her. "Well, if you honestly want my opinion, I think that less is more. Where I'm from, the women wear too much make-up, too much perfume and not enough clothes. I think you're pretty the way you are right now."

"Ronnie, you're so kind. I hope Shenzy gets the chance to know you like I do."

"You don't have to say that." I stared down at the floor.

"I didn't mean to make you uncomfortable Ronnie. I won't mention it again."

"No, it's fine. But today is about you and Luca. I'll let you freshen up and I'll go do the same."

"See you downstairs in ten minutes?"

"Sure."

I walked down to my room and closed the door. I wanted to relax a little before the picnic. I lay down on the bed and shut my eyes. But all I could see was his eyes staring back at me. Shenzy was now a constant fixture in my mind and the worst part was that I really didn't know that much about him.

"Snap out of it." I told myself out loud. I had to stop myself from continuing this childish obsessing. I'm a grown woman and a professional. I needed to start acting like it. I got up off the bed and went into the bathroom to wash my face. I put on a little lip gloss and brushed my hair.

Then I headed downstairs to the dining room. Kalani brought the picnic basket in and set it on the table in front of me. I thanked her as she disappeared back into the kitchen.

"Are you dating Rocco now? You're a fast worker." Don said with his usual unwelcomed sarcasm.
"You must be bored; no foreheads to kiss before lunch."
"So, you've been talking to my sister about me."
"No, I haven't. I have two eyes Don. I've seen your handy work for myself."
"See anything you like?"
"I can't say that I have." I grabbed the picnic basket and carried it out into the foyer, hoping that Shelby would show up soon.

Just as I reached the front door, Shelby emerged from the study. She met me at the door and we walked out in front of the house. I glanced out towards the open field where I could see Luca and Rocco approaching.

"Should we walk out to meet them?" I asked.
"Yes. That's a good idea." Shelby answered back.
We walked out of the gate and headed towards the field. Shelby looked like she could hardly contain herself. It made me smile. When we reached the guys, Luca spoke first just as before.

"Hello ladies, how are you doing?" Luca was staring directly at Shelby.

"We're great," I said. I must have sounded like I was twelve.

"I'm so glad that we could have lunch together." Rocco chimed in.

"Should we get going?" Shelby said shakily.

"Yes. Let's go." Luca reached out to take the picnic basket from her hand.

We walked the rest of the distance across the field and kept going past Shelby's house. I was actually able to find the path on my own. As we walked along, I stared out ahead of us. I realized I hadn't seen any animals roaming about. I turned to ask Shelby about that but I noticed that she and Luca were holding hands and whispering to each other. I decided not to bother her and asked Rocco instead.

"Rocco, have you ever seen a Lemur out here?"

"Yes. I have. The last one I saw was about this big and he looked like he weighed about three hundred pounds." He opened his arms up wide.

"Really? Where were you when you saw it?"

"I was right around here, actually." He stifled a laugh.

"Rocco, don't scare her that way. She thinks you're telling the truth." Luca couldn't help from laughing.

"Ronnie, Lemurs are very small and harmless. And they're actually quite friendly. If we came through here at night, you might see one." Shelby gave Rocco a stern look before smiling herself.

We kept walking along the trail and making small talk. When we finally reached the cluster of baobab trees, I could hardly resist the urge to start running toward the lake. I didn't understand why the others were not affected by it as I was. I decided to mask my enthusiasm by pretending to seek out a good spot for our picnic.

"I'll look for a good place for us to set up," I said casually.

"You don't have to do that Ronnie. Let the men handle it." Rocco said with a smile.

"Ok, if you say so."

Luca walked over to a level area not far from the water's edge. He opened the basket and pulled the blanket from the top fold. Rocco came over to him and grabbed the other end.

Within minutes, the blanket was laid out and our lunch was ready to be served. Luca took Shelby by the arm and helped her down to sit on the blanket. Rocco did the same for me. I couldn't help but take a nervous glance around to see of Shenzy might be watching.

There was nothing around us but the trees and bushy white clouds overhead. The sounds of the lake made a beautiful melody that played while we enjoyed the delicious food and wine. While it was very light and sweet, the wine was making me a little lightheaded. I couldn't say for sure, but it might have been affecting the others as well. We were all talking and laughing with one another. Before I could break into a giggling frenzy, Luca hopped to his feet.

"Shelby, there is something that I need to say to you and I can't think of any better time than now." Luca's expression was serious.

"What is it?" She asked nervously.

He pulled her up to her feet and got down on his left knee. Rocco stood up as well.

"You know how much I care for you and I don't think any man could love you more than I." Rocco pulled a small white box from his pocket and handed it to Luca. "Shelby Alana Misson, will you be my wife?"

He opened the box to reveal a red diamond ring. It was a marquee cut stone with a gold band. The band had a beautiful flower pattern around it. Shelby was shocked into silence. I don't know if she actually saw the ring because she was staring into Luca's eyes.

She slowly nodded her head and said, "Yes." I could see tears streaming down her face as Luca placed the ring on her finger. He stood up and kissed her passionately. I stood up as well thinking I might walk over to the lake and give them some privacy. Before I could, Rocco came over to embrace me. He kissed both sides of my face. Soon we were all overwhelmed with the joy of the moment. We were laughing and hugging each other.

Moments later, we decided to sit down and have another glass of wine. Luca and Shelby were kissing and holding hands while Rocco and I poured.

"I'd like to propose a toast, to the sweetest couple I know." Rocco practically sang the words.
"Here, here." I said.

"So what's the celebration?" Shenzy spoke from twenty feet away.
"Shenzy, come and have a drink with us. Luca and I are engaged." Shelby said as she got to her knees.
"I don't want to interrupt your celebration but congratulations to you both." He was talking to Shelby but his eyes drifted from me to Rocco. He turned to walk away and I got to my feet to follow him.
"Shenzy, wait. Can I speak to you for a minute?" I called to him but he did not slow down.
"I have to go," he said over his shoulder.

He went around behind the rocks that bordered the lake. When I finally made it to where I saw him last, he was gone. I walked back to our picnic area and tried to put a smile on my face. While I was happy for Shelby and Luca, I was sad that Shenzy might have gotten the wrong idea about me and Rocco. It was obvious that Luca wanted to have his brother there for this important moment in his life.

The only thing that made me feel better was the plan I devised for myself. I would come back tomorrow and explain to Shenzy what happened. He might not even care but I at least wanted to talk to him. After another hour or so, we packed up the picnic basket and departed the lake paradise.

When we started walking back, I looked over my shoulder a couple of times. Then I turned my focus back to our group. The walk back to the house went quickly. Luca and Shelby said their goodbyes and we headed into the house. Shelby ran into the study to see Chaunce. I could hear her trying to talk through joyful tears. I decided to give them some privacy so I went up to my room.

With a little time on my hands, I decided to call home. Lee was pleased to hear from me and that made me happy. We didn't talk that long though. He wasn't the type of man that went on talking all day. Gia, however, was a different story. She wanted to know everything I'd done from the last time we spoke. I couldn't really tell her anything. I just needed to assure her that I was alright. Convincing her did require us to stay on the phone for almost an hour.

I was trying to hang up with her when I realized I wasn't alone. I turned towards the door and saw Don staring at me as I lay across the bed. I sat up immediately.

"Gia, I really need to go. I promise I'll call you back soon." I turned away from him in hopes that he'd leave. It didn't work. When I turned to face the door, he was still there.

"Are you going to come to dinner on your own or do I need to carry you?"

"I can walk just fine, thank you." I walked towards the door and tried to move around him. He moved to block my path.

"I think we got off on the wrong foot. Tell me how I can make it up to you?"

"For starters, you can let me pass."

"Of course." He moved aside allowing me only a small space to get by.

When I got down to the dining room, Shelby and Chaunce were already there. Shelby was showing him the engagement ring and he was examining it with a careful eye. When I looked at it, I only saw beauty. I didn't know that red diamonds even existed. This was just another example of one of the million things I was clueless about.

Chaunce took both her hands in his and kissed them one by one. Shelby was trying hard to minimize the smile that made her look about twelve years old. It made me smile too.

But what delighted me most of all, was what Shelby said to me next.

"Ronnie, I know we haven't known each other long, but I would love for you to be my maid-of-honor." She smiled at me as if she were waiting for a response.

"Are you serious? Yes, of course I'll do it."

She leaned over and hugged me as Chaunce looked on. He smiled at both of us. I felt so warm and welcome at that moment, and I was so happy for Shelby.

A few minutes later, Don strolled into the room looking almost apathetic. He didn't say any kind words to his sister about her engagement. But I shouldn't have been surprised by that.

Kalani made a special dinner that night consisting of Shelby's favorite foods. She served *poulet sauté a la Bordelaise* which was a delicious sautéed chicken dish. We drank ginger beer and for dessert we had sliced fruit covered in a sweetened vanilla cream sauce.

After we finished eating, we stayed at the dining room table talking about the day's events. Don excused himself early which didn't seem to bother anyone. But after another hour, I started having trouble keeping my eyes open. I was next to head upstairs for the night.

I changed into my pajamas and brushed my teeth. I was still a little thoughtful about today. I couldn't help my mind from wandering back to Shenzy. When I shut my eyes, all I could see was his face.

Chapter 12

I woke up the next morning feeling refreshed. I was so excited to be going to the lake to see Shenzy. I got up and got dressed quickly hoping to get out of the house before anyone else woke up. I peeped out of my bedroom door to make sure I didn't hear anyone and then darted down the stairs.

I was delighted to see that no one was up; Kalani wasn't even in the kitchen yet. I grabbed a banana from the fruit bowl on the kitchen island and headed out the front door. I could feel my pace picking up as I made my way around the side of the house. The sun was directly overhead but it didn't bother me much. In fact, I don't remember the temperature ever being too hot. It was always perfect.

Once I reached the path, I started thinking of something clever to say for why I was visiting Shenzy again. Or maybe I would just tell him the truth. I would tell him that I liked him and that I wanted to spend some time with him. It sounded pretty simple in my mind but I didn't know if it would go so smoothly when I reached the lake. I had no idea how he felt about me.

It didn't take long for me to get there which was a good thing. But once I approached the edge of the trees, I needed a few seconds to gather my nerve. At least if he rejected me, there would be no one around to see. That seemed to give me a margin of comfort.

I walked through the giant trees and headed toward the lake. The emerald green water always caught my attention. But I had to make myself focus. I wanted to see Shenzy. I thought about where he might be and then I remembered that he liked to meditate on top of the cliff. There was only one way to find out if he was up there.

Once I reached the base of the cliff, I removed my shoes. When I put on my ballet flats this morning, I didn't factor in the need for climbing. I found a good hand hold and started my ascent. I was getting better at this climbing thing. Perhaps it was because of what I hoped was waiting for me at the top.

After a few sweaty minutes, I made it up to the top of the cliff. I just sat there catching my breath and wondering what my next move would be. He wasn't there. I crawled over to the edge closest to the lake. I sat up and stared out in every direction. Where could he be?

Now I was sitting on top of this cliff with only two options. I could jump off the cliff into the lake or I could climb back down the way I came. I decided climbing was a better idea since I didn't know for certain where I would land or how deep the water was. I got up and walked to the other side of the cliff.

I turned my body around and swung my legs over the cliff side. I slowly stepped down to the first indentation. I figured it wouldn't be so bad as long as I took my time. But after I'd taken a few steps down, I got a cramp in my left foot. I tried to shake it out but the pain just intensified. I knew I had to keep moving before the pain became too great. I stepped down again with my right foot and then I tried to move my left.

When I put my left foot in the new recess it slipped out and I completely lost my footing. My hands were already sweating and I knew that I was losing my grip. Fear overtook my body as I felt myself falling backward. I tried to get my feet under me but everything happened so fast; I blacked out.

When I woke up, all I could hear was screaming. It took me a few moments to realize that the screaming voice was my own. The pain was everywhere but the deep burning was focused down the left side of my body. I felt like I was about to lose consciousness again when I saw his face. Shenzy was talking to me but I couldn't hear his voice through the pain. He leaned over to pick me up and the movement was more than I could stand. I passed out again.

When I awoke, Shenzy was cradling me in his arms. And there was something else. I felt the glistening tingle of the lake water all over my body. When he noticed that my eyes were open, he spoke to me again. This time I could just make out what he was saying.

"Ronnie, can you hear me?" He spoke in a controlled tone.
"Yes."
"I need you to drink some water. It'll help you."

He carried me to the side of the lake and laid me gently on my back. He pulled a water bottle from over his shoulder and twisted off the top. He put his hand under my neck and put the water bottle to my lips. Then he poured a little water into my mouth. It tasted cool like menthol and I could feel the water's affect moving through my body. The pain I was feeling started to subside and was replaced by a tingling sensation. It wasn't painful at all which was good. But it did feel strange.

"Don't try to talk. I'm going to take you somewhere to rest." Shenzy spoke calmly again.

I don't think I could have spoken if I wanted to. I was just glad that the horrible pain was gone. But the pain meant something. I'd probably broken some bones or suffered other serious injuries from the fall. He started walking toward the jagged rocks on the opposite side of the lake. I closed my eyes as we neared a massive baobab tree.

I don't know if it was the motion from him carrying me or the water but I just couldn't stay awake. I drifted off again.

I woke up to the sound of Shenzy's voice. He was in another room but I could still hear him speaking clearly. The tone of his voice was not the calming tone I remembered from earlier. He was talking on a two way radio and he was obviously upset. It didn't take long for me to figure out who he was talking to.

"You're about as subtle as a raging bull." Shenzy spoke into the radio. "I'll take responsibility for her being here. Over"
"That may not be your decision. Over" Don spoke in a venomous tone.
"She'll remain here until tomorrow. I won't move her before then. After that, you can do what you wish. Over"
"Alright. I'll contact you in the morning. Over and out" Don said reluctantly.
"Over and out"

I heard him put the radio down. He started walking towards me so I closed my eyes. I don't know why I didn't just let him know I was awake. He came over to the bed and slowly sat down next to me. I felt his fingers moving the strands of hair from my face. He sat there for another few moments and then he got up. He was about to leave the room when I spoke to him.

"Where am I?"
"You're safe. How do you feel?" He turned around and walked back over to me. This time he remained standing.
"That's an interesting question. I feel pretty good. What did you give me?"
"I gave you some water."
"But that water isn't like regular water. There's something special

about that lake isn't there?"

"It's not the lake itself. It's the fountain that feeds into the lake. We don't know exactly how it works but it does."

"You used it to heal me. How badly was I hurt?"

"Well, I'm not a medical doctor so my assessment might not be completely accurate. As best I could tell, you broke your left arm, your left leg and probably your collar bone. I'm not sure what internal injuries you sustained. What the hell were you doing up on that cliff?"

"Where are we?"

"You didn't answer my question."

"I think we're in the no questions phase of the conversation. Why won't you tell me where you're holding me?"

"Oh now you're a hostage?"

"You tell me."

"I probably just saved your life. Are all Americans this ungrateful?"

"And now you insult me. Isn't this an exciting turn of events? Do you have anything to eat in your bat cave?"

He smiled and immediately got up to leave the room. "I have soup for you. But don't expect it to taste good. I'm not Kalani."

"I don't expect anything. I'm an American remember. We're all jaded from birth."

"Oh yes. I almost forgot."

Once I heard him puttering around in the kitchen, I started to focus my attention on my surroundings. I was lying on a bed in the center of a lightly furnished room. The walls were covered in a faded blue paint. There was a small, wooden chest of drawers in the corner. On the left side of the bed, there was a rocking chair that looked like it had never been used. Next to the rocking chair was an old fashioned coat rack. It took me a minute to realize that the white romper I'd been wearing was draped over the coat rack. I looked down at my body which was covered by a thin blanket. And underneath, I was wearing only my bra and panties.

A few minutes later he came back into the room with a food tray. He sat it down on the chest and pulled a napkin from the corner. He picked up the water bottle and removed the lid. He poured some of its contents into a plastic cup on the tray.

"Why did you take off my clothes?" I asked inquisitively.
"Your outfit was soaking wet. I was trying to get you dry and make you more comfortable."
"Did you see anything?"
"Yes, I saw a ridiculous girl who'd fallen off a cliff. What were you doing up there?" He seemed a little irritated.
"I'm hungry. May I have the soup now?"
"Yes. You may."

He grabbed the other two pillows that were on the bed and put them behind my back. He moved the bowl of soup closer to the edge of the tray and put the napkin in front of me. He picked up the spoon and began to swirl it around in the bowl. He got a good spoonful of soup and leaned it over towards my mouth. He fed me almost all of it before he offered me water.

"Why does the water make me sleepy?" I asked.
"Well, we assume that because our bodies regenerate while we're sleeping that the water's healing properties work best when we are asleep as well. Drink a little of this and then you can rest some more."

He gave me a few sips from the cup and I could feel the tingling sensation envelope my entire body once more. The last thing I remember was staring into his eyes before I drifted off to sleep.

I was awakened by a familiar urge. I had to use the bathroom. I opened my eyes to find Shenzy sleeping uncomfortably in the rocking chair next to the bed. I tried to think of a gentle way to wake him but nothing came to mind.

"Shenzy, are you sleeping?" I said in a loud whisper.

"I'm not now." He replied rather dryly.

"I have to use the bathroom."

He opened his eyes and looked at me with a rather perplexed expression.

"Ok. Don't move. I'll carry you."

"And then what?" I asked in a playful tone.

"And then I'll leave you. You can at least take care of yourself for five minutes without my help, right?"

"I'll do my best."

"How do you feel? I mean are you in any pain?"

"I'm fine. I just really need to go."

"Alright."

He got up slowly from the chair and came around to the right side of the bed. As he carried me to the bathroom, I couldn't help but take in his scent. He smelled like soup and honey. He flipped on the bathroom light and sat me down on the little stool in the corner. I flinched at the brightness of the light.

"I'm going to leave you here. When you're done, call me and I'll come back to get you."

"Ok. I think I can handle that."

He walked out of the bathroom and shut the door behind him. I stood up and pulled the blanket from around me. I used the bathroom as quickly as I could and washed my hands. I was looking around for something to dry my hands with when I caught my reflection in the mirror. I looked even better than before. My complexion was flawless.

And then I thought about what Shenzy had said about the fountain. Suddenly it all started to make sense. What would the rest of the world do if they knew about this place? If they knew there was a healing fountain tucked away on an island off the coast of Africa.

This place would go on the auction block; sold to the highest bidder. Or worse, it would be claimed by every government that ever visited this island. I was debating the horrors in my mind, when Shenzy knocked on the door.

"Ronnie, are you alright in there?"
"I'm fine. I'm just washing my hands." I hurried over to the stool and put the blanket over me. "I'm ready."

He came into the bathroom and looked at me quizzically. He didn't say anything though. He just picked me up and carried me back into the bedroom. He put me on the bed and went back to sit in the rocking chair.

"Are you going to sleep there?" I asked quietly.
"Yes. If you prefer, I can go into the front room and sleep at my desk."
"No, that's not what I meant. I was going to say that you can sleep here. This bed is large enough for both of us."

He opened his eyes and looked at me before closing them again. "That's ok. I'm fine here."
"Well, suit yourself. You're going to be the one soaking in the lake tomorrow. Your back will be twisted up in knots from sleeping in that chair."

I wrapped the blanket around me and moved over a bit to show how much space was left on the bed. I closed my eyes and took a deep breath. After a few moments, he got up from the chair and lay quietly on the bed next to me. Right away, I could feel the heat emanating from his body. I couldn't help but be affected by it.

"Am I making you uncomfortable?" He asked.
"No, not at all." I turned slowly towards him. I could just make out his face in the darkness. His eyes were closed and his breathing was rhythmic.
"I can feel you staring at me," he said.
"I am not." I turned away from him.
"Go to sleep. You need your rest."
"I've had enough sleep."
"Well, I haven't." He replied quickly.
"Goodnight."
"Goodnight."

There was no way I was going to sleep. I felt like I could run a marathon. I had so many thoughts running through my mind but all of them led back to Shenzy. After a few minutes, I felt his body relax and his breathing deepen. He was asleep. I turned to face him again. I enjoyed watching him and every time I did, I saw more about him that I liked. His sun-kissed skin, his serious eyes and his lean body were all a joy to behold.

And then there were his lips. What I wouldn't give for one kiss from those lips. I don't know if it was the water or just the opportunity, but I had an overwhelming urge to kiss him. I've never been so bold but something stirred in me. Maybe if I was gentle enough, he wouldn't even notice. I'm sure he was tired from taking care of me. I moved out of the covers very slowly trying not to shake the bed. I held my breath and leaned towards his face.

"Don't," he said without opening his eyes.
"I wasn't doing anything." I leaned back and turned away from him.

I couldn't believe myself. This guy was being so nice and taking care of me and I was trying to molest him in his sleep. What the hell was the matter with me? I really needed to get it together.

At least I could get up tomorrow and act like nothing had happened. I'm sure he wouldn't bring it up again and neither would I. It took a while but I finally went to sleep. And wouldn't you know it, I dreamt that I kissed him and he kissed me back.

Chapter 13

When I woke up the next morning, I'd almost forgotten what happened to me. Other than my damaged ego, I felt pretty good. Running that marathon was still in the realm of possibilities. Shenzy had already gotten up, of course. I could hear him in the other room moving around. I sat up and ran my hands down the lengths of my legs. All of the tingling was gone so I thought it was safe to get up.

I tested my legs by walking over to the coat rack. I put on my romper and then walked into the front room. Shenzy was making peanut butter and jelly sandwiches. He was wearing a pair of jean shorts and a t-shirt that read 'Close Encounters of the Third Kind'.

"Hi. Do you have an extra toothbrush?" I tried not to make eye contact with him.
"Good morning. Yes, there are spares in the bathroom cupboard. There's a full pack unopened. No one ever comes out here." He seemed amused.
"Thanks."

I went into the bathroom and pulled out the unopened pack. I brushed my teeth and washed my face as slowly as I could. I didn't really feel like facing him after what I did last night. But I knew I couldn't hide in the bathroom forever. I took a deep breath and headed back into the front room.

"I made you two sandwiches. I didn't know how hungry you were. I got you some orange juice too. I figured you'd had enough water."
"Thanks. I like orange juice." I ate my sandwich and just sat there.

"Are you alright? You were a little weird last night." He sounded genuinely concerned which made me feel that much worse.

"Ok, I tried to kiss you. It's not like I'm a rapist. I'm not usually like that."

"Maybe it was the water then." He still sounded amused.

"Has that happened before?" I saw a light at the end of my shame filled tunnel.

"You mean, where people try to kiss strangers in the dark? No, not at all." He laughed under his breath.

"I'm sorry, alright." I stood up and started pacing the room. "You saved me and you took care of me. I was grateful."

"A simple 'thank you' would've sufficed."

"Wow, I actually thought I couldn't feel any worse than I did last night." I turned away from him as the tears pooled in my eyes.

"Hey, I was just teasing you." He walked over to me and turned my body to face him. "Please don't be sad."

Before I could move away from him, Shenzy pulled me into his arms. His body was warm and comforting. I wrapped my arms around him as the tears continued to flow.

I don't think it was my embarrassment so much as everything that had happened in the last eighteen hours. He just held onto me; neither of us spoke a word.

I'd finally stopped crying and Shenzy stared at my damp face. Unexpectedly, he leaned down and gently kissed my lips. His lips were so soft and inviting. He started to pull away but I wouldn't let him. I put my arm around his neck and pulled him towards me.

When our lips touched for the second time, I couldn't resist the urge to lean into him. His lips were hot but his breath was cool. I reveled in every part of our exchange. He was so gentle but yet there was something urgent in his kiss.

I started playing with the hair at the nape of his neck and he kissed me even harder. Shenzy caressed my body and I could feel the heat emanating from both of us. I was lost in the moment and what a wonderful moment it was. But as luck would have it, the radio started to chirp. It was Don.

"Don Juan to pool boy, over" Even through the radio, his tone was irksome. "Don Juan to pool boy, over"

Shenzy let go of me and I moved away from him. I headed straight for the bedroom thinking that might make a good hiding place. Things had gotten a little more heated than I'd intended, and I know he felt the same way. He picked up the radio but when he spoke his breathing was a little labored.

"Shenzy here. What is it? Over"
"So how she is doing? Queenie is asking again. Over"
"She's fine. We just ate breakfast. I need to check everything here and then we'll be starting out. Over"
"Ok. Good. Let me know if there's any change. Over and Out"
"Over and Out"

I heard him put the radio down and then things got quiet. I went to check on him even though I didn't know what I was going to say to him. There was another doorway off the front room and I walked through it. Shenzy was standing in front of three very large computer screens and surrounded by some other high tech equipment.

"What is all of this?
"You have a child-like curiosity." He spoke without turning around.
"And you have a man size libido," I said jokingly.
"So is that what this was, some kind of test?" He turned to face me and leaned against the desk. "Did Don put you up to this?"
"Put me up to what? Whatever you're thinking the answer is no."

He seemed satisfied with my answer so he turned his attention back toward the screens.

"So what is all this stuff?" I walked further into the room and stood near one of the large monitors.

"This is how I keep an eye on everything." He started moving levers and pushing buttons.

"Why do you have to keep an eye on anything?"

"Someone has to make sure we don't get any unwanted visitors. Ronnie, you've seen how we live and what we have. You know what's at stake."

"I get it. I do. But how can you keep people out? What if the government comes snooping around here?"

"We don't fall under the sovereignty of any nation. We're a separate state. And we have ways of keeping people away. Our protection grid makes it impossible for aircraft to fly above our air space. It's similar to the field that exists over the Bermuda triangle."

"How could you possibly create something like that without people knowing about it?"

"As I said, we have our methods. We've been developing this technology for quite some time. I have a doctorate in electrical engineering among others. I keep everything functioning properly."

"That's impressive... so now what do we do?"

"Now I get you back to the house. You've already seen too much here."

"Whatever you say doctor Shenzy." I forced myself to smile. I really didn't want to leave.

I turned and walked toward the door. When I got there, I saw him put a small touch screen device in his pocket. He turned off the large monitors and walked toward the door behind me.

"Do you want to use the facilities before we leave?" He said with humor in his voice.

"I'm fine, thank you. I'm ready to go when you are."

"There is one thing though. I have to blindfold you before we go out."

"Are you serious? Oh whatever, let's just get it over with."

He put the blindfold on and lifted me off my feet. I actually enjoyed being close to him again. He started walking but I had no idea in what direction. After a few minutes, he slowly put me down on my feet and removed the blindfold. We were standing by a baobab tree just out of range of the lake. I needed a few seconds to get my bearing and it was so bright outside compared to Shenzy's cabin.

I started walking towards the lake but my right foot seemed to have caught in the grass. Shenzy grabbed me before I fell. He helped me over to the water's edge and we sat down.

"Let's just wait here for a few minutes until you've adjusted."

"Ok." I couldn't help but smile.

"Ronnie, I don't think you should come back here. It's not safe for you." He spoke without looking at me. "And that goes for any other sightseeing trips you might be considering. You could get lost or hurt out there."

"I knew you were going to say that."

"That's because you know it's true." He turned to face me. "Will you tell me something? Why did you come out here yesterday?"

"I came to see you. But you're right. It's silly of me to think..." I paused before speaking again. "I'm just being silly."

"What do you mean?"

"I'm being silly thinking that we could be friends."

"After what happened in my bat cave, I'd think we're friends by now." He smiled at me.

"I guess you're right." I'm sure my face was beet red.

"Do you feel like you can walk now?"

"Yeah, I can."

We started walking down the path towards the house. I kept stealing glances at him trying to get an idea of what he was thinking. He didn't give anything away. I figured the best way to find out was to just ask.

"I've got a penny for your thoughts." I said with an awkward laugh.

"What?"

"It's just what someone says when they want to know what you're thinking about."

"Well, I was thinking about what happened this morning." He stopped walking and looked back towards the baobab trees. "I would be very embarrassed if Chaunce found out about that."

"Oh, so you want me to keep it a secret." I said with a questioning frown.

"I just wouldn't want him to think I was trying to take advantage of you because I wasn't."

"Well, you could just tell him that the wayward, older woman tried to seduce you last night. That would probably get you off the hook."

"That wouldn't work but he might find it funny." He laughed out loud.

I'd finally heard him laugh. It was like music and his smile made me weak in the knees. I had to look away from him for fear that I would fall where I stood. At that moment, I was completely grateful. I was grateful that Garland didn't want to be with me. I was grateful that I didn't spend my vacation in Greece. And I was grateful that I got to spend the night with him.

For the first time in my life, I thought I might have a glimpse of why my father loved my mother so much. I realized how much I liked him and that made me nervous. I started walking as if I could escape from my own thoughts. As I picked up my pace, he walked faster to catch up to me.

"You're angry about something?" He asked as he searched my face.

"Well, I don't want to be anyone's secret."

"Are you seriously comparing this situation to your past relationship?" He stopped walking and I turned to face him.

"Well, if the shoe fits..."

"Nothing could be further from the truth. You just don't understand our culture here. I don't want to dishonor you or myself."

"You didn't."

He stared at me for a moment and then started walking again. "Let's get going. You may get tired soon."

We walked on for a while in silence. I didn't want to talk about what happened at the cabin anymore but I was still curious about the lake. I wanted to know more about how they kept people away.

"So what happens if someone reaches the settlement on foot? How would you know about it?"

"There are motion sensors all around our borders. If anyone gets within a hundred miles of this valley, I'd know about it."

"That little gadget in your pocket tells you."

"It's just a hand held device that transmits data from the system at my cabin."

"So what if someone gets close?"

"We have several defense mechanisms in place. It would be very foolish for someone to approach this valley."

I didn't like the way that sounded so I decided not to ask any more questions. We continued on in silence after that. He seemed to be getting more apprehensive as we got closer to the house. When we reached the area where I knew he would stop, I turned to face him.

"Don't worry. I won't say anything. We can both just act like it never happened."

He turned to face me but I couldn't read his expression. Just when I was about to ask him about it, Shelby came running toward us.

"I'm really sorry about what happened." He turned away from me and started walking back towards the lake.

"I'm not." I said it loud enough for him to hear. He turned to glance at me for a moment and then he kept walking.

Shelby caught up to me and grabbed me around my neck. She was holding me so tightly that I was having trouble breathing. Right away I noticed that she didn't have a bandage on her forehead. It was probably healed the same day we arrived from Greece but it certainly wasn't worth mentioning now. Too much had happened.

She'd been crying and I tried my best to assure her that I was alright. We headed towards the house and I started feeling fatigued. The events of the last twenty-four hours had finally caught up with me.

Minutes later, Chaunce came down to meet us. He picked me up and carried me to the house. I told him that it wasn't necessary but he insisted. Chaunce carried me up to my room so that I could relax and that's when I noticed my new shadow. Shelby was right there beside me. When I went to get a bath, she insisted on running the water.

The bath was nice but it did little to calm my mind. All I could think about was Shenzy. The way he looked at me, the way his kiss felt on my lips and the way he touched me. It had been a while since Garland and I were together.

But Garland never made me yearn for him this way. My entire body felt like it might burn up. I leaned back in the tub and shut my eyes. I actually started to relax until I was interrupted by a knock at the bathroom door.

"Ronnie, are you alright in there?" Shelby asked.
"Yes, I'm fine. I was just finishing up."
"Ok. Well let me know if you get hungry or something."
"I will. Thanks."

I finished washing up and got out of the bathtub. I looked like a prune but I was a well rested prune. I pulled my freshly washed hair back into a ponytail and threw on a t-shirt and jean shorts.

I knew that when I got downstairs everyone would be asking a ton of questions that I didn't feel like answering. I thought it best to prepare for the onslaught. I took a deep breath, and headed down to the dining room.

When I got downstairs everyone was sitting at the table making polite conversation. Even Don was on his best behavior. I kept waiting for him to say something foolish but he didn't. Kalani came in and brought me a sandwich and some orange juice. She caught me off guard when she uncharacteristically spoke to me about something other than food.

"You gave us all quite a scare my dear." Kalani spoke quietly to me and then headed back into the kitchen.
"I'm sorry everyone. I didn't mean to be a bother." I managed a faint smile.
"I wasn't going to discuss this now but I might as well." Chaunce spoke almost in a fatherly tone. "I must ask that you not visit the lake again. I would never forgive myself if something happened to you that could not be addressed."
"I understand. You've been very gracious to allow me to stay here." I felt like a teenager being scolded for sneaking out of the house.
"We're just concerned for you my dear." Chaunce spoke softly to me.
"I know."

Shelby smiled at me and squeezed my hand under the table. And for extra fun, Don started staring at me again. I guess even his semblance of self-control fizzled away. I just ignored him. I would probably never understand what made that guy such a prick.

When we finished eating lunch, Shelby and I went out and sat in the open field. It was becoming one of my favorite places. I could see the sky and I could feel a slight breeze blowing. I leaned back on the grass and let the sunlight shine in my face. Shelby leaned back too but it was probably so she could speak quietly to me.

"Ronnie, you must be wondering why I didn't tell you about the lake before now."

"No, I get it. I mean, how do you tell somebody something like that? I understand why Don was so weird about me coming here." I sat up as I was talking.

"But this situation is special. After what happened at the airport in Greece and since you've been here, I really feel like I can trust you. We all do."

"I'm glad. After my experience at the lake, I realize how special it is. Your secret is safe with me." I laughed to myself. "I mean who would believe me anyway?"

Shelby started laughing too. But I knew it was only a matter of time before she would start asking questions.

"So what did happen out there?"

"Shenzy saved me and he took care of me." I couldn't help smiling.

"How did you fall?"

"I was looking for him on top of the cliff. I don't know what made me do something so stupid."

"He was worried for you. Because you haven't had the water in your system that long, he wasn't sure if you would heal quickly." She looked away as she spoke. "We were all worried."

"Well, not everyone. I'm sure Don was probably making some sarcastic remark when he found out." I rolled my eyes.

"You know what, I think you're right." She laughed and so did I.

"He and Shenzy are so different it's scary." I said.

"I agree." Don said from behind us.

"What are you doing sneaking up behind us? Don't you have anyone else to annoy?" Shelby said angrily.

"Well, don't the two of you have something better to do then sit around giggling like two school girls? It's really pathetic."

"Oh, I get it. You have to be aggravating because you don't have any friends of your own." I responded sarcastically.

"Well, maybe I'll make you my new friend and then I'll find out what all the fuss is about." Don barked back.

"In your dreams."

"Well, judging by your demeanor my little brother didn't seal the deal last night. You might want to spend some time with a real man." He laughed and started walking back to the house.

"Shelby…"

"Yes. You have my permission to kill him."

Shelby and I stayed out in the field a little while longer. We weren't doing a lot of talking but it was nice to just hang out together. Shelby was so easy to be around.

We were about to head back to the house, when we saw Claudia. She appeared to be heading towards the town square. I don't know if she saw us but I was glad we didn't have to talk to her. There was something about her that rubbed me the wrong way. And once Shelly told me more about her, I realized that my instincts were right.

Shelby told me about the broken engagement between Claudia and Don. The marriage was meant to bring the families together but unfortunately a rift was created that has never been healed. The worst part was the damage Claudia caused between Don and Shenzy.

"Shelby, was she involved with Shenzy too?" I asked quietly.

"That's been debatable for years. She got mad at Don for having a fling with a girl he'd met while on vacation in Italy. The next thing we know, she winds up in Shenzy's room half naked. Shenzy swore he'd gone to bed alone but Don didn't believe him."

"And let me guess, that started the tension between Don and Shenzy."

"No. That didn't start it but that didn't help the situation either. Our families have struggled a little bit but that will all change when Luca and I get married."

I saw her staring towards his house. I knew that she wanted to go and be with him but she felt the need to keep an eye on me.

"Shelby, I'm fine. You can go and see Luca. I'll probably go take a nap anyway."

"Are you sure? I feel bad leaving you."

"Shelby, you have a totally hot fiancé waiting for you. Go be with him." I motioned for her to get up.

"Ok. I'll see you later."

She gave me a quick hug and jogged off towards Luca's house. I was glad that I convinced her to go. She was off on a romantic rendezvous, and I was off for a nice afternoon under house arrest. I suppose I only had myself to blame after my last stunt, but it was worth it.

When I walked in the front door, I had every intention of going to my room and relaxing. Unfortunately, Don had other ideas.

"Ronnie, you've had a busy couple of days, right?"

"Don, what is it? I need to go and call my dad." He was blocking me from going up the stairs.

"What happened when you were out at the lake? What did my little brother tell you about us?"

"Don, I'm really tired. Please let me pass."

"Sheldon, is there a problem?" Chaunce came out of the study. He looked at Don and then at me.

"No sir. I just wanted to make sure Ronnie was alright."

"Thank you Don. But I really just want to go and rest." I stared past him as I was speaking.

"I think that's a fine idea." Chaunce turned his attention back to Don. "Sheldon, I could use your help in the study."

I would need to get Chaunce a fruit basket before I left Seulmonde. He had perfect timing. I went up to my room and shut the door behind me. I pulled the satellite phone out of my closet and turned the power on. I noticed that the voicemail light was flashing again. I cautiously hit the button and put the phone to my ear.

"Hello Ronnie, it's Garland again. I spoke to your friend Gia and she said that you've called her several times since you've been gone. I guess that means you're intentionally avoiding me but I don't know why. I just want to talk things over with you. Please call me when you get this message. I miss you. Goodbye."

I hit the power button on the phone and sat it on the nightstand next to the bed. I couldn't understand why he was still calling me. Maybe he thought that I was still in the dark. There was only one way to set him straight once and for all. I picked up the phone and dialed his number.

"Ronnie, is that you?"

"Yes, it's me Garland. What do you want?"

"Ronnie, I've been so worried about you."

"Garland, we broke up remember? You didn't want to take the next step and I did."

"Ronnie, I told you that things were complicated and they still are."

"Well, I'm happy for you. Oh, but I did want to congratulate you on your new niece and nephew."

"Ronnie, is that what you're upset about? That has nothing to do with us." He hesitated. "Ronnie, we had some good times right?"

"Yes, we did. But I'm looking for something more. I just want you to leave me alone."

"Ronnie, you're not making any sense. Where are you? Let me come and get you and we can talk this out."

"Garland, we don't have anything to talk about anymore. When I get back to the states, I'll make sure you get your phone back. Goodbye Garland."

I hung up the phone and put it away in the closet. I couldn't make any more calls. I knew how I'd sound and I didn't want to upset anybody. I just lay across the bed and covered my face with my arms. I was still digesting what had happened to me yesterday. I was tired both mentally and physically. After laying there for a while, I was somehow able to fall asleep.

Chapter 14

"Ronnie, are you in there?" Shelby called through the door.

"Shelby, come on in. I'm here." I said mostly into my pillow.

"Are you ok?" She sat down on the bed next to me. "How long have you been up here?"

"I don't know."

"Are you hungry?"

"Yeah, I am. Did you eat yet?"

"No. I just took a shower and I was on my way downstairs."

"I actually need a few minutes. Can I meet you down there?"

"Ok."

I went into the bathroom to wash up. I don't know why Garland's call bothered me so much. Maybe talking to him just reminded me of what a fool I was to let our so-called relationship drag on for so long. The good news is that it's over now. I never have to see him again and now I'm open to find a real relationship.

I headed downstairs feeling better about things at home. Now I just wanted to focus on enjoying the rest of my time here. When I got down to the dining room though, my anxiety quickly returned. Chaunce was nowhere to be found and Luca and Rocco were sitting at the dining room table. I didn't know what was going on but I had a strong feeling that Don was behind it.

He was seated at the head of the table which confirmed for me that Chaunce wouldn't be joining us. I just sat down and drank a big gulp of water. I noticed that Don was drinking too but instead of water, he was drinking champagne. I had no idea what he was celebrating but I'm sure he would think of something.

"Shelby, you didn't tell me we had dinner guests." I said trying to put a smile on my face.

"That's because I didn't know. When I came downstairs, they were here." Shelby said looking uncomfortable too.

"I decided to surprise you both. We're going to be family soon so we might as well get used to having dinner together." Don said and flashed a toothy grin.

"So where's Chaunce this evening? Isn't he joining us for dinner too?" I asked.

"No, he won't be joining us. He had to go to town for a business matter." Don added happily.

Once everyone started eating, the room was much quieter. I was hoping that it would stay that way, but I should have known I was asking too much.

"Ronnie, I hope you don't mind, I sort of invited myself along tonight." Rocco looked a little nervous. "When Don came over and invited Luca to dinner, I insisted on coming as well. I wanted to see for myself that you were alright."

"Rocco, I appreciate your concern but I'm fine." I said quietly.

"Oh, I forgot to mention that part Rocco. She spent the night at the lake with Shenzy. He nursed her back to health. Isn't that right, Ronnie?" Don spoke with a sardonic tone.

"May I use your restroom?" Rocco asked as he abruptly rose from the table. He seemed a little bothered.

"Ronnie, will you be a dear and show him the way?" Don replied.

"Of course." I got up slowly and walked toward the doorway.

Rocco followed me out of the dining room and into the foyer. We walked under the staircase and headed towards the powder room that was directly across the hall from the grand ball room.

"You didn't have to walk me out, you know. I've been in this house many times." Rocco said playfully.

"I know. I just wanted to get out of there for a minute."

"Don can be a bit much to take sometimes."

"That's an understatement. He's the only part of my visit that I haven't enjoyed; well and my accident."

"Is what he said true? Did you spend the night with Shenzy?"

"It wasn't like that." I tried to sound convincing. "He found me after I fell. I'm grateful to him for that."

"Well, in that case would you like to accompany me to the engagement party?"

"What engagement party?"

"Oh, that's right. We were talking about it before you came downstairs. Luca and Shelby are having an engagement party next Saturday night."

"Rocco, I appreciate the offer but I'm not ready to date yet. My last relationship ended right before I got here and it didn't end well."

"I understand. But let me know if you change your mind. Otherwise I might have to ask my sister to come with me."

"Ok. Well, I'm heading back to dinner."

"Ok."

I started back towards the dining room and I could feel his eyes watching me as I walked away. I really needed to have a chat with Shelby. Was I really upstairs that long that I missed the planning of an entire party? When I sat down at the table, I noticed that Don was finishing off his personal bottle of champagne. Shelby and Luca were totally engrossed in conversation. They didn't appear to notice that Don was unraveling by the minute.

When Rocco came back to the table, I decided it was a good time to excuse myself for the night. Unfortunately, my desire to leave only caught Don's attention that much sooner.

"Ronnie, where are you going? The night is young." Don spoke with slurred speech. "Let's get another bottle of champagne."

"Don, don't you think you've had enough to drink? Maybe you should go lie down." I said with a concerned tone.

"Listen to her. She even sounds like our mother." Don spoke to Shelby but looked in my direction. "Now she wants to tell me what to do. It didn't work for Maggie and it won't work for you little girl."

"Don maybe you have had enough to drink." Shelby was staring at him but he wouldn't look back at her.

"Queenie, did you ever think about why you're so drawn to her? Maybe she reminds you of Maggie too."

"Don, why don't you shut your mouth? You're making everyone uncomfortable." Shelby replied angrily.

"Perhaps Rocco and I should leave." Luca stood up and looked down at Shelby.

"That's a good idea. I'll walk you out. Ronnie, can you come with us please?" Shelby was trying to compose herself.

We all got up and left Don sitting at the table. He was pouring himself another glass of champagne as we were leaving the room. Shelby and Luca walked ahead of me. Instead of stopping in the entry way, they kept going outside. They were talking in hushed tones but I could tell they were arguing about something. Rocco and I just stood in the doorway. The awkward silence was more than I could stand.

"Rocco thanks for coming to dinner. I'm calling it a night."
"Alright. It was really nice to see you again Ronnie. Hopefully, Chaunce will be back before too long." He stared back towards the dining room as he spoke.
"I hope so too. Goodnight Rocco."
"Goodnight."

In an effort to avoid seeing Don again, I walked quietly across the foyer and ran up the stairs to my room. When I got inside, I shut the door behind me and locked it. I sat down on the bed and closed my eyes for a few seconds. I was seriously considering getting the hell out of here. It was obvious that Don didn't want me to be here and I just didn't feel comfortable around him. Lee and Gia would be happy if I came home now anyway.

Since it was still early, I decided to make some phone calls. I pulled the satellite phone out of the closet and powered it up. I was about to dial my dad's number when I heard loud voices in the hallway. I put the phone down on the bed and walked over to the door.

"Don, you have embarrassed me for the last time. Just wait until Chaunce gets back." I could hear the anger in Shelby's voice.
"You're such a drama queen. But of course you're just avoiding the real issue."

Their voices were getting farther away. But I could still hear them arguing. I opened my bedroom door just in time to see Don following Shelby into her room. He slammed the door behind him.

I didn't want to snoop but I had to know if they were talking about me. I opened my door and crept down the hall so that I could hear more clearly. I was too afraid to go all the way down the hall, so I stopped about halfway between her bedroom and mine. I could hear Don's voice loud and clear.

"What do you think is going to happen? How long do you think you can continue this charade?" Don barked.
"Why don't you just stay out of it? It's not like you care."
"I'm just stating the obvious and if you cared about her, you'd tell her the truth."
"I told you to mind your own business. I'm going to tell her when I'm ready. This has nothing to do with you."
"Is that right? Ok. When this thing blows up in your face, I'll be the one standing there saying 'I told you so'."
"You're drunk and I'm tired of this conversation."
"You know that I'm right." He came out of the room so quickly I didn't have a chance to react.
"What are you doing out here? Were you listening to us?"
"I wanted to make sure Shelby was alright."
"Of course you did." He looked up at the ceiling and then spoke out loud to no one in particular. "I'm going to bed."

He started back down the hall towards his room. I could still hear him talking to himself when he turned down the other hallway. Shelby came out of her room and saw me standing in the hall. I tried to disguise the fact that I was listening to them.

"Shelby, are you alright? I could hear your voices down the hall."
"I'm fine Ronnie. Don and I were just having a difference of opinion for the ten thousandth time."
"Do you want to talk about it?"
"No thanks. I'd rather just get some rest."
"Ok. Well, I need to call my dad before I go to sleep."
"Goodnight."
"Goodnight."

I went back to my room and shut the door. I had no idea what they were talking about and I'm not sure I wanted to know. I walked over to the bed and picked up the phone. I called Lee just as he was about to go out for a walk. We talked for just a few minutes but that was enough to help me feel a little better. He even got me to laugh.

My call with Gia was a little different. She started asking questions I didn't want to answer. When she sensed my hesitation, it just made her more curious.

"Ronnie, I feel like you're hiding stuff. You won't tell me where you are, who you're with or when you're coming home."
"Gia, I've told you everything. I'll be home next month just like I planned."
"I just hope you know what you're doing." She hesitated for a moment. "But if that guy comes by here one more time, I'm gonna scream."
"You mean Jim?"
"Yes. He came by yesterday afternoon. The worst part is he just comes out of nowhere. I never see what he's driving."
"Really?"
"Yes really. I'd like to get a license plate or something but I never have the chance. Ronnie, I'm starting to think that there's more going on with that guy than you're telling me."
"I can't sneak anything past you, right?" I tried to sound amusing. I don't think it worked. Gia knew me too well. "Gia there's no big conspiracy. He's just a guy and he's a non-issue. You'll see when I get back."
"If you say so. Well, I'm gonna go. I have to get back to work. Call me in a few days, ok?"   "I will. You be good. Goodbye."
"Bye."

I hung up with Gia and put the satellite phone back in the closet. I felt like I was still dating Garland. It just didn't make sense to me that he kept dropping by Gia's place and asking her questions about me. Hopefully, our last chat was enough to make him go away quietly.

As usual, thinking about Garland always led to thoughts of Shenzy and that was pointless too. I didn't know if I'd see Shenzy again at the lake. I was feeling better but I knew that Chaunce was serious when he told me to stay at the house. I lay on the bed and drifted between restlessness and boredom until I finally drifted off to sleep.

That next morning, I didn't get out of bed right away. I just stared up at the ceiling trying to make sense of my thoughts. My first thoughts were of course about Shenzy. But I also couldn't forget about the argument between Don and Shelby last night. It was obvious they were talking about me. I considered asking Shelby about it but a part of me was afraid to. If there was one thing I knew about Seulmonde, there were certainly a lot of secrets here.

I showered quickly and got dressed. When I came downstairs to breakfast, the only person there was Shelby. She didn't appear to have gotten much sleep which I found odd. We ate pretty much in silence and I worked hard to relax. I kept expecting Don to burst into the room but he never did. I was drinking the last of my orange juice when Shelby finally spoke to me.

"Ronnie, I need to talk to you about something. I don't know how you'll take it but it needs to be said. Can you come up to my room for a few minutes?"
"Sure. Do you want to do it now?"
"Yes. I do."

She got up from the table leaving most of her breakfast behind. My anxiety began to build as I followed her upstairs. When we walked inside, she closed the door behind me. She offered me a chair next to the bed and then she sat down in her chaise. Her face looked really sad and I could tell she was having a hard time with what she was about to say.

"Ronnie, there's something else you need to know about the lake and the people who live here. I know you've experienced the healing properties of the fountain first hand. But there's another side effect of drinking the water."
"What do you mean side effect? Is there something wrong with me now because I drank the water?"

"No, nothing's wrong. Just hear me out. After drinking the water for some length of time, the aging process is interrupted. We've seen regression in some cases but not many."

"Regression? What are you talking about?"

"We don't age." She looked at my face to discern my reaction. "At least not entirely."

"What do you mean you don't age? Everybody gets old. There's no way to avoid it."

"We have found a way. I know it sounds incredible but it's true."

"So how old are you exactly?"

"We don't really count in years. We count in cycles."

"Cycles? So how many cycles have you lived?"

"Almost three." She hesitated before speaking again. "One cycle equals twenty-five years."

"I don't believe you." I stood up almost as a reflex. "Why are you saying this?" I thought it had to be a joke but she was serious.

"Ronnie, I know this is a lot to take in." Shelby stood up and started toward me. I moved back against the wall so she returned to her chaise. "Ronnie, I have proof if you don't believe me."

She claimed to have a copy of her birth certificate that would prove her age. It was down in Chaunce's study and all I needed to do was follow her downstairs. I was pretty numb but I agreed. What else could I do?

When I came into the room, Shelly had exposed a safe situated behind a book shelf. I'd never seen a secret compartment like that. When she closed the shelf, it looked like any other book shelf in the study. She was holding the birth certificate in her free hand. She motioned towards the sofa in hopes that I would sit down. I wasn't in the mood to sit so she sat down instead.

"There's one more thing," she said cautiously.

"Let me guess, Peter Pan is your first cousin?"

"No, it's about Chaunce." She hesitated before speaking again. "He's not just my guardian; he's my father."

"Your father?" I walked into the far corner of the room across from the doorway. It was the farthest point from where she was sitting.

"I'll give you a minute." She placed her birth certificate on the desk and walked out of the room.

I walked over to the desk and picked up the certificate. I just stood there staring at it. Either it was a brilliant fraud or she was telling the truth. I didn't know what to say. I just sat the page down on the desk.

I felt my hands shaking. I was afraid but I didn't know of what. The people of Seulmonde were still regular people; they just lived a lot longer than the rest of us.

I panicked; I walked as quickly as I could out of the study and headed for the stairs. By the time I made it to my room, my heart felt like it was beating out of my chest. I just couldn't wrap my mind around what Shelby had just shown me.

I locked the door and went to sit in the window. I just stared out at the bright blue sky thinking about how safe it usually made me feel. But there was no comfort for me. I thought if I pinched myself maybe I would wake up. But this was no dream. I was wide awake and scared silly.

For all intents and purposes, I was thousands of miles away from anything remotely familiar. I didn't even know how to leave. I tried to comfort myself in the idea that I wasn't in any danger. But the picture was now crystal clear about just how secret this place was. Shenzy mentioned that they had ways of keeping people out.

And just that quickly, I knew what to do. I had to see Shenzy. But how could I get to the lake? They were never going to let me go there now. I would just have to wait for the opportunity to present itself. I sat there in the window for about an hour and a half.

Nobody bothered me so I started to relax a little. The only issue was that I was getting hungry. Before I could start to panic, I heard a light knock at the door.

"Who is it?" I said with a shaky voice. But no one answered. I tiptoed over to the door and put my ear to it. I listened for a few seconds but I didn't hear anyone.

I unlocked the door and slowly opened it enough to stick my head out. I didn't see anyone so I started to shut the door. Right before I closed it, I saw the food tray on the floor in front of the door. I picked it up and quickly closed the door again.

I put the tray down on the bed and took the cover off. There were two grilled cheese sandwiches and some apple sauce on the plate.

There was also a small carton of orange juice. "What am I seven years old?"

I guess compared to the people on this island it must have seemed that way. And I was way too hungry to complain. When I finished eating, I put the tray on the floor and sat down on the bed. I leaned back and stared at the ceiling. I immediately thought about Shelby. I tried to think of the situation from her perspective. She took a big risk bringing me here.

She could have just left me in Greece to fend for myself. That's certainly what Don had in mind. Who could blame him? They had no idea who I would tell once I finally got home. After my reaction, would they let me leave? I had no idea. A sudden knock at the door would bring answers to all of my questions.

"Who is it?" I said with a small voice.
"It's Chaunce." He paused as if he was about to say something else but he didn't.
"Come in." I got up off the bed and moved back to my place by the window.

As usual, he came into the room and remained standing near the door. But this time he did shut it quietly behind him. The look on his face was one of sadness. I found it hard to keep hold of the fear I had felt so completely only moments ago.

"Ronnie, I'm so sorry that you had to learn about our…" He hesitated before speaking again. "…longevity without my being here. You must be very confused and frightened."

"Yes, I am."

"Let me start by saying that your reaction is understandable. We don't normally interact with the outside world for that very reason. We know that our existence depends on our ability to remain hidden."

"I just don't understand how it's possible. I mean, if I wasn't healed by the water myself, I wouldn't have believed it."

"Ronnie, the fountain water somehow reverses any form of damage to human cells, thereby preventing aging and death."

"You make it sound so simple." It was starting to make sense but I had more questions. "So if you're old when you drink the water, will you become young again?"

"The answer to that question is complicated. If a person repeatedly consumes water directly from the fountain, their body will start to regress meaning they will look younger. This is not a practice of ours because we have not discovered a way to control the rate of regression. There can be negative effects as well."

"Like what?"

"Well, adolescents aren't permitted to drink from the fountain until they have completed the first cycle of their lives. And women who are with child aren't allowed to drink either. Nature has certain fundamental processes that we cannot disturb. When we violate these laws, there have been catastrophic results."

"So what will happen to me? Shenzy gave me fountain water to heal me."

"You're perfectly fine. But you probably won't need a flu shot this year." He smiled but it didn't reach his eyes.

"Do you have any special abilities from drinking the water?"

"Ronnie, the effects of the water are not supernatural. They are biological. Heightened physical strength, agility and intellect are attainable but they must be cultivated."

"That's interesting."

"The fountain can make you better. But it also gives you time to be more of what you are."

I looked out the window as a thought suddenly occurred to me. I didn't want Chaunce to see my face.

"Are you thinking about your mother? The answer is yes. The fountain probably could have saved her. But Ronnie, there is a delicate balance to nature. There is a balance to the world. Can you imagine what would happen if we tried to save every person on earth from sickness and old age? The world would run out of resources within two generations."

"Is that why you let your wife die?" I asked without thinking.

"My wife didn't die Ronnie." He walked over to sit on the bed. I couldn't see his face.

"She left on her own about twelve years ago. You see, she wasn't born here. She'd fled Ireland with her brothers in the 1920's during the Irish Civil war. They were accompanied by about twenty other brave souls sailing around the Cape of Agulhas on the clipper route."

"They ran into a storm and their ship was badly damaged. They made it to the island but many men were lost including her two brothers. When the survivors happened upon our valley, she decided to stay. I fell in love with her almost immediately. It took her a little while to warm up to our way of life though."

He turned to smile at me. "We were happy for a long time. We had three beautiful children together. But about fifteen years ago, she became sad. She said that we weren't meant to cheat death and she was ready to join her brothers. We built a small vessel for her and she sailed towards Ireland."

"So you have no idea where she is?"

"When she first left, I assumed that she would perish at sea. It seemed to be what she wanted."

"What about the rest of your family? Where are they?"

"They are scattered around the world. My parents decided to leave after Shenzy was born. With my father's duty fulfilled, he wanted to lead a normal life outside of Seulmonde."

"Does that happen a lot?"

"It happens often enough. We don't have a population problem here but we might one day."

I was trying to process everything Chaunce had told me. I just couldn't help thinking about his wife. She'd left of her own free will which must have been so difficult for him to accept.

"Well Ronnie, I hope you're feeling a little better about all of this. I'll give you some time to yourself." He reached down and picked up my lunch tray.

"Thanks for taking the time to talk to me. I think I will lie down for a little while."

"That's a fine idea." He walked towards the door. When he opened it, he smiled over his shoulder at me and then closed the door behind him.

As soon as he left, I started to think about how I could get out of the house without anyone seeing me. I knew that going downstairs was out of the question. I remembered that Shenzy's bedroom was at the back of the house and suddenly I had an idea. I grabbed the blankets off my bed and walked over to the door. I opened it very slowly and looked in both directions. It sounded like everyone was downstairs.

I went out into the hall and practically ran down to Shenzy's bedroom. I went inside and closed the door behind me. I put my blankets down on the dresser and went over to his bed to get his. I was momentarily thrown off track by thoughts of him asleep in bed. I picked up his pillow and put it up to my nose. I inhaled deeply. If I pulled this off, I would be experiencing the real thing soon enough.

I grabbed the blankets off the dresser and put them all in a pile on the floor. I connected the blankets end to end making sure they were triple tied and secure. I opened the window closest to the dresser to take a look at how far down I had to go.

I picked up one end of the blanket rope and tied it to the bottom post of Shenzy's huge four poster bed. I picked up the rest of the blankets and draped them out of the window. The length ran down the side of the house with plenty to spare at the bottom.

I said a quick prayer to myself and crawled out onto the window ledge. I kneeled down and got a good grip onto the blanket rope. I started to climb down the wall very slowly. I tried not to think about the cliff at the lake.

When I made it to the ground, I felt a huge wave of relief flow over me. But just as quickly, I felt a rush of fear that someone would see me. I broke into a sprint across the back lawn. I scaled the stone fence and headed for the path.

Chapter 15

When I arrived at the lake, I was once again taken in by its beauty.
But I also had the memory of my fall. I tried to put it out of my mind
as I looked around for Shenzy. I didn't know how to find his cabin,
so I decided to sit down and wait for him to show up. But after a few
minutes of waiting, the allure of the water was more than I could
resist. I took off my shoes, rolled up my pant legs and started walking
towards the water. I froze when I heard his voice behind me.

"I was wondering when you would get here." Shenzy spoke with a
playful tone.
"You were expecting me?" I turned to face him a little surprised.
He was wearing a pair of cargo shorts and an Alphaville T-shirt that
read 'Forever Young' across the front.
"Nice t-shirt. So it's good to know you have a sense of humor."
He just smiled at me and shook his head.

"So how did you know I was coming?"
"Don told me. I asked him to wait a little while before he came to
bring you back."
"Why did you tell him that?"
"Because I wanted to talk to you; I wanted to make sure you were
alright." His mood suddenly turned serious.
"I'm fine. I mean I just found out that everybody here has a big
secret. I don't know what to make of it."
"Why do you have to make anything of it? There's nothing different
except for your perception."

He looked away from me and started walking around the edge of the
lake. I knew where he was headed but I wanted to stay where I was.

When he'd gotten about half way to the cliff, I willed myself to follow him. I would be safe with him there. When I reached the back side of the cliff, he was leaning against it with what looked like a belt in his hand.

"It certainly took you long enough," he said with a smile.
"You didn't ask me to follow you."
"Come here. I want to show you something."

I felt my pulse quickening as I walked toward him. When I was in arms reach, he grabbed me by my waist and wrapped his arms around me. It took me a few seconds to realize that he was attaching the belt around my waist. He turned his back to me and grabbed a rope that was hanging from the side of the cliff. I hadn't even noticed it was there. He attached the belt around my waist to the rope.

"This will keep you from killing yourself. Come on."
"You expect me to climb up there after what happened to me?"
"Ronnie, I won't let you get hurt." He looked at me intently. "Do you trust me?"
"Yes, I do."
"Alright. Let's go." He gave me a wide grin.

Shenzy showed me how to start climbing while adjusting the rope. It took longer for me to take each step but I did feel more secure. He was also waiting at the bottom just in case I slipped. When I reached the top, I signaled to him. He seemed to be standing next to me in mere seconds. I'm sure he'd climbed this cliff a thousand times before so I wasn't impressed with his climbing ability. Or at least that's what I told him.

"So why are we up here, anyway?"
"I wanted to show you the rope and I like the view." Shenzy stared out over the lake.
"Oh, well how do I get down?"
"I'm going to show you. That will be lesson number two for today."
"So now you're my teacher?"

"Something like that."

"Can I ask you a question?"

"Technically you just did. But go ahead."

"How old are you?"

"How old are you?" He asked and looked at me with one raised eyebrow.

"I asked you first."

"I'm asking you now." He paused before continuing. "Why does it matter so much?"

"Oh, forget it. You're obviously not going to tell me." My voice came out a few octaves higher than I wanted it to.

"Yeah, you're probably right."

I sat down on the edge of the cliff facing the water. Shenzy came over and sat down next to me. It really was a breathtaking view of the lake and the giant baobab trees. I couldn't imagine myself getting tired of it.

"So I hear you have an admirer." Shenzy didn't look at me as he spoke.

"Who told you that? Luca and Rocco came for dinner. That's all."

"So do you like him?"

"Yeah, he's nice." I paused before speaking again. "But I don't like him the way I like you."

He finally turned around to look at me. I couldn't tell by his expression what he was thinking but he abruptly got up and walked to the other side of the cliff.

"You know, Rocco is a pretty nice guy." Shenzy spoke over his shoulder.

"If you think so maybe you should date him."

"Where did that come from?"

"I just told you that I liked you and you bring up some other guy."

"Well, what do you expect me to say?"

"I don't know Shenzy. I wouldn't want to put words in your mouth."

"Ronnie, you don't understand." He turned away from me. "My life is complicated."

"Well, I've heard that before." I stood up and stared at the lake below. "I shouldn't have come out here."

I suddenly felt a twinge of embarrassment. I guess I read too much into what happened in his cabin. I was ready to go back to the house and I didn't feel like climbing down the cliff at a snail's pace. I quietly removed the belt from around my waist and let it slip from my hand.

"How deep is this lake?" I asked.
"It's pretty deep in the middle. Why do you ask?" Shenzy still had his back to me.

Before I could give him a chance to catch on, I jumped off the cliff into the lake. As soon as I hit the water, I felt an exhilarating rush of effervescence all over my body. I was under the water for only a few seconds but as soon as I came up, I could hear Shenzy calling my name. I started swimming towards the shore when I heard him enter the water not far from where I landed.

I stopped swimming about twenty feet from the shore where the water was about waist deep. When I stood up, I could see Shenzy approaching me and he didn't look happy. I tried to ignore the sensations I was feeling from the water so that I could deal with him.

"Ronnie, why did you jump? Are you losing your mind?"
"Yeah, I guess I am. That's my secret."
"Well, I have a secret too."

Before I could say anything, he grabbed me around my waist and covered my mouth with his. He kissed me so passionately that it took me a few seconds to get over the shock. In that one instant, he'd confessed to me what he couldn't say up to that point.

I put my arms around his neck and held him as tightly as I could. He'd taken off his t-shirt before he jumped in the water which only added to my enthusiasm. We were both starting to breath heavily and I could feel his excitement building. I ran my hands through his hair and caressed his neck. I relished in the feeling of his lips on mine as he moved his hands up and down my body.

After several intense moments, I felt him start to pull away from me. He was trying to do the honorable thing but I had other plans. I pulled my tank top over my head and let it fall into the water. He looked like he was torn between what he thought he should do and what his body wanted.

I decided to help him with his decision so I moved towards him. He stayed where he was but he shut his eyes. I reached out my hand and gently touched his face. Then I put my hand around his neck and pulled his face to meet mine. He kissed me very tenderly. I couldn't decide which one of his kisses I enjoyed the most.

He reached down and grabbed both my legs and I wrapped them around his waist. Our skin on skin contact excited me to no end. I could feel the hard lines of his stomach against mine. He started kissing my cheek and then he trailed down to my neck. The intensity between us was undeniable.

He found my mouth again and our passionate kiss served as a prelude to something we both wanted. If we were the only people on earth at that moment, it would have been fine with me. Unfortunately, we weren't alone. Don was standing on the shore watching us.

I felt Shenzy's body tense and he let go of my legs. He turned me around so that his body was between me and Don. Then I remembered that I wasn't wearing my tank top and I had no idea where it was. Shenzy started looking for it all around us in the water. Finally he found it where it was floating a few feet from us. He wrung it out for me and I slipped it over my head.

"Please don't stop on my account. It was just getting good." Don said with a sarcastic smile.

"I am beyond embarrassed." I said under my breath.

"Why? Are you ashamed of me?" Shenzy replied almost in a whisper.

"Of course not." I started walking towards the shore but then I stopped and turned to him. "You said you had another secret. What is it?"

"I don't want you to go out with Rocco; even if he asks you nicely."

"Then I won't." I said as I started walking away.

This was the second time I'd made out with him. And this time was even better than when we were in his cabin. I think it was safe to assume that we liked each other. I didn't know what that meant and I certainly wasn't going to ruin it by over thinking it.

I walked past Don without looking at him. I didn't want to contemplate how awful the walk back to the house would be. I picked up my track shoes and just carried them in my hands. The path was smooth enough that I didn't really need to wear them. I walked quickly hoping that he would let me walk ahead without trying to talk to me; no such luck.

"Well, you might be uncomfortable around the rest of us but you certainly aren't afraid of my baby brother."

"Captain obvious strikes again."

"So you admit it. Just what do you see happening between the two of you?"

"Why do you care?"

"I'm just asking. Is it so wrong for me to want to know what your intentions are?"

"Don, I'm not answering any more of your questions."

"You must really like him to rappel down the side of the house like that. I thought it was pretty funny but Chaunce was less amused."

I ignored him for the rest of the walk back to the house. It still took him a few minutes to shut up but finally he did. As we got closer to the house, I started to get nervous. What if Chaunce really was angry with me? He might send me away and that was exactly what I didn't want to happen.

As we neared the house, I tried to calm myself. After the way I'd snuck out, I shouldn't be surprised by anything Chaunce said. I walked inside the gate and into the front door. The light was on in the study so I assumed Chaunce might be in there working.

I quietly walked across the foyer and started up the stairs. It reminded me of when I was a teenager and I was trying to sneak past my dad. It never worked then and it didn't work now.

"Ronnie, is that you?" Chaunce called to me from inside the study. "Yes, it's me."
"Can I speak with you?"
"Sure."

I already knew what he was going to say. Listening to the disappointment in his voice was hard enough. But the look on his face was the worst part. I felt embarrassed that he needed to have this conversation with me again. I knew that he was concerned about my well-being.

When we were done talking, I slowly walked out of the study and headed up the stairs. I had so many thoughts running through my head. And even though Chaunce was probably ready to blindfold me and put me on the next plane, I couldn't help relishing in the time I'd spent with Shenzy. I knew that he liked me and that made me very happy. I didn't know when I'd see him again, but I wouldn't worry about that now.

I went into my room and took off my wet clothes. I put them in the sink and hopped in the shower. As the water washed over me, I thought about the lake. And when I closed my eyes, Shenzy's face appeared in my mind. His smile was all I needed to brighten my day. And for the rest of my vacation, I would spend as much time with him as I could.

I'd just finished getting dressed when there was a knock at the door. "Who is it?" I asked.

"It's me. Do you mind if I come in?" Shelby sounded nervous as she spoke through the door.

"Come on in." I went over and sat down in the window seat.

"Hey, I wanted to see how you were doing." She sat down on the bed closest to the door.

"I'm fine, really. I just needed a chance to take it all in."

"I understand." She stopped talking but I could tell she wanted to say more. She glanced at me quickly and then looked down at her hands. "I wanted to find out if you were still comfortable with staying."

"Yes, I am. And I appreciate your concern. I just hope I'm still welcome here after today."

She tried to hide her amusement. "I didn't know what to expect when Kalani said that the sheets were missing from your bed. We had no idea that you'd escaped out of an upstairs window."

"I don't know what I was thinking. Chaunce was so angry with me. I thought he would ask me to leave."

"I don't think you have that to worry about." She lowered her voice before she spoke again. "Don't tell him I said so, but he couldn't stop laughing when he heard."

"Really?"

"Yes. Don offered to go look for you. We had a good idea where you'd end up."

"I really wanted to talk to Shenzy. But I promised Chaunce that I wouldn't go to the lake again and I meant it."

"Ronnie, I know that you like each other but your safety has to come first."

"I realize that." I looked out the window not wanting to face the reality of what she was saying.

"Ronnie, I just want you to know that you have nothing to fear from us."

I stared at her intently for a moment. "But there's something you're not telling me."

"Well, you know that Luca and I are having an engagement party. I wanted to get it out of the way."

151

"Alright. That sounds reasonable."

"Well, we're going to have it here at the house next Saturday. I wanted to make sure you were comfortable."

"You mean so I don't make a fool of myself."

"Well, that too." She said and smiled at me. "I just want you to become a little more familiar with our customs."

"That actually sounds like a good idea."

"Ronnie, I'm really glad you're staying." She smiled at me and got up off the bed. "Well, I'll give you some time to yourself."

"Alright. I'll see you in a bit."

She left the room and headed downstairs. I was really glad that she came up to talk to me. All in all, Shelby was a lot like me. There were times she seemed unsure of herself and times when she just needed a friend. She'd told me things she hadn't told anyone else. I'd told her things too. We were friends and as strange as this place was, I didn't want to leave right now.

Since I wasn't going downstairs yet, I kicked off my shoes and lay across the bed. I started thinking about Shelby's party. I would see all of the people who were affected by the fountain in one room. I'd have no idea who was a twenty something post adolescent and who was a grandmother in her seventies. I'll just smile a lot and not ask questions.

I was caught up in my thoughts when there was a knock at the door.

"Come in," I said expecting to see Shelby.

"Ronnie, how are you?" Don chided.

He came into the bedroom and sat down on the bed. I immediately walked back to the window to put some space between us.

"Don, can I help you with something?" I refused to look at him.

"Actually, I was hoping I could do something for you." He looked at me in a way that made me uncomfortable. "With the party on Saturday, I realized you don't have anything to wear."

"Well, that's true. I haven't had time to think about a dress."

"You don't need a dress dear girl, you need a gown. And as a peace offering, I'd like to get one for you. What do you say?"

"Don, that's very kind of you. But where are you going to get a gown for me?"

"Don't you worry yourself. I just wanted to make sure you were on board before I made the effort."

"Thank you Don. I appreciate your help and I'd like us to get along better."

"Then it's settled. I'll have it for you in a day or two."

He stood up and quickly left the room. I felt some relief but also confusion. What would suddenly cause him to have a change of heart? I couldn't be sure. But with Shelby making me her maid-of-honor, I needed to make a good impression. I'd have to accept that maybe he was trying. Shelby's marriage was a good reason to make a change.

If Don could try harder, then so could I. I would start at dinner tonight. I pulled on my shoes and headed for the door. When I got downstairs, Shelby, Don and Chaunce were already in the dining room. I sat down and joined in on the conversation. After a few minutes, Kalani started serving a delicious shrimp dinner. I started eating and was once again surprised when she spoke to me.

"Ronnie, I'm so glad to see that you're alright." She whispered to me as she filled my plate.

"Thanks Kalani. I'm fine." I tried to give her a reassuring smile.

When we finished eating, we all went into the study to review Shelby's party notes. I was glad that the focus wasn't on me anymore. Shelby perked up as each detail was discussed. I pictured her as a wife and mother and the thought made me smile.

"Ronnie, there is one special matter we need to address," Shelby said matter-of-factly.

"What's that?"

"There is a traditional dance that takes place as part of the celebration." Shelby glanced around the room. "And we have just enough people to practice."

"We do?" Don asked.

"Yes, we do." Chaunce replied quickly.

"Alright, let's go to the ballroom." Shelby practically skipped out into the hall.

We all followed her out the door and down the hall to the ballroom. This was my second visit to the ballroom and it overwhelmed me once again. The room was shaped like a large rectangle with two gigantic crystal chandeliers hanging from the vaulted ceiling. The marble floor was a true complement to the antique white walls and the large columns that stood in the far corners of the room. The crushed velvet draperies were pulled aside filling the room with the light of the setting sun.

Shelby didn't seem to be affected by the beauty of it. She'd probably been in this room more times than she could remember. She turned on the overhead lights and switched on the compact disc player that rested on a high table in the corner. She'd selected a whimsical melody that I'd never heard before but I liked it.

Shelby joined the rest of us in the middle of the room. We assumed the first position and I watched carefully to see what movements Shelby was making. Chaunce stood next to Shelby and Don stood next to me. She looped her arm into Chaunce's and Don reached for my arm. After we repeated the dance steps a few times, I was able to do them without staring at my feet.

We kept in rhythm with the music and turned to face each other. I was trying hard to ignore the look of indifference on Don's face and I hoped that I wouldn't have to look at it much longer. When we finished the pattern for the fourth time, I got my wish. Shelby and I changed dance partners.

As soon as Chaunce took my hand, he beamed at me with a kind and playful smile. I smiled back at him. The more I stared at him, the more he reminded me of Shenzy. A little twinge of pain etched in my chest. I tried to laugh through it but it was still there. Even though I enjoyed the dancing, I was glad when it was over.

Shelby switched off the music but she continued to practice a few steps. Chaunce excused himself and headed back to his study. Don mumbled something about an appointment and he slipped out of the room. Shelby started talking to me about where the guests would come in and where they would be standing. I tried to pay attention because I knew she was really excited. I guess I wasn't doing a very good job because after a few minutes she brought the conversation to a close and started turning off the lights.

"Hey Shelby, do you think Shenzy will come to the party?"
"I'm not sure. I'd like him to come and I know you want him there."
She got quiet again. Her facial expression changed from excitement to concern. "I'm sorry Ronnie. I've just been going on and on. I haven't even asked you how you're doing."
"I'm alright. I was just wondering when I'd see him again. I feel so at ease when I'm around him."
"I understand. Shenzy is a sweetheart and I'm not just saying that because he's my brother."
"Well, I'm heading upstairs to get some sleep."

I excused myself and headed upstairs to my room. I had a feeling that Shelby might visit with Luca tonight and I didn't want to dampen her spirits. I went into my room and actually put on a nightgown. I was just about to climb into bed when I heard laughter in the hallway. I went to the door and put my ear against it. It didn't sound like Shelby and I couldn't imagine who else it could be.

I slowly opened the door and walked down the hall. When I got to Shelby's room, I noticed that she wasn't there. I kept walking until I reached the adjacent hallway. I peeped around the corner to see a blond girl walking next to Don. I couldn't be sure but she looked a lot like Mira; the young woman I saw in town. She was laughing at Don and shaking her head. When she turned to face him in the doorway, I got a good look at her. It was definitely Mira.

He started talking in her ear and she nodded slowly. But right before he pulled her into the room, he kissed her forehead. I ducked my head back around the corner and walked towards my room. I'd seen more than I needed to.

I went to my room and got in bed. I tried to focus on Shenzy instead of what Don was doing in his bed room. I tried to imagine Shenzy's eyes staring at me; through me. And within minutes, I was asleep.

Chapter 16

The next few days went by in a blur. I didn't even chance a trip to the lake so I just tried to keep myself busy with Shelby. I understood that they were concerned for my safety but it was getting ridiculous. I mean, what was safer for me than to be with Shenzy? Or maybe that was the problem. I was distracting him from what he was supposed to be doing. I knew it was an argument that I wouldn't win so I decided not to have it.

Shelby had reviewed the details of the party until they were air tight, and then she turned her attention to me. I suppose she worried that I might freak out at the party because of what I'd just found out. I told her that I was fine; at least I thought I was.

She just stressed that she wanted me to be comfortable. The main facet of my comfort was in her opinion, the guests. She wanted to prepare me for who I would be meeting. Because of the youthful inclination of practically everyone, it would not be easy to identify the heads of each family.

She reminded me of the Tew's that I had met a few days after I arrived. But what I didn't know at the time was that Ruth and Fenton were the parents. And when I thought back to that night, I remembered that they never explained how they were all related. In the coming days, I would probably have more moments with details coming together that didn't make sense before.

When Saturday finally arrived, I was surprised at how relaxed everyone was. When we sat down to eat breakfast, I might have thought it was any other day. I didn't have much of an appetite but I didn't want anyone to know. I thought they might get the wrong idea about why I was feeling uneasy.

I was actually worried about fitting into the dress that Don got for me. And that was partly because I hadn't seen it yet. I decided to nonchalantly bring it up.

"Don, I was wondering if you could give me a little hint about the dress. I'm just so curious." I tried not to sound accusing. "Relax Ronnie. You're going to be the most beautiful girl there, well, next to my sister of course." He smiled but never moved his attention from his breakfast.

I didn't trust him as far as I could throw him so I decided on a back-up plan. I would borrow something of Shelby's in case Don didn't come through. We finished eating breakfast and everyone seemed to scatter.

Don and Chaunce went into the study to talk about some business matters. Shelby said she was going to Luca's house and invited me to come along. I declined, opting instead to do some personal grooming.

I went upstairs to my room and pulled my makeup bag out of the closet. I got a little nervous thinking about how I would do my hair and makeup. Without Gia, I was almost helpless. I decided to focus on what I could handle on my own.

I changed my nail polish, shaved my legs and cleaned my face with Gia's homemade facial scrub. I was having a true girly moment all by myself. And before I knew it, I ran out of things to do. I decided to go and see if I could help Kalani with anything.

As usual, she was happy for the extra pair of hands. I found her in the ballroom setting up candles on the tables. Chaunce was supervising a small group of volunteers who came to help arrange the tables and chairs. Don was supposed to be helping too but he was missing in action. Wherever he was, I hoped he was getting my dress. We worked efficiently for the next few hours. Chaunce's group even set up the buffet tables.

It was early afternoon when we finished. Kalani just made us some sandwiches because it was the quickest thing to make and we were hungry. Don came strolling into the dining room and sat down. Chaunce looked at him with a questioning stare but he pretended not to notice. I just shook my head and kept eating. When I was done, I headed upstairs to my room to rest.

I didn't realize it at first, but helping set up the ballroom took a lot out of me. I figured with the party tonight, I better take a quick nap. I definitely wanted to be at my best. I took off my shoes and lay across the bed. Within minutes, I was asleep.

I awoke to a knock at the door. It took me a few minutes to realize that the sun had gone down. I wondered how long I'd been asleep.

"Who is it?" I asked with a sleepy voice.
"Ronnie, it's me. Can I come in?" Don said almost in a whisper.
"Sure. Come on in." I quickly sat up on the bed.

Don walked in with a long garment bag. He hung it in the closet and walked over to sit on the bed next to me. A few seconds later, Mira walked into the room carrying a large, brown bag. Before I had a chance to ask any questions, he started talking.

"Ronnie, I have your dress. We don't have a lot of time so we need to make this quick." He pointed at Mira and she waived at me. "She's going to help you with your hair and makeup."
"Are you serious? I don't know what to say." I was so relieved. I'd thought so many bad things about Don and now I would have to take them back.
"I know. You can thank me later. But right now, you need to get ready. The guests have already started to arrive."

And just like that, he was gone. I was sitting there waiting for instructions. Mira picked up the bag and placed it on the dresser. She started removing the contents of the bag and setting them up on the dresser.

"You might want to go and get a quick shower. If you shower after we're done, we'll have to start over."
"Alright. I'll be right back."

I practically ran into the bathroom. I didn't want to leave her alone for too long for fear she might wander off. I brushed my teeth and showered quickly. When I came out of the bathroom, she was sitting at the edge of the bed smoothing the makeup brushes.

"Ok, let's get started." She smiled at me and motioned for me to sit where she'd sat a moment ago.
"Pardon my rudeness, but how do you know Don?" I asked quietly.
"We're friends." She said as she started applying my makeup. "I work at the school and I see Don when I can."
"What do you mean?"
"You know what I mean." She smiled at me and shook her head.
"Do you want your hair up or down?"
"What do you suggest?" I really didn't have a preference.
"I think definitely up."
"Ok. Up it is."

She finished my makeup and moved on to my hair. And for some reason, I started thinking about last night when I saw her outside Don's bedroom. I couldn't understand why so many girls were willing to give themselves to him so freely. I must be missing something.

"Ok. There you are; pretty as a picture." She handed me the mirror she'd taken from her bag.
"Mira, I don't know how to thank you. It's lovely."
"You're very welcome. Don told me how important this night was. I know how it feels to want to make a good impression."

She grabbed all of her makeup and hair accessories and packed them into her bag. Then she winked her eye at me and headed out the door. Once she was gone, I ran to the door and locked it. I grabbed the garment bag out of the closet and put it on the bed. I unzipped it and pulled out the gown. It was absolutely beautiful. The full length, white, taffeta gown was covered with beading and an intricate flower pattern. It was also strapless which I loved.

I gently pulled the gown on and zipped it up on the left side. It fit perfectly. The sweetheart neckline and natural waist complemented my figure. I picked up the garment bag to put it away and a square box fell out of it. I picked it up and hung the garment bag in the closet. When I opened the box, I couldn't believe my eyes. There was a gold and diamond necklace inside with a small piece of paper. I sat the box down and read Don's hand written note.

Dear Ronnie,

I hope you enjoy tonight and maybe this will help. It's just a loaner so don't get too carried away. It's worth more than you know.

Hugs, Don

I put down the note and picked up the necklace. Then I went into the bathroom and put it on. It was stunning. I looked at myself in the mirror and was almost moved to tears. I'd never felt more beautiful than I did at that moment. I took a few deep breaths to calm down because I didn't want to ruin my makeup. I walked back into the bedroom and put on my shoes. I was finally ready to go to the party.

I headed downstairs to a quiet house. Everyone was in the ballroom. I hoped that Shelby wasn't upset that I was late. When I reached the ballroom doors, I stopped and took a deep breath. I tried not to think about how everyone in the room would be staring at me. But nothing could have prepared me for what I saw when I walked inside.

I opened the door and walked full speed into the room. I was looking around for Shelby and that's when I saw the unthinkable. Everyone in the room was dressed in black. The women were wearing dresses and gowns of all shapes and sizes. But the one common thread was the color. As people started to notice me, I heard several gasps of shock at my apparent ignorance of the customary hue. It took a few moments for me to find Shelby's face. The look she had was a mix of shock and pity.

Then my eyes found Chaunce. He was furious. It was obvious that this little gown trick was an attempt by Don to either humiliate me, to be humorous or some combination of both. As my private terror mounted, I became fixed where I stood. I wanted to run from the room but I couldn't. I tried to look away from everyone but two familiar faces caught my attention. I noticed the shocked faces of Claudia and Ariana Tew as they stood by the bar.

I looked down at the floor and wondered how I could get out of this predicament. I heard the door to the ballroom open and close and I couldn't help but turn around. Shenzy was standing behind me with a playful grin on his face. But it wasn't just his smile that lightened my mood. He came and stood next to me wearing a light gray tuxedo with a white shirt and tie. He looked like a Calvin Klein model.

In a room full of black tuxes and LBDs, we stood out entirely. The icing on the cake was when he asked me to dance. I was so happy to see him that I gladly obliged. He took my hand and led me towards the open floor. We started dancing slowly as the music dictated.

"You look beautiful." Shenzy whispered in my ear.
"So do you." I whispered back. "I'm so glad that you're here."
"I wouldn't miss this for anything."

All of my embarrassment from the last few minutes seeped away as we danced. I saw Don watching us out of the corner of my eye. Instead of wearing his usual sarcastic smile, he looked surprised that Shenzy was with me. Chaunce abruptly ushered Don from the room. I wanted to waive goodbye to him as he left. Just as I was enjoying Don's misery, Shenzy commanded my attention anew.

"Ronnie, where did you get that necklace?" He asked cautiously.
"Don loaned it to me. Let me guess, it's stolen."
"Not exactly; it belonged to my mother."
"Wonderful. I should have known he was up to no good. I mean why would he ever try to play nice with me?"

"Well, don't blame yourself. That just shows who you are. You try to find the good in people."

"I really must thank you for rescuing me."

"It was my pleasure."

"So judging by your choice of tuxes, you knew what he was planning."

"There isn't much that goes on here that I don't know about. I didn't want to confront him because he would have just come up with some other trick."

"Well, maybe you could have clued me in."

"Why would I do that? You look stunning. Besides, I'm glad that you're not like everybody else here. It's refreshing."

"Thank you. You look very handsome yourself. However, I do prefer the shirtless version of you better."

"Are you trying to make me blush? It won't work. I can make you blush far more easily."

I couldn't think of a witty reply. I started blushing before he said another word. Luckily for me, he decided to change the subject.

"Ronnie, do you know our traditional dance?"

"Yes, I do. Shelby showed me."

"That's good because it's almost time to begin. Let's go find our places."

"Alright."

We lined up just the way Shelby showed me. She and Luca were to the right of us. She looked over and gave me a reassuring smile. Claudia and Nicholas Tew were directly in front of us. When Nicholas caught my attention, he smiled at me and bowed his head ever so slightly. Claudia must have noticed too because she rolled her eyes at him.

When the dance finally started, I was impressed at how well Shenzy moved. And I could tell he was enjoying himself. When we reached the point in the dance when we were supposed to turn around together, he picked me up instead. Shenzy turned me around in the air which surprised everyone including me. He brought me down slowly disrupting the dance and my breathing pattern.

When we got back in place, I caught up to Nicholas who was my new partner. He was a pretty good dancer too but I was glad when we switched back. I wanted to be with Shenzy every moment I could. When the music slowed down, everyone started clapping their hands and moving towards the tables in the back of the ballroom.

We followed Shelby and Luca to the main table. We were soon joined by Claudia, Nicholas, Ariana and Don. I didn't look in Don's direction because I didn't want to lose my composure. Ariana couldn't stop staring at my dress and she wasn't alone. I was trying to ignore the looks that were coming from the tables around us.

I reached for the bottle of champagne in the middle of the table but Don beat me to it. He shot me a silly grin which I ignored. Shenzy must have caught the exchange because he motioned to me to follow him to the buffet table. All of the food looked wonderful. I decided to get a small sample of almost every course. It was delicious and I probably drank more champagne than I should have.

I realized this at no better time than when I was about to make my toast to Shelby and Luca. I'd watched Chaunce get everyone's attention by clinking his glass with a knife. I picked up my glass so that I could do something similar. I tapped my spoon on the crystal flute and waited for everyone to look in my direction. I was surprised at how clear and firm my voice sounded.

"Hello everyone. I'm very pleased to be speaking to you tonight and very honored. A few weeks ago, I met a very special woman under less than ideal circumstances. And since then, she has become like a sister to me; the sister I never had. Soon she will be taking the next steps in her life with Luca by her side. It's so easy to look at the two of you and see how much in love you are. Maybe one day we might all be so blessed. So I make this toast to you. May you both live as long as you want and never want as long as you live. To Shelby and Luca."

Everyone repeated the words "To Shelby and Luca" and then we all drank from our flutes. I could tell that Shelby was really touched by my toast. She came over and hugged me around my neck. Before she let go, she whispered in my ear. "You really do look beautiful."

Luca came over and kissed me on both cheeks. After that, everyone started kissing each other and hugging. When Don approached me, I started to run in the opposite direction but there were too many people behind me.

I was cornered. I even considered stabbing him with my butter knife but that would ruin the evening for everyone. And I had already made enough of a spectacle of myself with my gown.

"Ronnie, no hard feelings right?" Don smiled at me but I looked away from him.
"Don, I won't let you ruin this party for me or for your sister. Now why don't you run along?"

I turned my back to him and continued engaging the other guests. After a few moments, he walked away. I didn't see what direction he went in and I didn't care. Shenzy came back to sit down next to me and my run in with Don was all but forgotten.

When dinner was over, the music changed to a low and sultry melody that was perfect for dancing. Shenzy and I found our way back to the dance floor. Being close to him this way was more than I could have hoped for. We weren't doing a lot of talking so his question surprised me.

"So is this our first official date?" He whispered the words.
"I suppose it is."
"So will there be other dates?"
"Definitely."

We continued dancing in silence. I closed my eyes so that I could focus on remembering everything about him. The smell of him; the way I felt in his arms. There was no place else in the world I'd rather be. Unfortunately, everyone did not share in my enthusiasm. Much to my chagrin, we were interrupted.

"May I cut in?" Rocco asked gingerly.
"Yes, of course." Shenzy replied and he took a step back from me.

I tried to smile as I watched Shenzy walk away. He went over to talk with Chaunce and Fenton Tew. I could tell that Rocco was watching my every move so I tried to spark up a conversation.

"So Rocco, are you enjoying the party?"
"I am now. What about you?"
"I must admit I'm having a pretty good time. Even with my wardrobe malfunction, the night's going well."
"Don't worry about it. It didn't take anybody long to figure out who was behind the whole thing. And you do look beautiful in that dress."
"Thanks Rocco. That's very sweet of you to say."

We went on dancing without a lot of conversation. I was enjoying myself but after a few minutes, I started getting a little antsy. I tried to crane my neck over Rocco's shoulder to find out where Shenzy was. When I finally spotted him, he was by the ballroom door locked in a heated conversation with Don. It appeared that at any moment, they were going to start throwing punches. Luckily, Chaunce saw the same thing that I did because he moved quickly to where they were.

He was trying to defuse the situation but it wasn't going well. A few moments later, Shelby joined them. She started talking directly to Don but he didn't seem to be getting the point. She started crying which only caused the tension to escalate. Don through his hands up in the air and walked out of the ballroom. Chaunce followed behind him.

Shenzy reached out to Shelby and put his arm around her shoulder. As I was watching them, Shenzy caught my gaze. He flashed me a quick smile and headed out the door with Shelby in tow. I wished I knew what was going on but I was stuck there with Rocco. I figured they were dealing with family business right now and it wasn't a good time for me to intrude anyway. When the song ended, I thanked Rocco for the dance and headed back to the table.

I was only there for a minute when Luca came over and sat down next to me. He had a worried look on his face.

"What the hell was that?"
"I don't really know." I replied cautiously.
He kept staring at the ballroom doors. "I'm going to find Shelby."
"That's a good idea."

Luca got up and headed for the door. I waited a few minutes and then I walked out behind him. When I went into the hall, I didn't see anyone. I walked around to the study but the door was closed. I knocked and waited for someone to answer. Chaunce opened the door so that I could come in. He smiled at me but I could tell that he was still upset about whatever happened earlier.

"Hi Shelby, I just wanted to make sure you were alright." I walked over to her and sat down on the sofa.
"I'm fine. I'm just trying to understand why my twin brother wants to ruin my life."

Chaunce motioned to Luca to follow him out. I guess he thought Shelby could use some girl time.
"Shelby, I'm going to go say goodnight to the guests. Why don't you just relax here?" Chaunce was in full support mode.

They left the room and shut the door behind them. I didn't know what to say to help her but I had to try.

"Shelby, I think Don is really happy for you. He just doesn't know how to show it. And all of the champagne he drank didn't help."
"That's exactly my point. Why does he do it?"
"I really don't know." I didn't think I was doing a good job of making her feel better.
"I'm surprised you can say anything nice about him. Look at what he did to you."
"Actually, my humiliation was short lived. Shenzy thought I looked beautiful."
"I saw how relieved you were when he walked in. You looked great together."

"Where did he go anyway?"

"I think he went up to bed. He was pretty upset with Don and he didn't want to make a scene in front of everyone."

"Oh, he's staying here tonight?"

"Yes, he is." She gave me a wide grin.

"Maybe I should go check on him. Will you be alright for a few minutes?"

"Of course I will. Just take your time." She gave me a sly smile.

"Shelby!" I tried to sound offended. "I just want to make sure he's OK. After the way he helped me tonight, it's the least I can do."

I left the study quite sure that I'd embarrassed myself. I took a deep breath and climbed the stairs. I tried to think of what excuse I could use for checking on him now. As I walked down the hall, I was still drawing a blank. I stood in front of his bedroom door feeling my heart rate quicken.

I didn't know when I would have this opportunity again so I needed to man up. Well, you know what I mean. I knocked three times and stepped back. A few moments later, he answered the door wearing only his tuxedo pants. I tried not to stare.

"I was wondering when you'd show up." He had a teasing smile on his face.

"Is that right?" I smiled back.

"Yes. I've been waiting for you."

"Sorry I'm late."

He leaned over to me and kissed my forehead very gently. I couldn't help but laugh as he pulled me into his room.

Chapter 17

The next morning I woke up in a wonderful haze. I just lay there for a few minutes thinking about everything that happened last night. Shenzy and I spent most of the night together before I snuck back to my room. With the party going on last night, I doubt if anybody checked on me.

I was nervous about seeing him though. I know that sounds silly after we'd just spent a very intimate night together. I'd be having breakfast with Shenzy and his family in mere minutes. I just didn't want to do what I normally did which was to over think every detail. I willed myself to pull it together and get dressed. With all of the analysis I was doing, I was missing out on the opportunity to see his handsome face.

When I walked into the dining room, Shenzy gave me a warm smile. Everyone else was already there so I said good morning and sat down. Shelby glanced over at me and smiled but she didn't say anything. It made me wonder if she had in fact noticed that I wasn't in my room all night.

I was relieved when Kalani started serving breakfast. It gave me something else to do with my eyes. I tried not to look in Shenzy's direction but it wasn't easy. I kept thinking about last night.

To make matters worse, when he looked at me, I couldn't stop blushing. Even when he was talking to Chaunce about cloud patterns, he kept stealing glances at me. I just wanted to walk around the table and kiss him. It was safe to assume that everyone knew about us and they seemed to be cool with it. Well, everyone except for Don. He stared at me suspiciously and I immediately looked away from him.

"Ok, that's it." Don belted out to no one in particular. "I've had enough."

"What's your problem?" Shelby asked.

"Am I the only one that can see what's happened here?" He glanced from Shenzy to me.

"What are you talking about Don?" I spoke in a louder voice than I intended to.

"You and Shenzy. You've been grinning like idiots since you sat down."

"Sheldon, let's just enjoy our breakfast. Shall we?" Chaunce chimed in.

"Fine, but if I have to watch this excuse for puppy love, my food might not stay down."

We finished our breakfast in silence. I didn't look at anyone. I needed to give my face a chance to return to its normal color. When I was finished eating, I finally looked up to see Shenzy staring at me. I chuckled under my breath.

He suddenly got up from his chair and walked around the table to me. He nodded towards the door and held out his hand to me. I almost knocked over my chair trying to get to my feet. Shelby laughed and helped me steady my chair. I even caught a hint of a smile on Chaunce's face. I was glad that I could entertain everyone at my expense. But it lightened the mood in the room which was a good thing.

"Where are we going?" I asked him as we reached the front doors.

"We're going somewhere fun. Are you up for that?" Shenzy smiled at me and took my hand.

"Of course I am."

By the time we reached the open field, I started to relax. I felt the cool morning breeze on my face and when I looked up towards the sky, I saw pieces of gray mixed with bright blue. There were storm clouds forming overhead but not even that could ruin my mood. If it did rain, it would be the first rain since I'd arrived.

"Ok Shenzy, where are we going?" I asked in a playful tone.

"We're going on a date."

"Really? What kind of date?"

"The normal kind; we're going to an art class."
"That sounds like fun."
"Well, we'd better hurry up if we don't want to get wet."
"Lead the way."

We picked up our pace as we walked along the path to the town square. We were still holding hands when the first drops of rain came. I could see the group of buildings in the distance and we must have gotten the same idea. We took off running at a fairly decent pace. If we weren't laughing so hard, we might not have gotten soaked before we reached the school.

We ducked inside the door and I couldn't help laughing as I took in the sight of our drenched clothes. Shenzy just smiled at me and shook his head. I pulled my wet hair back into a knot as Shenzy led me through the halls toward Pierre's classroom.

When we arrived, the class had already begun. Pierre motioned for us to find an empty station so we did. As I listened to him address the group, it reminded me of when I was in college.

Pierre gave us one object to focus on. It was a tiny baobab tree that sat in a pot at the front of the room. We were to draw the tree using whatever painting style we preferred. In this exercise, we would show the instructor our skill levels and what type of painting we enjoyed. I had no idea what I was doing but I was having fun.

I kept looking to see what Shenzy was painting. His painting was very good but it was more a construct than a picture of a living thing. My painting almost resembled a tree. I saw Shenzy glance at it and then quickly turn away. He was trying hard not to laugh so I leaned over and pinched him on the arm. He jumped and almost knocked over his easel. That got everyone's attention around us. We both tried to pretend that we weren't making the ruckus.

I kept working but my painting wasn't getting any better. I started looking around at what others were doing and I suddenly had the feeling I was being watched. When I looked over by the window, I saw Rocco. I'd forgotten that he signed up for the class. He waived at me and smiled. I gave him a quick wave and went back to my work. I don't know why I felt weird seeing Rocco here but I did. And now I was trying hard not to look in his direction. I started to wonder if coming here today was a good idea.

When the class was almost over, Mira walked to the front of the room and gave us direction on what to do with our paintings. Our eyes met for a moment and then she hastily looked away. I didn't understand why though.

We were putting our paintings on the back ledge of the room, when she approached me.

"Ronnie, may I speak with you privately?" I could tell she was nervous.
"Sure, do you want to go outside?"

Shenzy smiled at me and then walked over to speak to Rocco. Mira and I walked across the hall and into an empty classroom. She had her arms wrapped around herself and she was looking at the floor. I was relieved when she finally said something.

"Ronnie, I'm really sorry about what happened at the party. I had no idea what Don was planning with your dress." She looked like she was about to cry.
"Mira, I don't blame you for what happened."
"Don uses people. He uses them and then throws them away."
"Mira, he can only use you if you let him."
"Well, I'm not seeing him anymore. I'm done with Don Misson."
"Good for you. You know, I'm glad we saw each other today."
"Really, why?"
"I never properly thanked you for helping me get ready that night. If it wasn't for you, I don't know what I would have done."
"You're welcome." She finally smiled. "And if you ever need my help again, just let me know."
"I'm definitely going to hold you to that." I smiled back at her as we walked into the hall.

"Ok. Well, I'd better get back in the room. We have another class coming and I have to organize the stations."
"Ok. I'll see ya later."

Mira walked into the classroom and I made my way to the front of the school to look for Shenzy. Once I got outside, I saw that he and Rocco were standing just off the main path in the square. I wondered what they were talking about. When Shenzy saw me, he motioned for me to come over and Rocco just walked away.

When I reached him, he kissed my hand and we started walking towards the path. We walked about ten yards and I looked back to see that Rocco was watching us from the steps of the school. I didn't know what to make of it, but I was definitely going to ask Shenzy.

We'd put some space between ourselves and the town center, but I still couldn't discern his mood. He was holding my hand but he didn't look at me.

"I used to be amused by Rocco's interest in you," he said matter-of-factly.
"And now?"
"Not so much." He tried to smile. "I'm not used to these jealous feeling."
"You have no reason to be jealous of him." I really needed to know what they were talking about. "What happened while I was talking to Mira?"
"Well, he told me that he asked you out a little while after you got here."
"Yeah, I remember that." I tried to sound nonchalant.
"What did you say to him?" He finally looked at me. "He conveniently left that part out."
"I turned him down gently." I stopped walking and turned to face him. "Shenzy, I really like you. Even before last night, I had no intention of spending time with anyone besides you."

That made him smile. He put his arm around my neck and we continued on our way. I hoped that his mind was at ease because what I told him was the truth. Well, I left one thing out. But I thought it was too soon to tell him that I was falling for him.

After a while, we reached the open field. I tried to slow our pace as I realized we might have to face our biggest cheerleader, Don. Shenzy must have noticed my apprehension. He leaned toward me and gave me a reassuring kiss on my forehead.

We continued walking toward the house in silence. As much as I tried not to, I started thinking about what would happen between us. I was developing strong feelings for him. I knew that on some level, he felt the same way about me. I just didn't want to ruin it by obsessing about it. I wanted to enjoy him as much as I could.

When we walked into the house, I realized I would have to share him with the rest of his family too. Shelby told me on numerous occasions that she missed him hanging around. I wanted to be selfish but I couldn't.

"Shenzy, is that you?" Shelby called to him.
"Yes, I'm here."

We walked into the study to find her and Chaunce looking at some drawings on the desk. There were still so many plans to make for the wedding. Any decorations or food stuffs they ordered from outside the valley was a logistical hat trick to bring in.

"Did you both enjoy the class?" Shelby asked.
"Yeah, I think I need a lot more practice with my technique before I actually try to paint something."

Shenzy was trying to hide his amusement but I pretended not to notice. However, I couldn't ignore when Don strolled into the room and joined in the conversation.

"So have you come to help us with planning the wedding Shenzy?" Don walked over and draped himself over the sofa. I'm sure he was only here because Chaunce insisted.
"Sure. But I need to get the paint off my hands." Shenzy replied.

"Me too. I have paint up to my elbows." I followed him out of the room.

"Oh this is just great. Now they have to go to the bathroom together." Don whispered to Chaunce as we were leaving the room.

We walked upstairs to my room and I ran into the bathroom first. I turned on the water and started soaping up my hands. Shenzy came up behind me and put his arms around me. I thought he was going to hug me but he didn't. He reached down and started soaping up his hands with mine.

He massaged my hands between his very slowly. Then he started rubbing his fingers in between mine. I glanced up in the bathroom mirror and saw that he was watching my reaction to his movements. I had to look away.

He started rubbing the lather farther up my arms. I wasn't sure if he was trying to get the rest of the paint off or if he was trying to excite me. In all honesty, he was accomplishing both.

He rinsed the lather from my arms and his hands and then he reached for a towel to dry us both. When I turned to face him, my insides were ablaze. He started massaging my arms again and then he moved up to my shoulders and then my neck. My skin was warmed by his touch.

He smoothed his hands up to my face and gently pulled my chin up so that my lips met his. I put my arms around his waist and held him to me. He covered my mouth with his and everything intensified. He suddenly picked me up and carried me over to the bed.

He laid me gently on the bed and then lay down next to me. He pulled off his t-shirt and shorts and hugged me again so that I could feel his skin on mine. But I wanted to feel more. I slowly unbuttoned my dress and tossed it onto the floor.

Shenzy looked at me with those deep, piercing eyes. I couldn't help but feel slightly self-conscious. The daylight flooded into the room and my body was completely exposed to him.

"What's the matter? You look nervous," he said softly.

"You can see me; all of me."

"Of course I can see you. That's a good thing. You're beautiful Ronnie." He pulled me up so that I was straddling him.

I felt the weight of his gaze as his eyes travelled along my body. I couldn't help responding to him. The way he looked at me now made me feel beautiful; desired.

I leaned over to kiss him and he met me half way. He started to massage my body as if he were memorizing ever contour of it. I felt like we were learning each other in a way that made our movements almost instinctual.

When Shenzy grabbed hold of my hips, I knew exactly what would happen next. He held me closely to him as we started a sensual rhythm. The sensations coursing through my body were just short of overwhelming. I only hoped he enjoyed our encounter as much as I did.

He slowly moved his hands up to my face so that he was looking into my eyes. But I soon realized that his dark stare was more than I could stand. With each passing moment, I felt myself unraveling.

I noticed the same excitement in his gaze. I stroked his hair and then kissed him hungrily. We became electric for a few sweet moments.

We fell back on the bed in sweet exhaustion. Shenzy held me in his arms and stroked my hair. I felt so close to him; so contented. I closed my eyes so that I could savor those moments. He gently kissed my cheek and it made me smile. Then he went back to stroking my hair and I just couldn't stay awake.

When I woke up, there was a blanket over me and the sun was setting outside. I looked over at Shenzy and noticed that he wasn't asleep.

"What are you doing?" I asked him.
"I'm making a memory," he replied calmly.
"A memory of what?"
"Of you, of course."
"Did you fall asleep too?"
"I slept for a little while. But then I woke up and saw you looking so peaceful."
"I feel peaceful. I'm so happy that you're here with me."
"So am I."
"What would you be doing if I wasn't here?" I asked rather boldly.
"I'd probably be at the lake doing nothing in particular." He got a faraway look in his eyes.

I watched him for a few moments. I wanted to make a memory too. I finally had to look away when he stared back at me with those penetrating eyes of his. There was no end to how sexy he was.

A little while later, he got up off the bed and headed for the bathroom. When he was halfway there, he turned to face me.

"Are you coming?"
"Coming to the bathroom with you?" I asked cautiously.
"Well, yeah. We need to take a shower."
"Oh, right. That's a good way to conserve water."

I picked up the blanket that was on the bed and headed for the bathroom. When Shenzy saw it he started laughing.

"Where are you going with that thing? Are you showering with the blanket on?" He asked sarcastically.
"Very funny."

I tossed the blanket back on the bed and followed him into the bathroom. We showered together for the first time. I hoped that no one could hear us laughing and playing. They might start to have serious doubts about my maturity level since I was doing most of the laughing.

I got dressed in the bathroom because Shenzy just wouldn't leave me alone. Every time I buttoned a button he would undo it. Then I brushed my hair back in a quick ponytail. It was obviously time to eat dinner and my grumbling stomach was prompting me to hurry up and get ready.

I asked Shenzy to go downstairs ahead of me. I don't know why I was trying to conceal that we were together but I wasn't used to being in a house with my boyfriend and his entire family. I decided to go downstairs and just play it cool but that was easier said than done.

I couldn't deal with the look on Don's face. And to top it all off, we had dinner guests. When I walked into the dining room, Claudia, Rocco and Luca were smiling up at me from around the table. Shelby had a concerned look on her face and Chaunce was nowhere to be found. I glanced over at Don who was sitting at the head of the table. That meant that Chaunce definitely wouldn't be having dinner with us.

"So happy you could join us Ronnie." Don chided.
"Well, thank you Don. I wouldn't miss a chance to have dinner with such fine people." I tried to sound genuine.

I would just be as cheerful as I could and try to make it through dinner. I was pretty hungry after all. By the time everyone started eating though, I had relaxed a bit. I still felt a little uncomfortable about Rocco. After all, the exchange that he and Shenzy had was about me.

Don added his own course to the meal with a couple bottles of champagne from his private stash. With Chaunce out for the evening, I wondered how long it would take him to get plastered and ruin dinner. And of course, his favorite target was yours truly.

"Shenzy, I don't mean to be rude, but what is it with you two anyway?" Don was already getting warmed up after only two glasses. I decided it was a good time to have a glass myself.
"What are you talking about Don?" Shenzy tried to look innocent.

"I'm talking about you and her." Don pointed at Shenzy and then at me.

"We're friends. We're very good friends." Shenzy winked his eye at me. I wonder who else noticed.

"Well, I don't think I approve of your friendship." Don snapped back.

"Don, I really don't care what you think." Shenzy's tone had both humor and sarcasm in it.

Everyone turned to look in my direction. After drinking some of Don's champagne, I didn't much care either. I just hunched my shoulders up and kept on drinking. Shelby was laughing pretty hard by this time which didn't give Don the affect he was looking for.

Everyone around the table started drinking champagne and otherwise trying to ignore Don. His desire to ruin dinner and make everyone uncomfortable had failed. He suddenly got up and headed out into the foyer. He made sure to grab one of the champagne bottles before he left the room.

"Where is he going?" Claudia was trying to crane her neck to see where Don had gone.

"I think he's going into the ballroom," Shelby said as she reached for her champagne. "He sometimes goes in there to dance by himself."

"To dance?" I couldn't help laughing. "I've got to see this."

I got up and headed for the ballroom. Shelby and Luca were right behind me. After a few minutes, we were all tip toeing down the hall to try and sneak up on Don. It didn't work. We were all laughing at each other and trying to keep an eye out for anyone who might fall to the floor. When I reached the ballroom door, I could hear 'Walk This Way' playing inside.

I swung the door open and danced my way into the room. Don didn't seem to notice the intrusion. Shelby and Luca started dancing too. Pretty soon, we were all cutting up on the ballroom floor. Well, everyone except for Shenzy. He was standing on the side watching us and laughing. When Don finally noticed we were there, he just blended in with us and kept on dancing.

Don had a really cool play list of music from the sixties, seventies and eighties. Some of the songs I hadn't heard in years and some of them I'd never heard before. But even the music, couldn't keep me on my feet all night. After a while, the champagne started wearing off and I was running out of steam. I slowly walked over to Shenzy and stood in front of him. He looked down at me and started smiling.

"You're tired, aren't you?" He asked.
"Yes. But why didn't you dance with me?" I replied in an infantile tone.
"I don't really like to dance. I prefer to watch you."
"So you're never going to dance with me again?"
"I didn't say that. There will be other occasions."
"Like what?"
"Like my sister's wedding." Shenzy laughed to himself.
"Is that right?" I poked him in his chest.
"I'm just kidding." He grabbed my hands. "Are you ready for bed?"
"Yeah, are you?"
He nodded his head. "I'll tell Shelby that we're going up."
"Alright."

I stood there and watched him walk over and hug Shelby. He even spoke to Luca and Rocco before coming back over to me. I was glad to see him engaged in polite conversation with Rocco. I didn't want to be the cause of any unnecessary tensions that might continue after I was gone. I waved goodbye to everybody and Shenzy and I left the room. By the time we made it to the stairs, my feet were giving out on me. Shenzy must have noticed that I was struggling because he walked up behind me and swept me off my feet; literally.

He carried me up the stairs and down the hall past my room. I knew where he was taking me and I didn't protest. I felt more comfortable in his room primarily because of its location. It was at the back of the house. My room just seemed too accessible. He laid me very gently on his bed. I pretended to be asleep; not that I was far from it. I watched him undress and put his clothes on the chair in the corner. Then he walked over to me and touched my shoulder.

"Ronnie, wake up. You shouldn't sleep with your clothes on."
"OK."

I lay there while he helped me out of my clothes. He pulled the covers over me and swept my hair back from my face. Then he turned off the lights and slid under the covers with me. I felt him kiss my forehead very gently as I started drifting off to sleep. I might have been dreaming but I thought he uttered three words very quietly.

"I love you."

Chapter 18

Over the next few weeks, Shenzy and I spent every moment together that we could. I don't remember another point in my life when I'd been so happy. There were times when Shenzy had to go to the lake but I would wait for him to return. Chaunce still wasn't comfortable with me going with him and deep down I understood. Shenzy probably wouldn't give his full attention to his work if I went with him. And there was still the concern about my safety.

When Shenzy was away, I kept myself busy with Shelby. There were still plans to be made for the wedding and she insisted on making me feel like a full-fledged maid-of-honor. We pored over fashion magazines with Claudia since she was the resident fashionista. We looked at dresses and shoes and talked about squeezing all of Seulmonde into the ballroom for the wedding.

But all of my worries went away when Shenzy returned. When we were together, there was only us. The rest of the world just faded into the background. I could be myself around him and that meant a lot to me.

He showed me more of Seulmonde and I loved it. It truly was a self-sustained city. They grew most of their own food, maintained viable energy sources and functioned quite well without the outside world.

The people seemed quite fascinated by me as well. It was getting better though. They didn't stare as much. After a while, they seemed to accept Shenzy and me. Whether we were strolling about the valley or sitting in on Pierre's art class, we were treated like any other couple.

The only person who wasn't on board was Don. He still gave us disapproving looks when he saw us canoodling. We didn't care though. We just focused on our time together because we knew we didn't have long. I just didn't realize the enchantment would end as soon as it did.

Shenzy and I had gone for a walk one Saturday morning. We'd eaten an early breakfast and wanted to get out of the house for a while. We walked to the far side of the valley where most of the other inhabitants lived. The cottages were cozy and filled with country charm. Most of them had small gardens in front and flower baskets in the first floor windows.

Beyond the cottages were the fruit and vegetable gardens. Shenzy insisted on showing them to me but I'd never made it all the way to that part of the valley. Something else would always get my attention. Today was no different.

I was distracted by a construction crew making a repair on one of the cottages. I'd never seen a crew that made use of all materials; they didn't waste anything. But after a couple hours, I started getting tired. Shenzy offered to carry me back to the house but I wanted to walk on my own.

We started back across the valley at a leisurely pace. It did take a while for us to reach the house. When we arrived at the front gate, Don came barreling down toward us.

"We have a serious problem." Don glared at Shenzy and then let his gaze rest on me.
"What is it Don?" Shenzy asked.
"Why don't you come and see for yourself?"

Don turned back toward the house and we followed him in. What made me uncomfortable was when Don asked me to wait in the foyer while he and Shenzy went into the study. While I was standing there, Shelby called to me from inside the dining room. Her face looked sad or maybe concerned. I couldn't decide which it was.

"Ronnie, please sit down," Shelby said and motioned to the chair next to her.
"Shelby, what's wrong? You're scaring me."
"Someone has breached the perimeter of Seulmonde."

I didn't know how to respond to her or if I should. But I knew it wasn't good news. If someone discovered this valley, it would be detrimental to everyone here. I knew what needed to be done, but I didn't want to admit it to myself.

I was running through the horrors in my mind when Shenzy came into the dining room. He didn't look happy. "Ronnie, I need to show you something. Can you come into the study?"

I got up and followed him. Shelby was right behind me. When I walked into the study, Don was holding the hand held device that Shenzy usually carried with him.

"Do you recognize this man?" Don turned the device around and showed me an image of a man with wind torn hair and a sallow expression. It was Garland.

"Where did you get that picture?" I could barely speak.
"Do you know this man?" Don yelled at me.
"That's Garland Malloy. He's my ex-boyfriend."

Shenzy got up and ran from the room. A few seconds later I heard the front door open and close. Shelby sat down hard on the sofa. She looked like she'd eaten something distasteful.

"How the hell did he find this valley? What did you tell him about us?" Don growled at me.
"I've spoken to him once since I've been here and I told him nothing about Seulmonde." I couldn't help sounding defensive.

He looked thoughtful for a moment. "Well if you didn't bring him here, he must have tracked you somehow. Perhaps that satellite phone is the key. He figured out a way to trace it."
"Is that even possible?" I turned to face him.
"I don't know." Don replied dryly.
"So what happens now?" I asked with a shaky voice.
"Chaunce will decide but most likely we'll have to bring your boyfriend here so he doesn't get himself killed out there."

I sat down next to Shelby on the sofa. I started feeling sick myself.

"He's not my boyfriend" I yelled back. "I don't know why he's here."
"Is that what you're going to tell my brother? Good luck with that. I have to go. This situation won't end well. I can just feel it." Don strode out of the room and closed the door.

Shelby glanced at me but she didn't say anything. As much as I hated to admit it, I agreed with Don. I knew that whatever happened after this, the time I enjoyed with Shenzy was over. I didn't want them to bring Garland here but I knew they didn't have a choice.

All of the time that Don had spent being cruel to me and reminding me that I didn't belong here was validated. I just sat there feeling sorry for myself. A part of me wished that I'd never left Columbia at all. Maybe I wasn't meant to have somebody care for me the way Shenzy did.

"I know what you're thinking Ronnie and you're wrong." Shelby finally spoke.
"Am I?" I couldn't look at her. It was too painful. "Don was right. I should never have come here."
"Ronnie, don't say that."

I got up and walked out of the study. I went up to my room and lay across the bed with my eyes closed. I didn't want to deal with this situation and I certainly didn't want to see Garland again. I'd finally moved past our so-called relationship and now he was destroying the happiness I'd found here.

But I had to do something. I needed to talk to Shenzy and make him understand. He was too important to me and I wouldn't give up so easily. Whenever he returned to the house, I would talk to him alone.

I tried to feign at least a glimmer of hope. It worked for about five minutes. The tears started coming and they wouldn't stop. After I ran out of tears, my strength left me as well. I shut my eyes and took a few deep breaths. I didn't intend to fall asleep but that's exactly what happened.

I don't know how long I slept but I was awakened by the sound of voices in the hall. Before I had the chance to discern who it was, the door to my room swung open. I couldn't believe my eyes.

"Ronnie, here you are. I've been so worried." Garland came running over to the bed and sat down next to me.
"Garland, please get a grip." I sat up on the bed trying to focus my eyes on who was in the hall.
"Let's give them some time alone." Don walked out of the room and closed the door behind him.
"Garland, what the hell are you doing here?" I stood up and walked over to the window. I didn't want to look at him.
"Ronnie, I came to find you. Is this where you've been all this time?"
"Garland, you have to leave. You have no idea what you've done." I started pacing the floor. I wanted to strangle him so I kept my distance.
"Ronnie, you're not making sense. And where the hell is here? You know, I think they drugged me. I woke up a few minutes ago on the floor of an office downstairs."
"I can't tell you anything. The only thing you need to know is that you're lucky they didn't leave you out in the wilderness."
"I'm really glad to see you." Garland got up and walked over to me.
"Please don't." I stepped back from him. "Garland, I really wish that you hadn't come looking for me."
"I can't believe you're saying that. We were just on a break and..."
"Are you fucking kidding me?" I lost it. "We broke up Garland. I wanted a real relationship and you didn't. Case closed. End of story."
"That's not true. It wasn't as simple as you make it sound; I tried."

"Well, I'm really happy for you. Maybe the next time you have a girlfriend, you'll figure out what you want before the relationship ends." I turned my back to him again. "I'd like you to leave. I want to lie down for a little while longer."

"Well, where do you expect me to go? Don told me I had to sleep in here with you."

"The hell you are. I'll be right back."

I went downstairs to find Shelby, Don and Shenzy in the dining room. It wasn't hard to guess what they were talking about. Shenzy wouldn't look in my direction and I didn't feel like dealing with him right now anyway.

"Don, did you tell Garland that he was sleeping in my room?"

"Ronnie, where else is your boyfriend supposed to sleep?" Don asked sarcastically.

I saw Shenzy cringe when Don mentioned my boyfriend. I wanted to scream at him at the top of my lungs. But I wouldn't add to Don's enjoyment. I quietly left the room. I was halfway up the stairs when Shelby came running behind me.

"Ronnie, wait. Can I speak to you for a minute?"

"Sure." I turned to face her on the stairs.

"Let's go into the study."

I followed her back down the stairs. She walked in the room first and closed the door behind us.

"Ronnie, I know that you're upset. We all are. And Shenzy, well he's confused. Don has been filling his head with a lot of information. I hope you aren't angry with Shenzy."

"Of course I'm not angry at him. I just wish he would talk to me." I felt like I would cry again so I turned away from her.

"Ronnie, I think you should know what Garland has been saying about the two of you."

"I can only imagine." I tried to brace myself.

"He told Don that you were still together. He said that you just had a fight and that's why he came looking for you."

"And Don believes him?"

"Yes, he does."

"What about Shenzy? Does he believe Garland too?"

"He doesn't know what to believe."

"What about you?" I still didn't face her.

"I believe you Ronnie. I didn't think you'd have to ask."

"I'm sorry. This has just been the worst day."

I turned to her but I kept my eyes down. She came over to hug me and I struggled not to start sobbing again. I was glad that I had her to talk to and that's when I thought of a way she could really help me.

"Shelby, I need to ask you a big favor."

"Sure, what is it?"

"Do you mind if I sleep in your room? Mine is a little crowded."

"I don't mind at all." She smiled at me. "In fact, I insist."

"You're a life saver." I said to her and smiled back.

We left the study and Shelby headed back into the dining room. I slipped upstairs hoping that no one would see me. I'd almost made it past my room when Garland came walking out.

"Ronnie, there you are. I really want to finish our talk."

"Garland, please just leave me alone." I just couldn't deal with him.

I walked down to Shelby's room and shut the door behind me. I tried to ignore the pain in my chest and the sick feeling in my stomach. I wasn't sure if I would even be able to go to sleep. But as usual, I surprised myself.

When I woke up, the room was quiet. The sun was still up and I was starving. I guess the rest of my body had forgotten to remind my stomach of how sad I was. I slipped my shoes back on and headed downstairs.

I didn't see anybody which was a good thing. I went into the kitchen and grabbed a banana. It was either that or a whole cake. Since I didn't have any cake, the banana would have to suffice.

I ate my banana and was pleased to find that it actually stayed down without any trouble. Then I headed outside. As large as the house was, I was starting to feel confined. Perhaps it was the presence of the newest house guest. I walked out the front door and to the open field.

When I felt like I'd walked far enough, I sat down in the grass. I closed my eyes and let the sun wash over me. Being out there helped a little. A few minutes later, I heard someone walking up behind me. I turned to see Shelby's smiling face.

"Feeling better?" She said as she sat down next to me.
"I'm alright. Thanks for asking." I tried to smile back at her.

We sat there for a while not saying anything. In that way, she reminded me of Shenzy. The smile that I forced a few moments ago wouldn't stay.

"You're in love with Shenzy, aren't you?" Shelby asked without looking at me.
"Yes, I am." I stared up at the sky.
"You know that he loves you too, right?"
"If you'd asked me that question yesterday, I would have said yes. I'm not so sure now."
"What are you going to do about it?"
"I don't know. I figured I'd just sit here until something came to me."
"That's a really good plan." Shelby said playfully.

We sat out there for a while making small talk. I knew that we'd have to go inside soon but I wanted to put it off for as long as I could. Shelby must have figured that I was stalling but she didn't say anything. As the sky began to darken, I accepted the obvious.

"We'd better go in." I said reluctantly.

Shelby helped me up off the ground and we headed back towards the house. She grabbed my hand and started swinging it back and forth the way children do. It made me smile but only for a moment. When we reached the house, Don was waiting for us in the doorway. I started to take off running but I knew that I wouldn't get far without food or water. I just had to suffer his gloating face as we walked into the house.

We went into the dining room and I noticed that Garland was seated next to my normal chair. I decided to sit on the other side of the table two seats down from Shenzy. I figured if I sat any closer, he might get up and leave. I didn't want to push it. I did see him glance at me when I sat down.

Don strolled into the dining room and glanced around the table at us. He was the only one who looked happy to be there. Even Garland's face was fixed in a cheerless expression. We started eating dinner and I thought that might prevent anyone from talking to me. At least that's what I thought.

"Ronnie, is there something going on here that you need to tell me?" Garland asked quietly.
"Garland, why don't you just eat your food? We can talk later." I said just as quietly.
"Ronnie, you should be a little nicer. If Garland wants to talk, I think you should hear him out." Don said sardonically.
"I think you've imposed you're views enough for one day Sheldon." Chaunce spoke from the doorway.

Don snapped his neck around in surprise. I think we were all pretty shocked to see Chaunce there but also relieved. That meant that Don would be reined in at least until Chaunce had to leave again. I found my food more palatable just knowing that Chaunce was in the house. And if I got the chance, I would speak with him as well. I didn't want him to have the wrong impression of me.

Garland looked really confused. I for one thought that was a good thing. The less he knew the better and the sooner he was gone, the better. I just hoped that I would have time to straighten things out with Shenzy before it was time for me to leave.

Chaunce walked into the dining room and sat down next to Shenzy. It was a little weird to see him sitting there but I guess he didn't want to embarrass Don by asking him to move to another chair. He made small talk with everyone including Garland. As usual, Chaunce practiced a statesmanship that was unparalleled.

Dinner went well but I was still glad when it was over. Shenzy left the room first. I started feeling down again as I realized this was normally the time that he and I snuck away to be together. This was about the same time I noticed Garland staring at me. But it was more than just a stare. It was more like he was undressing me with his eyes and he didn't seem shy about it. I'm sure if I noticed, everyone else did too.

Shelby came to my rescue yet again. I made a mental note to thank her later when we were alone.

"Ronnie, why don't we go upstairs and move your things down to my room. That way Garland will be more comfortable after his ordeal today."
"Yes, that's a great idea." I finally had something to smile about.
"Ronnie, you don't have to go through any trouble for me." Garland piped up quickly.
"It's no trouble at all. Besides, what would your father think of you shacking up with someone like me? He has such high expectations for you." I replied gingerly.

I followed Shelby out of the room. I couldn't wait to get upstairs and move my bags. I didn't even try to be neat about it. I just threw my clothes into my suitcase haphazardly. Once I was in Shelby's room, I let my guard down.

I couldn't stop thanking her for letting me sleep in her room. I don't know what I would have done otherwise. I don't think I could handle Shenzy slamming the door in my face.

Shelby tried to make me feel better. But I just couldn't see the silver lining. I was having a hard time adjusting to me and Shenzy not being together. Shelby tried to offer a solution but I wasn't so sure.

"I have an idea. Hear me out before you say no." She continued. "Beggars can't be choosers, right?"

Shelby jumped up and ran over to her closet. When she came back, she was carrying a fancy box covered in red cashmere. "What is that?" I asked inquisitively. "This is the fun box." Shelby replied with a giggle. "What's in it?" "It contains some of the gifts that Luca has given me over the years." "Can I see?" "Only if you promise to pick something out; that's the deal." "You want to give me something that your fiancé gave you as a gift?" "Believe me Ronnie, you need this more than I do right now." "Ok, fine. Let's see what's in the box."

She dumped the contents on the bed in front of me. I had never seen so many different colors and styles of lingerie in my life. Some of them would have made Gia blush. I started picking them up one by one.

"I will never look at Luca the same way again." I laughed uncomfortably. "Stop stalling and pick one. They're all new; never worn." She replied flatly. "Wait a minute. I just realized something. Do you expect me to seduce your brother with one of these?" "Do you have any better ideas?" "No, I don't." For a moment I was angry. Why did I need to seduce Shenzy? I didn't do anything wrong. But I thought for a minute if the situation had been reversed. I would feel exactly the same way he does. "Ok. Give me that purple one." "Great choice; that's his favorite color." "I'm going to take a shower before I change my mind about wearing this thing." "Good luck. I'm going downstairs to see what I can find out. I won't wait up."

I was glad that she was so optimistic or maybe she was acting that way for my benefit. Either way, I appreciated it. I showered, brushed my teeth and put on some lip gloss. I had to move quickly so that I didn't lose my nerve. That was a definite possibility.

I put on the little purple number and then looked at myself in the mirror. It was low cut in the front and made almost exclusively of lace. I did feel sexy wearing it and I doubted Shenzy could throw me out dressed like this. I pulled on my robe and took a quick look both ways down the hall. I didn't see or hear anyone so I dashed down to Shenzy's room and knocked on the door.

"Who is it?" He said sleepily.
"It's me, Ronnie."

I didn't hear him answer so I twisted the doorknob. The door wasn't locked so I went inside. When I walked in, he got up off the bed. He didn't look comfortable which made my heart sink.

"I wanted to talk to you alone." I wanted to break the silence in the room.
"Ronnie, I don't think this is such a good idea."
"What isn't a good idea?"
"That we're in here alone like this with your boyfriend down the hall."
"He's not my boyfriend. You are."
"Ronnie, I don't know what's going on..."
"Well, let me explain it. I'm not with Garland anymore. I care about you and I want to be with you."
"I really don't know what you expect me to say. He's just telling a very different story about what happened between you two."
"So you don't believe me?"
"Ronnie, I think you should go. I need to get some sleep and so do you."
"Well, I'm not leaving. I'm sleeping here with you just like I've been doing."
"I don't think that's wise but whatever; I'm going to sleep."
"Fine, go to sleep then."

He lay back on the bed, put his hands behind his head and stared up at the ceiling. I slowly took off my robe and dropped it on the floor. I hoped it would get his attention and it did. His eyes were drawn to the robe and then he glanced at me. He couldn't help but do a double take but I pretended not to notice. I didn't look in his direction as I walked over to turn off the light. I wanted to give him time to get a good look at me.

I sat on the edge of the bed and took off my slippers one by one. I could tell he was watching me and that was exactly what I wanted him to do. I leaned back on the bed next to him and I didn't get under the covers. I wanted to tease him as long as I could without appearing to try.

"What are you wearing?" He asked quietly.
"It's my nightgown."
"That is not a nightgown."
"Well, it's the only nightgown I have. Do you like it?"
"Of course." He looked uncomfortable. "Purple is my favorite color."

He closed his eyes apparently trying to calm himself. It didn't appear to be working. I lay there next to him feeling my own body temperature rise. He opened his eyes and stared at me. He couldn't turn away.

"You can touch me if you want to." I said staring back at him.
"You know that I do."

He leaned up on his elbow facing me. His dark eyes were surveying my entire body using only the moonlight. I closed my eyes giving him license to explore. His hand trailed down my face, to my neck and then he caressed my breast. He moved his hand down to brush my hip and then worked his way back up again. It was more than I could stand. I tried to pull him to me but he hesitated.

"Ronnie, I'm so confused."
"I know you are and I'm sorry."
"Everything is different now." He sounded so unhappy.
"Not for me."

Shenzy didn't need a lot of convincing because moments later he got up and locked the bedroom door. I could hardly wait for him to get back in bed. He lay down next to me and pulled me into his arms. The feel of his skin against mine excited me beyond words. I responded to his every touch and movement.

We made love over and over again. I couldn't get enough of him. We couldn't get enough of each other. My body was starting to ache but I didn't care. It was better than the ache in my heart at the thought of losing him.

It was probably around midnight when we collapsed on the bed. Our entire bodies were covered in sweat. We just kissed and held each other tightly. Neither of us wanted to let go. When I finally felt myself falling asleep, my Shenzy spoke softly in my ear.

"I love you."

Chapter 19

When I woke up the next morning, Shenzy was gone. I can't say that I was surprised. Garland's presence in the house was more than he could stand. I missed him already. And I wondered if last night was the last time that we would be together.

It was pretty early when I got up so I decided to take a shower in Shenzy's bathroom. I didn't want to disturb Shelby before I had to. When I finally decided to go and get my clothes, I saw that she was awake and already dressed for the day. I said good morning to her and started looking through my bag for something to wear.

"How are you?" Shelby said in a low voice.
"I'm alright. Shenzy's gone."
"I know. I spoke to him before he left."
"You did? What did he say?"
"Not much. He just said he was going to the lake and he would be back when he was needed."
"That was all?"
"Well, yes. But there's one more thing."
"What is it?"
"Well, it's about Garland. It seems he's been asking a lot of questions and Don is really concerned. He wants to get Garland out of here as early as tomorrow."
"I think that's a great idea. Is there anything that I can do to help?"
"They're hoping that you can convince him to go back to Greece quietly of course."
"Sure. I'll do whatever I can."
"Alright. Let's go get some breakfast. Perhaps you can talk to Garland afterwards."
"Ok. I just need a few minutes."

I went into the bathroom and got dressed. Then Shelby and I headed downstairs. I walked into the dining room and was surprised to find that only Chaunce was at the table. I figured this was a good opportunity to speak with him about Garland. Apparently Shelby agreed because when we sat down, she motioned toward him.

"Chaunce, I wanted to talk to you." I spoke quickly. "I know that Garland being here is a major issue but I don't think you've been given all of the facts."

"Ronnie, you have nothing to explain. I've heard what Garland is alleging. And my issue with his story is simple. What man would let the woman he loves travel overseas alone? If you two had simply had a lover's quarrel, than he would have travelled to Greece with you."

"Exactly my point. He's delusional. I mean, why put on this show?"

"He seems like the type of man who's accustomed to getting what he wants. And he's not able to understand that you sincerely wanted to leave the relationship."

"As far as I'm concerned, our involvement is over. I just want him away from here."

"That would be for the best."

"What would be best?" Don said as he strolled in with Garland in tow.

"Getting our friend back to where he belongs." Chaunce said matter-of-factly.

"Yes, that would be nice." I said coldly.

Garland followed Don around to the other side of the table which pleased me until I realized he would be staring in my face all through breakfast. I just focused on my plate until I was done eating.

I looked up to meet Garland's gaze and I realized that I felt nothing for him. I'd spent so many months trying to make something happen between us that didn't exist. I'd spent about a month with Shenzy that had fulfilled me more than I could have imagined. I decided that this was a good time to deal with Garland once and for all. He had to realize by now that I wasn't interested in him anymore.

"Garland, can I speak to you outside?" I spoke softly.

"Yes, of course." He replied happily.

I got up and headed towards the front door. He followed me outside and I kept walking once I realized he was right behind me. When we were a good distance from the house, I stopped walking and turned to face him. I needed him to understand how I felt but I still wanted to be civil about it.

"Garland, I know that you came looking for me and I appreciate that. But now that you've found me, you can see that I'm fine. I need you to go home."

"You expect me to leave you here alone?"

"I'm not alone. I'm with friends here."

"Friends, really? Which one of them are you friends with?" He spoke with a sarcastic tone.

"I'm friends with all of them. And just what business is it of yours anyway?" I turned away from him before I let him see how angry I was. "We ended our little masquerade, remember?"

"No, you ended it. I didn't end anything."

"Yes, I did end it. You wouldn't take our relationship seriously. Do you have any idea how that made me feel?" I turned to look him in the face. "Did you even care?"

"You know that I cared and it was more complicated then you're making it seem."

I took a few steps away from him and then sat down in the grass. The conversation wasn't going as well as I'd planned. I was over him and he wasn't accepting that fact. He came and sat down next to me but he didn't say anything right away. We sat there in silence for a few minutes. As much as I would miss Shenzy when I left, it felt good that I wouldn't have to deal with Garland anymore. And that made me smile.

"You don't get it do you?" He said sardonically. "I'm not leaving without you."

"I'm not going back with you Garland."

"Well, if you're not leaving than neither am I."

"You don't mean that."

"Yes, I do. Ronnie, I know that you're angry now but I think we can still salvage this."

"There's nothing to salvage." I laughed to myself. "Garland, the thing between us should never have dragged on as long as it did."

"You can't mean that."

"No, but I do. Do you know how it feels to not have to lie to my father anymore? I can go home and reconnect with my friends. I can be a whole person and work on making connections with people that are real."

"Oh, you mean like the people here. Ronnie, do you know what I had to go through to find you? No one on this island would bring me anywhere near this valley. They think this area is cursed or haunted. They say people who come out here never return home."

"Well, maybe that should have told you to stay away."

"I'd already come too far to turn back. My guy is waiting for me in the capital. I told him to give me three days and if I didn't return that he was to send a search party."

"Well, then you need to call him now. Tell him that you're alright."

"Maybe I don't want to do that."

"And why not?"

"Maybe everyone needs to know this place exists. There's something special here, admit it. You've been here for a while and you look amazing. I've never seen you more beautiful than you are now."

"Maybe this is what I look like happy." I got up and started walking back towards the house.

"Ronnie, I'm not leaving without you."

I stopped walking for a few moments and then kept going. He got up and started following me. When we walked into the house, Don was still sitting in the dining room. He called to me and Garland but I kept going up the stairs. I wasn't really sure where to go. I wanted to be alone for a while so I kept going down the hall. I went into Shenzy's room and shut the door.

I lay down on his bed and buried my face in the pillow. I could still smell him. I felt that familiar tingle in my nose when I was close to tears. I tried to remember last night as vividly as I could. His touch on my skin, the feel of his body against mine and the words he whispered in my ear. What if I never experienced those things again? Just as I was entering the first wave of my pain spiral, I heard the bedroom door open. Shelby walked over to the bed and sat down next to me.

"I figured I'd find you in here." She said solemnly.
"He won't leave." I sniffled loudly. "He won't leave unless I go with him."
"He told you that?"
"Yes. He's delusional."
"What if you refuse him?"
"He's threatening to expose everyone. He has two days to report to his contact in the capital or they'll send a search party out here."
"That would be disastrous." Shelby got up and started pacing the floor.
"Don't worry though. I've decided to go with him."
"Ronnie, there must be another way." She walked back over and stood by the bed.
"This is the only way that everyone will be safe. It's my fault that he's here. Once we get back to the states, he'll forget all about this place."

I hoped that my words would become reality. My one focus was getting Garland away from Seulmonde. I had to do this one thing for the people that I cared about.

I couldn't stay in the room anymore. I didn't want to argue with Shelby and have our last memories of each other to be bad ones. I headed back downstairs to find that Garland and Don were still sitting in the dining room. Chaunce had joined them too. I figured this was a good time to get everyone up to speed.

"Garland, I've decided to go back with you. We leave in the morning."

I quickly walked away so that I didn't have to deal with the looks on everyone's faces. I went back upstairs to Shelby's room and started organizing my clothes in my suitcase. I wasn't surprised when I heard her come in. I really didn't know what to say to her.

But instead of talking, she started helping me get my clothes together. I had some toiletries in the bathroom and she went to collect them for me.

I knew that she was sorrowful and so was I. In the time that I'd been in Seulmonde, we'd become so close. She and Shenzy were so much alike and I loved them both. I was packing my toiletries when I noticed her staring at me. I reached out to her and she took my hand. We hugged for a few moments and then she ran from the room.

I had my bags packed up so I decided to take them down to Shenzy's room. I knew he wouldn't be there but that was where I wanted to spend my last night. I tried to think of some positive spin I could put on this whole experience. That would've been easy to do if I could stop focusing on what I was about to lose.

I was sitting in the window when Don opened the door and walked into the bedroom.

"Don't you know how to knock?"
"I didn't think you'd invite me in. Look, I've just spoken to Shenzy and we have a problem. The Malagasy authorities are looking around out where we picked Garland up. We can't get you out yet. We need to wait until they leave the area."
"And how long will that take?"
"It'll probably be another couple days."
"Well, that's just perfect." I turned away from him and stared out the window.

For once Don didn't feel the need to agitate me. I heard the bedroom door open and close. I was so relieved that he'd left without a fight. I already felt like I was being tortured just having Garland here.

A few minutes later, there was another knock at the door. I thought it might be Don again. I was never happier to be wrong.

"Ronnie, may I come in?" Shelby said through the door.
"Of course; it's not locked."

"Hey there, Ronnie. I wanted to bring you something to eat. I figured you'd be getting hungry by now."
"Thank you. I really appreciate it."

It was so thoughtful of Shelby to bring me dinner. I really didn't want to look at Garland's face at the dining room table. She carried in a tray with soup for me and a salad for herself.

Prompted by Garland's presence in Seulmonde, our dinner conversation surrounded some of the encounters they'd had with visitors over the years. I got the feeling she was leaving out some of the details. To be honest, I didn't want her to tell me more. Shenzy gave me a pretty good idea of what would happen if someone got too close to this valley.

After we finished eating, Shelby gathered up our dishes and put them on the tray. I could tell she wanted to say something but she was having trouble forming the words.

"Is there something else?" I asked cautiously.
"I don't want to sound selfish at a time like this but I was thinking about the wedding. I hope that you'll still attend. I need my maid-of-honor."
"Of course I'm coming. I wouldn't miss it for anything."

I wanted to run to Shelby and squeeze her tightly but I was already an emotional wreck. She smiled warmly at me and carried the tray out of the room. I was glad that she came to eat with me because I had a feeling I wouldn't see her any more tonight. I'm sure she was going to see Luca. And with Garland around, they'd want to limit his contact with everything and everyone here.

I changed into my nightgown and climbed into bed. I was finally letting the reality of the situation wash over me. I felt so helpless. I wished there was something that I could do to change things.

I was relieved when I finally started to drift off to sleep but it wasn't a restful sleep. I dreamt that the police had found a way through Shenzy's defenses and they were storming the valley. They'd started bulldozing the giant baobab trees that protected the lake. And the last image my mind created was that of Shenzy being lost in the destruction.

I woke in a cold sweat. I jumped up out of bed and ran to the window. In the early morning light, I could just make out the tops of the trees. The sun seemed to shine on them with extra care.

I sat down by the window imagining I was out in the valley. There was still so much of Seulmonde that I hadn't seen. And to be honest, I was becoming a little stir crazy inside the house. A beautiful cage is still a cage. I needed to get outside; at least for a little while.

I showered and dressed in comfortable clothes. I even remembered to put on two pairs of socks for comfort. I'd be doing a lot of walking. I moved quietly around the room even though I doubted anyone else was awake. I grabbed my backpack and headed downstairs.

I went into the kitchen and grabbed whatever finger food I could find. I found Emerson crackers in the bread bin and fruit in a large bowl on the counter. I also found an empty container with a lid that I filled with water. I put everything in my backpack and scurried out the front doors.

Once I walked out of the stone fence, I felt a hint of panic. I knew which direction I wanted to go in but I was worried someone might see me. I took a deep breath and started jogging away from the house. I tried to block out everything around me and just focus on reaching the baobab trees on the far side of the field.

I was closest to the Tew's house now and I glanced nervously over my right shoulder. I wanted to make sure that no one from their house spotted me either. I didn't think anyone would feel comfortable with me roaming around the valley after the trouble that had followed me here.

When I reached the trees, I wasn't as tired as I thought I'd be. It had to be the effects of the water on my body. I slowed my pace now but

I didn't stop. I finally let myself enjoy my surroundings a little. I walked amongst the large baobabs and the smell of their flowers made me smile.

As I walked on, the trees became more sparse until they ended completely. Before me were rolling hills and grasslands. The view from where I stood was breathtaking.

I decided to rest a minute and have some breakfast. Then I just sat there and let the sunlight bathe my skin. It was quickly exchanged with a wisp of morning air that was just as calming. I definitely needed this time to myself. I felt so much better now than when I started out this morning.

I continued walking across the grasslands. Once I got closer to the hilly area beyond the trees, I realized that the mounds were larger than I expected. I was getting a pretty good workout as I traversed the peaks and valleys. It was a welcome departure from my endless thoughts of Shenzy.

I approached the largest of the hills I'd seen. And I felt a real sense of accomplishment that I'd come so far on my own. But as I reached the summit and observed what lie beyond the hill, my frame of mind dramatically changed.

The hill sloped down into a completely baron stretch of land. And beyond the lifeless terrain, was a huge thicket that seemed to go on for miles in either direction. I just had to get a closer look at it.

But the closer I got to the briars, the more ominous they looked. They were dull and lifeless with vines that intertwined at various points along their length. They were so close together that moving between them would be impossible.

I was about twenty feet away from the wall of vines when I smelled something rancid. It was a smell that I would never forget. It was getting so strong that it stopped me in my tracks.

Immediately I thought that something had gotten caught in the vines and died and I became keenly aware of the fact that I was out in the middle of nowhere and I was alone. Fear started to engulf me as I started to slowly back away from the vines.

I had the worst feeling in my stomach and my first impulse was to take off running. As I turned to break into a sprint, I ran smack into someone. I lost my balance and was about to fall when he caught me by the arm.

"What the hell are you doing out here?" Shenzy was holding on to my arm as he glared at me.

"Where did you come from?" I was so surprised to see him.

"Answer the question or are you planning to martyr yourself?" He let go of my arm.

"I needed to get away for a while. I needed some time to think on my own."

"Did you really believe you'd get this far without anyone knowing you were gone?"

"I guess I didn't think that far ahead."

"Why does that not surprise me?" His words were harsh but they didn't match the sad look in his eyes. "Your little field trip is over. Turn around and go back."

"Will you walk with me?" I asked quietly.

"I can't. I'm still monitoring the police activity south of here. So you see I don't have time to chase you around this valley."

"Alright. I'll go." I turned away from him as the tears welled up in my eyes.

I walked for a few minutes in silence. I thought he might watch me until I was well away from the briars. But when I turned around, he was gone. I walked the rest of the way back to the house feeling so alone.

When I got inside the house, I could see that the light was on in Chaunce's study. I didn't want to face him so I hurried up the stairs. I was on my way to Shenzy's room when Garland walked out into the hall. He was definitely the last person I wanted to see.

"Ronnie, is everything alright? They said you'd gotten lost."
"Garland, I'm fine." I kept walking past him. "I just need to lie down."
"I'm here if you want to talk."

I walked into Shenzy's room and shut the door. I let my back pack fall to the floor as I headed for the bathroom. All I wanted right now was a long, hot shower and to go to sleep.

I put on my nightgown and lay across the bottom of the bed. I could see clearly out of the bedroom window. The sun was setting in the distance and I was alone again with my thoughts. But for once, my thoughts didn't rest on Shenzy. I couldn't stop thinking about the menacing, network of vines that ran along the borders of Seulmonde.

And more than anything, I remembered the fear I felt as I approached them. Perhaps it was the look of the vines that scared me most or maybe it was the smell; I can't be sure. I was lost in my thoughts, when there was a knock at the door.

"Who is it?" I asked cautiously.
"It's Chaunce. May I speak with you?"
"I'm not dressed. Can you give me a few minutes?"
"Of course; I'll be down in the study."

I went to my suitcase and pulled out a pair of shorts and a t-shirt. I didn't care what I wore. I had a feeling he was going to talk to me about my journey today. I knew I had it coming.

When I got down to the study, I noticed that the door was shut. I knocked and Chaunce invited me in. When I walked inside, I was surprised to see Shenzy leaning against the book shelf at the far corner of the room. I had no idea he was even in the house.

I tried to hold my composure after seeing him. I sat down on the couch and tried to focus my attention on Chaunce. He was sitting behind the desk with a rather peculiar look on his face.

"Ronnie, I wanted to speak with you about what happened today."
He glanced over at Shenzy. "But I thought you might feel more
comfortable talking to someone else."
"Ok." My voice sounded so small. I wasn't sure I'd said it loud
enough for them to hear.
"I'll give you two a few minutes to talk." Chaunce got up and quickly
left the room.

"So did you have fun today?" Shenzy said it as a joke but I could tell
he was angry.
"I wouldn't call it fun. I just needed to get away for a while."
"You need to be more thoughtful in your actions. With the police at
our door step and you running off, it's a recipe for disaster."
"Look, I get it. I messed up… again."
"Ronnie, I need you to promise that you'll stay near the house. I can't
watch out for you and give our borders the attention they deserve."
"Ok. I'll stay in the house."
"Good girl." He walked slowly towards me.

I stared into his dark eyes and it was almost too much for me to
handle. I wanted to reach out and touch him so badly. But I couldn't
risk having him reject me. I just stood there.

"I have to go," he said quietly.
"Shenzy, there is one more thing. When I was out there today, I
smelled something and it scared me."
"That's exactly why you need to stay close to the house. It was
probably just an animal stuck in a trap."

He gave me a reassuring glance and walked out of the study. I
followed him outside and watched as he walked out into the night.
When I reached the gate, I heard someone behind me. I turned to see
Don walking in my direction.

"Don't worry, I'm not going anywhere. I just needed some fresh air."
"You know, you're even more trouble than I thought you'd be." He
spoke behind me.
"You know Don; you never gave me a chance. Why is that?" I said as
I turned to face him.

"I don't know what you mean."

"You've been pretty horrible to me since we first met."

"That's not a true statement. You're just a very sensitive person."

"Tell me the truth. You don't think I'm good enough for your brother, do you?"

"Wrong again. I was just trying to save you both from heartache."

"What are you talking about?"

"Don't you get it? Shenzy has a responsibility to Seulmonde. It's his birth rite. I have a duty as well."

"And what is your responsibility Don? This should be good."

"I will take over for Chaunce. I'll be the next leader of Seulmonde."

I quickly realized that he was serious. "So what does that have to do with me and Shenzy being together?"

"You don't get it… Shenzy can't marry; he can't have a family."

"He'll be alone forever?"

"By the time he's free of his duty, you'll probably be dead." He almost looked sad. "So go home with Garland. Marry him and get on with your life. Forget about Shenzy."

"I can't. I don't want to forget him. And maybe if you'd ever loved anybody in your whole miserable life, you wouldn't even suggest such a thing."

I pushed past him and walked back into the house. I didn't stop to see if Chaunce needed to see me. I just kept walking up the stairs and headed for Shenzy's room. I just lay across the bed staring at the ceiling.

I couldn't stop thinking about him stuck out at the lake for the next fifty years or more. I wondered if he'd ever find happiness. Would he ever know the joy of having a wife and children? I didn't like the thought that he might never be loved again.

The more I thought about what Don told me, the more it made sense. That was why all of the women flocked around him. They were hoping to be the next Mrs. Seulmonde. My poor Shenzy was left with no one. As I lay in bed that night, I made a silent prayer for him. I fell asleep with his name on my lips.

It took another two days for the authorities to complete their search of the region below Seulmonde. When they moved out of range of Shenzy's equipment, he gave the ok for Garland to call his friend in the capital.

That phone call would serve two purposes. It would reassure the local police that a wealthy American hadn't perished on their island and it gave his contact the green light to go home. Everything was coming together.

That last evening before we left was bittersweet. I was happy that Garland would be away from Seulmonde but it also meant that I had to leave too. I felt like I was leaving my family behind but I knew it had to be done.

Chapter 20

I woke up early the next morning but I didn't get up right away. I wasn't ready to leave and I certainly didn't want to see Don's face. As I lay there on the bed, I heard voices in the hall. One of them sounded like Shenzy so I jumped up and put my ear to the door. He must have been heading toward his bedroom.

"She's in there?" Shenzy said in a low voice.
"Yes. She moved into your room when he came." Shelby replied in a low voice as well. "Are you going to talk to her?"
"No. It wouldn't change anything. She's leaving with him."
"But you know why; you're not being fair to her."
"Look Shelby, I know what you're trying to do and I love you for it. Let's just get downstairs."
"Alright."

I went back and sat down on the bed. I couldn't believe he was right outside the door and he wouldn't talk to me. I got up slowly and dragged myself into the bathroom to get cleaned up. Even though he couldn't face me, I wanted to pull myself together.

I picked up my suitcase and my smaller bag and carried them downstairs. I left them in the foyer and walked into the dining room. Everyone looked in my direction but the only person I saw was Shenzy. He smiled at me but it only lasted a moment.

When I sat down at the table, I noticed Garland staring at me. It made me uncomfortable so I just worked harder to block him out. Pretty soon, I was blocking everyone out. I was completely focused on Shenzy and nothing else really mattered. He was wearing a Rolling Stones t-shirt and he looked absolutely adorable. I stared from his hair to his eyes to his kissable lips. And just to throw everyone off, I would eat a mouthful of food every so often.

I would make a thousand memories at this breakfast table and they were all of him. It was going really well until Garland decided he needed to say something. I tried to hide my irritation at his blatant display of idiocy.

"Well, I don't know if this is a good time, but I want to say a few words."
"What is it Garland?" Chaunce spoke in his diplomatic tone.
"I just wanted to thank you for taking care of my Ronnie." Garland touched my arm as he spoke.
"Actually, we owe her a debt." Don said matter-of-factly. "She saved my dear sister in Greece."
"She didn't tell me," he said as he glanced from me to Shenzy. "It seems there are many things she hasn't shared."
"I need to get everything ready." Shenzy got up and left the room.

I glanced over my shoulder at him. He picked up my bags and carried them outside. When I turned back to face the table, I saw that Chaunce was also watching Shenzy. The look on his face was one of concern and it mirrored how I was feeling. I got up from the table and went outside. Then I ran down to the gate and looked to see which way Shenzy was going. He was walking down the left side of the house and I called to him hoping he would slow down. He didn't.

"Shenzy, wait a minute. I need to talk to you." I kept after him.
"What is it Ronnie?" He finally stopped but he didn't turn around.
"I just wanted to tell you that I'm sorry about all of this." I walked up and stood next to him.
"I'm sorry too." He spoke in a low voice. "But it doesn't change anything. It doesn't change who I am and it doesn't change the fact that you're leaving."
"I know why you're saying that. Don told me about your duty and I don't care."
"Ronnie, let's not make this harder than it has to be. Go back up to the house and say your goodbyes. It's almost time to go."
"And that's it? "You just want me to leave you alone?"
"Ronnie, I'm not the one who's leaving."

He walked away from me but I didn't follow him this time. I headed back to the house to say my goodbyes. Shelby was very emotional; we both were. Don and Garland ended up having to usher me out of the house. I never thought I would feel this way when I finally left. Instead of feeling like I was going home, I felt like I was leaving my home behind.

We followed Don down the left side of the house in the direction Shenzy had been walking. He didn't tell us how far we had to go. He just said to follow him. We probably walked half a mile or more before we reached a line of trees. The trees stretched out as far as I could see. And when I rounded the tree closest to us, I saw Shenzy sitting in what looked like a large roller coaster car painted to look like the surrounding trees. He was sitting in the driver's seat and Don motioned for Garland and I to get in the back. Don climbed in front with Shenzy and we took off.

We started off slowly but we sped up quite a bit. The ride was smooth and comfortable. I could tell that Garland was enjoying the ride by the look on his face. He tried to hold my hand but I moved it away. I thought he might protest the gesture so I started talking before he could.

"What is this thing? I thought you didn't have cars here." I spoke in Don's direction.
"It's a hydraulic car and its compliments of Dr. Shenzy," Don said in his sarcastic tone. "And you've been in it before. You were asleep though."
"I wondered about that. How did you get me to the house?" I asked quietly.
"Shenzy brought you." Don replied matter-of-factly. "You don't think I carried you and my sister, do you?"

At that moment, I was glad I couldn't see Shenzy's face. I wondered what he was thinking. So Shenzy had seen me before we met at the lake and he never told me. I wondered why. I tried not to react too much to what Don said because Garland was watching me. I didn't want him to start connecting all of the dots. I figured that changing the subject was probably a good idea.

"So Don, what happens after this?" I moved up in my seat so Garland couldn't look at my face.

"Well, once we get to the chopper, you and Garland will take a nice nap and you'll wake up in Athens."

"The chopper? You mean we have to get on a helicopter too?" I probably sounded like a twelve year old.

"Yes, that's how we get to the airport. Don't worry, Shenzy is an excellent pilot."

"He's the pilot? Wow, is there anything this guy can't do?" Garland chimed in.

"That's a good question. Ronnie, what do you think?" Don said with a sly smile on his face.

"Don, I really don't know what you're talking about so just forget it."

"What I mean is that you've road Shenzy before, I mean you've road with him, right?" Don wasn't letting go.

"I was asleep so I don't remember, remember?" I added quickly.

I didn't want to have to look at Garland's face. But that didn't stop him from opening his mouth. I wished that I could've gotten out of the car but we were moving so fast. After Garland started talking, I seriously considered jumping out as an option.

"Ronnie, is there something you need to tell me?" Garland whispered to me.

"Garland I have nothing to say to you." I whispered back.

"When we get to Greece, we really need to talk about what happened here. I need to know the truth."

"Garland, will you please shut up. We are in the no questions phase of this trip."

Even though we were trying to whisper, I knew that Don and Shenzy could hear everything we were saying and that really bothered me. Even though I was leaving, I didn't want Shenzy to think that I was leaving to be with Garland.

We drove the rest of the way to the helicopter pad in silence. The ride lasted about an hour. The tension in the air was palpable, but I still had time to notice just how incredible Shenzy's hydraulic car was.

He was the smartest, most fascinating person I'd ever met and I couldn't tell him. I just needed to get Garland away from here and that was more important than my infatuation.

We came to a stop about thirty yards from where the helicopter was positioned. I began to realize how carefully orchestrated everything in Seulmonde needed to be. I also realized just how dangerous this terrain could be. If they hadn't noticed Garland was out here, he would certainly have perished. I'm sure in his current state, that thought had probably escaped him. I would be sure to remind him later.

We waited near the hydraulic car while Shenzy started the helicopter. That's when Don pulled out a flask and handed it to Garland. He hesitated and I motioned for him to go ahead and drink. He handed it to me and I took a few sips as well. I gave the flask back to Don and I started feeling the effects right away. Garland hit the ground with a dull thud. Just as my eyes were closing, I saw Don reach out to grab me.

When I woke up, I had a slight headache. I couldn't tell where I was but I could see that the sun was going down. I sat up and looked around. I was in a hotel room but I had no idea where. The pale blue room was dimly lit and beautifully furnished. I thought I was alone until I heard Garland's voice behind me.

"So which one was it? Which one of them were you playing house with while I was risking my life to save you?" Garland was more animated than usual.
"Did I ask you to come looking for me? I was perfectly fine where I was."
"Well, that makes sense considering you don't find any of this strange. They drug us and drop us off in a hotel in Athens and you don't bat an eye."
"Is that where we are, Athens?"

"We're at the Hotel Grande Bretagne in downtown Athens. Our bags are here and our room is paid for the night. Over on the desk, I found two first class tickets for a flight home in the morning." He paused to look around. "Yeah, they thought of everything."
"I'm going to freshen up and then I want to go find something to eat."
"So that's it? That's all you have to say?"
"Yup, that's it."

I went into the bathroom and turned on the faucet. I sat on the side of the bathtub and felt a rush of fear come over me. I couldn't help but wonder if I would ever see Shenzy again. But at least I'd led Garland away. That was the important thing. I dampened a cloth and wiped my face with it. I knew that if I stayed in the bathroom too long, Garland would come knocking. I turned off the faucet and walked back into the bedroom.

I was pretty hungry by then so I walked over to the desk and picked up the phone receiver. I didn't see a menu anywhere but then this type of hotel didn't have such things lying about. As soon as I hit the button for service, a woman answered.

"Hi, can you tell me if your dining room is still serving dinner?" I spoke into the phone. *"Do you have room service at this hour? Oh, alright. Do you recommend anything? That sounds fine. We'll take two and a bottle of wine. That's fine. Yes. Please charge it to the room. Thanks."* I hung up the phone.

"Well, who are you?" Garland said as he stood up and walked over to me. "What happened to you out there? You've never taken charge and ordered for us before."
"We've never gone anywhere before," I said and walked over to the window to stare out at the darkening sky.
"Ouch. You're in a mood."
"Garland, it's been an interesting few weeks. I'm ready to get back to my life and figure out what my next move is."
"So what does that mean for us?"
"Garland, there is no us. I wish you'd realize that."
"Well, I've heard that before. We're alone now so you can just drop the act."

I turned and looked at him. He really believed this was another one of our episodes. I didn't feel like wasting my breath. He'd find out soon enough that I was serious.

For a while, I just stood there staring out the window. I wondered where Shenzy was at that moment. I would give anything to talk to him right now but I had no way to reach him. I was lost in my thoughts when Garland came toward me. He turned me to face him and covered my mouth with his. I pulled away from him and turned back toward the window.

There was a knock at the door that surprised us both. Garland hesitated for a moment and then went to answer it. Our dinner had arrived and not a minute too soon. Garland tipped the room service attendant and ushered him out the door. He turned to face me with a look of amusement on his face.

"We're alone in one of the most beautiful cities in the world and you're playing hard to get?"
"If you do that again, you're going to get arrested in one of the most beautiful cities in the world."
"Ronnie, don't be that way." He walked towards me again.
"Do not touch me again Garland. I mean it."

I was fighting back tears. I'd never felt so violated in my life. I walked into the smaller bedroom and shut the door. I officially claimed this room for my own. I started pacing the floor trying to compose myself. I knew that Garland wouldn't leave me alone for long though.

"Ronnie, come out and eat. You're food will get cold," he said quietly. "I'm sorry. I'll behave myself."

I waited as long as I could to come out but my stomach was starting to protest. I opened the door slowly and walked over to the table. Garland set out our food and poured wine into two glasses. The food smelled wonderful. The salmon was blackened to perfection and the broccoli looked like it would fall right off my fork. I sat down with a huff and put my napkin on my lap.

Garland looked pretty pathetic. Maybe he was sorry for what had happened. Either way, I was still angry with him. We ate dinner pretty much in silence. He tried to talk to me a few times but I just gave him one or two word answers. When we were done eating, I said goodnight to him and went into my small bedroom.

I didn't shut the door but I lay on the bed and turned to face the window. I heard Garland moving around so I looked over my shoulder. He was collecting my bags for me. As he approached, I turned my back towards the door again.

"Where do you want these?" he asked.
"Just leave them by the door. Thank you."
"I'm really sorry Ronnie. It's just that you never minded before."
"Things are different now." I didn't look in his direction again.
"Goodnight Garland."
"Goodnight."

I waited for him to go into the other bedroom. He shut the door and turned on the television. I felt a huge wave of relief wash over me. I decided that now might be a good time to call my dad and it might keep Garland from coming back if he heard me on the phone. I hadn't spoken to Lee in a few days with so much going on. I pulled the satellite phone out of my suitcase, powered it up and sat back on the bed. When I dialed the number, I was surprised that the phone rang several times before he answered.

"Hello." Lee answered the phone sounding tired.
"Hello Lee, how are you?" I replied.
"I'm doing fine; just fighting this summer cold."
"Have you been taking your vitamin C?"
"Yes, I have and I've been to the doctor as well. I'm as fit as a fiddle."
"Are those your words or the doctor's?"
"They're mine. I think I'm doing pretty well for a man my age. But enough about me, how are you doing young lady?"
"I'm ok. I'll be home in a couple days."

The conversation went better than I thought it would. Lee was excited to hear from me and excited to hear about my trip. I even told him about the new friends I'd made. I left out the part about falling head over heels in love with Shenzy but that was normal daughter withholding stuff. Even though I was worried about Shenzy, it felt good that I told my father about him.

After my phone call, I started getting tired. I figured a hot shower would help me sleep more restfully. I locked the door to my bedroom and got a nightgown out of my bag. I was headed for the bathroom when there was a light tap on the door. I put my ear up to the door and spoke as clearly as I could.

"Garland, what is it?"
"I want to talk to you for a minute."
"Alright; go ahead and talk."
"I was hoping to talk face to face. I promise to behave myself."
"Just give me a minute."

I put my nightgown on the bed and slowly opened the door. Garland was on the sofa in the sitting room. I walked in and sat down a comfortable distance away from him. I could tell that he was unhappy with my body language.

"Ronnie, I think we should clear the air before we get back to Columbia."
"About what?"
"Well, about us." He looked away from me before continuing. "In all honesty, I expected you to be happy to see me. I've never been so wrong before. You're so angry."
"Garland, I'm not angry with you. I've made peace with what happened between us and now I think you should too."
"So you won't even consider working things out with me?"
"Garland there's nothing to work out. I don't feel the same way I did before." I stared down at my hands before continuing. "I don't want to be with you."
"I see. Well, I appreciate your honesty."
"There's more."

220

He took a deep breath and stared at me intently. "What is it?"

"I'm not going back with you tomorrow. I've decided to stay here for the rest of the week."

"You want to stay here alone?"

"Yes, I do."

He hesitated for a moment and then stood up. "Well, I'm going to go get some rest. Tomorrow's going to be a long day for me."

"Alright."

I thought he was going to say something else but he didn't. He walked into his room and quietly shut the door behind him. I leaned back on the sofa and shut my eyes. I was glad that Garland and I had gotten everything out in the open.

I went into my room and changed my flight. Tomorrow morning I would get another room. I started feeling a little better after I decided to stay. There was just one thing left to do. I needed to give Garland his phone. He certainly wouldn't have a need to contact me now. I put the phone on the floor in front of his room door and quietly went back to my room.

I took a long hot shower and then slipped into my nightgown. I lay across the bed knowing that I would soon be asleep.

Chapter 21

I woke up with the sun shining directly in my face. I rolled off the bed, closed the satin curtains and lumbered into the bathroom to brush my teeth. I washed my face and then went to check on Garland. As a peace offering, I thought we might have breakfast together before he had to catch his flight.

But when I got over to his room, he was gone. I knew he wasn't coming back. He'd taken all of his things with him. He must have really been upset after we talked last night. I can't say that I blame him but it would have been nice if he had told me he was leaving.

As I walked back to my room, I looked down to see a handwritten note. He must have slid it under my door this morning and I hadn't noticed it when I came out. The note was short and to the point.

Ronnie,
I realize that I made a big mistake coming to look for you.
You were doing pretty well on your own. I guess it's true
what people say. You don't realize what you have until it's
gone. I just want you to know that I meant you no harm.
And I hope that one day you can think of me fondly as I will
think of you.
Yours Garland

As I finished reading the note, I realized that this might be the last I'd hear from Garland Malloy. I was alone in Greece but I wasn't afraid. This hotel was in a great location and I would take full advantage of that fact. I just needed to check back at lunch time to see if I could switch to a smaller room. But for now, I would get some breakfast and then do some exploring.

I started to feel a little of the excitement that I felt when I first decided to take this trip. And with Garland gone, the anxiety I was feeling had all but dissipated. I showered and dressed comfortably in shorts and track shoes.

I grabbed my purse and the card key that was on the table by the door. When I got out into the hall, I was ready to see Athens. Well, at least the part that was within a one mile radius of my hotel. I dared not venture out farther than that on foot. But that one mile radius included the Acropolis which was at the core of my interest.

After a delicious buffet style breakfast, I headed outside. The air was warm and the sun was shining overhead. I stood on the hotel steps for a few moments just taking in the sights and sounds. There were signs at the street corners but I couldn't read them from where I was standing. I took a chance and headed towards the corner that was most congested. It was a lucky gamble because one of the signs pointed in the direction of the Acropolis.

I followed the signs until I reached Theorias Street. The entrance to the Acropolis was just ahead on the left. I realized when I was planning my travel that this was the busy season but I was still surprised by the large volume of visitors. There were many tourist groups and families walking about. Some of them were carrying bottles of water which I had completely forgotten about. I knew that I wouldn't last long in the heat without some water of my own. Luckily for me, the sun wasn't at full strength.

As I entered the main archaeological site, I noticed the beautiful stone-paved paths. Each path led to ancient temples and monuments that I'd read about as a little girl. But I never imagined I would see them with my own eyes. I picked up a site map at the ticket window and I used it to get around.

When I reached the Parthenon itself, the view took my breath away. The sheer size of the columns was awe inspiring. I began to imagine what it was like before the destruction it suffered over five centuries ago. I walked around the perimeter of the temple for almost an hour and I had plenty of company. The Parthenon was the main attraction even though visitors weren't allowed to go inside.

I walked beyond the temple and looked out over the city. I could see all of Athens from here and then it hit me. This is what I travelled thousands of miles to see and I wasn't disappointed.

While I enjoyed my visit, it would've been nice to have someone to talk to. I saw very few people that were walking around alone and they were usually men. I started thinking about how worried my father was that I was travelling by myself. I would just have to be extra careful.

As I made my way back to the hotel, I began to feel the full weight of the sun. I picked up my pace as I rounded the last corner onto Constitution Square. The streets were still full of people who didn't seem too bothered by the heat. I was relieved when I finally reached the air conditioned lobby of the Hotel Grande Bretagne. I headed up to the front desk to request a smaller room when I received some surprising news.

"Ms. Adler, I show that you're checked out of the hotel."
"Excuse me? There must be some mistake. Perhaps I was already moved to another room."
"I just checked again. I show that you checked out and there is no other room reserved under your name."

"I think I can help solve the mystery." Don spoke from behind me.
"Excuse me for a moment." I said and smiled at the attendant.

I turned to see Don standing behind me. I walked over to him trying hard to maintain my composure. He was very amused by my efforts.

"Don what have you done and what are you doing here?"
"First things first. I've collected your belongings from upstairs and checked you into more appropriate accommodations."

"Why on earth did you do that?"

"Because I didn't think you would feel comfortable here alone. Now answer a question for me, why didn't you catch your flight?"

"I wasn't ready to leave." I immediately thought about Shenzy. "Are you here alone?"

"Shenzy isn't here with me if that's what you're asking."

I stood there for a moment trying to think of what I should do. But to be honest, I was glad to see a familiar face; even if it was Don's.

"Alright, I'll go with you."

"Excellent. I have a car waiting right out front. Let's go."

I walked out of the hotel and stepped into the noon day sun. For a moment, I thought my eyes were playing tricks on me. The car waiting out front was more limousine than car. For someone who should be keeping a low profile, Don certainly didn't mind attention.

There was a driver waiting and he opened the door as we approached. I smiled at him and stepped inside the car. Don stepped in after me and sat a little too close for my comfort. I crossed my legs and used that opportunity to move closer to the window. I could see him smile out of the corner of my eye. Everything I did amused him.

"So did you enjoy yourself this morning?" Don asked matter-of-factly.

"Yes, I did. I saw the Parthenon up close. It was better than I expected."

"I was actually given permission to go inside. Now that was exciting."

"Who'd you have to pay for that privilege?"

"Who said I had to pay? Maybe I just asked nicely." He was the most egotistical man I'd ever met. I started to second guess my decision to go with him.

For the first time since we met, I rolled my eyes at him. He always had to be one step ahead of everyone else. Why couldn't he ever let anyone else just enjoy a moment of recognition or accomplishment?

He must have detected my irritation because he left me to my thoughts for a while. I glanced out of the car window and saw that we were riding along the coast. The view from the car window was doing wonders for my mood. Even though I had no idea where we were going, I wasn't worried about it. Don could be a real jerk sometimes but I trusted him.

"I think I was a little hasty in my judgment of you." Don surprised me with his admission.
"Is that some sort of apology?"
"I guess it is."

I didn't say anything else during the drive and neither did he. We continued along the coast until we reached a secluded road. A few minutes later, we pulled into the drive way of a beautiful sand stone villa. From the outside, it appeared to have two levels.

When we got out of the car, I could barely wait to see inside. Don walked in the front door and held it open for me. Once inside, we were standing in the main room. It had large floor to ceiling windows that let in huge amounts of light.

Directly ahead of us, were two large patio doors that opened to a wrap around deck and a swimming pool that appeared to blend in with the Aegean Sea beyond. I walked out onto the patio and stared out over the water. The property even had a pier. This was perhaps the most inviting part of the house. I loved the comfy lounge area with huge white sofa chairs and a full size canopy. I was just about to sit down when Don joined me.

"Ronnie, come have some lunch. Rafael has prepared something for you. Once you eat and put your bags away, you can come back out here and relax."
"Who's Rafael?"
"He's our chef and Fedor is our butler."
"Why do you have a chef and a butler?"
"Their services come with the villa."
"This place must have cost a fortune to rent."

"Not really. Please come and eat." He ushered me back into the house. "Then you can go upstairs and pick out a room. Fedor will take your bags for you."

Fedor nodded his head to me and walked out to collect my bags. He looked about thirty five but he was well built with dark hair and eyes. He never looked directly at me which I found a little strange. I'd been in Greece for a little more than a day so I probably wasn't the best judge of normal.

I walked into the dining room which looked like no one had ever eaten in it. My eyes wandered over the extravagant furnishings but they came to rest on a plate of food at the edge of the table. I walked over and sat down. Don came in with a rotund gentleman who I assumed was Rafael.

"Hello Ms. I have prepared pastitsio for you. You will like it very much." Rafael replied energetically.
"Thank you Rafael. It smells delicious. But what is it?"
"It's like lasagna. You'll love it." Don chimed in.

Rafael went back into the kitchen apparently pleased with himself. I ate practically the whole thing before I took a breath. I was waiting for Don to comment on how much I'd eaten but he never did. I got up from the table and headed for the stairs. When I reached the landing above, I saw a furnished sitting room with a door on either side.

I walked in the door at the top of the stairs first. The room was furnished much in the same way as the sitting area. The king size bed had a canopy and netting above it. When I walked over to the window, all I could see was the driveway and part of the garage. I decided to check out the view in the other room.

When I walked into the second bedroom, I noticed that the television was on. I was surprised to find that the room was already occupied.

"What do you want Sheldon? I'm busy." Shenzy spoke with an irritated tone.

He was lying on the bed facing the television. I was so surprised to see him that I didn't say anything right away. I just stood there in the doorway holding onto the knob for dear life.

"Shenzy, it's me," I said quietly.

When he heard my voice he sat up immediately but he didn't turn around to face me.

"Now it all makes sense. That's why he didn't tell me where he was going this morning."
"He didn't tell me you were here either."
"So where's Garland?"
"I would guess he's somewhere over the Atlantic by now."
"So he left without you? Why?"
"Because I asked him to. Shenzy, the only reason I left with him was to get him away from Seulmonde. You have to know that."
"You spent the night with him." He didn't say it as a question but he was waiting for my reply.
"It was a two bedroom suite."
"So you didn't sleep together?"
"No, we didn't. Nothing happened between me and Garland last night."

I walked over and sat next to him on the bed. I didn't know if he wanted me to but I didn't care. He started talking so I took that as a good sign.

"I couldn't sleep last night. All I could think about was him touching you."
"Shenzy, I missed you from the moment I left. I wanted to talk to you so badly."
"I understand why you left but I still didn't like it. You have a history with him."
"Yes, we have a history together and that's all it is. Things didn't end well between us." I tried to reassure him.

"Garland travelled half way around the world to find you, Ronnie."
"And nobody knows accept you and your family. He certainly didn't tell his family or friends about me; even when he feared the worst. I could never be with him again and that's what I told him last night."
"What did he say?"
"He didn't say anything. He left this morning without saying goodbye."

He stood up and walked over to the window. I couldn't see his face but I thought he might be working out what to say to me.

"Are you going to stay here with us?"
"Since your brother checked me out of my hotel, I suppose I am."
"He can be so dramatic sometimes."
"I'm coming to realize that. Well, I'll let Fedor know to bring my bags upstairs."

I walked over to where he was standing and kissed him lightly on the cheek. He smiled down at me which made me feel a little better. Not as good as if he'd kissed me back, but better all the same. I went to leave the room but he called to me just as I reached the door.

"Ronnie, will you stay with me?"
"Yes, I'm staying."
He must have noticed my confused expression. "I want to know if you'll stay in this room with me."
"I'd like that. Besides, this room has the better view." I smiled at him as I walked out the door.

When I got downstairs, Don had a playful look on his face. Before I could say anything, he directed Fedor to carry my bags up to Shenzy's room. I just gave him a cross look as I stood there waiting for him to explain himself.

"Why didn't you tell me he was here?"
"I wanted it to be a surprise."
"And I actually thought you were trying to be nice to me."

"Well, that was part of it. I really needed to get you here. Shenzy blamed me for chasing you off so I had to try and make things right. When he gives you the silent treatment, it can be maddening."
"Well, I wouldn't know." I spoke in a teasing tone.
"I guess you wouldn't. By the way, is he still watching television?"
"I believe so."
"Maybe you can get him out of that room. Since we got here, he's been watching television and sulking."
"Really?" I felt horrible. He was like that because of me. "Well, I'll just ask him to go swimming with me."
"Ronnie, you're definitely wrong there. He spends all of his time at the lake. The last thing he wants to do right now is swim."
"Do you doubt my powers of persuasion? I can easily get your brother in that pool."
"I don't think so. Well, unless you pretend that you're drowning or something."
"I'm so not a damsel in distress. I'm just going to ask him nicely."
"This I have to see."
"Well, just wait a few minutes before you come out there. I don't want you to ruin it for me."
"You've got yourself a deal."
"Hey Ronnie..." Don called to me as I ran for the stairs.
"Yeah?"
"I'm really glad you're here." He spoke with sincerity in his voice.
"Me too. Thanks for coming to get me."

I continued up the stairs and walked into the bedroom to find Shenzy watching a game show. I walked over to my bag and pulled out my bikini. I caught Shenzy's attention and I knew it wouldn't be long before he said something.

"Going for a swim?" He said without looking my way.
"Yes and I think I'll take some pictures while I'm down there. You know, I haven't taken any pictures since I've been on vacation."

I walked into the bathroom and slipped out of my clothes. I put on my hot pink bikini and grabbed my sun tan lotion out of my bag. I put the lotion on and walked back into the room to see Shenzy looking out the window at the swimming pool.

"So do you think you can help me?"

"You mean with your pictures?"

"Yeah, or maybe someone else can help. I'll see what Don's doing or maybe Fedor." I grabbed my camera out of my bag and started toward the door.

"Not so fast." He jumped off the bed and followed me out the door.

When we got downstairs, Don was lounging in the main room reading a newspaper. But when he saw us walking toward the patio he peeped over the top of it and shook his head. I smiled as I watched his reaction but kept walking out to the pool. When we got outside, I handed Shenzy the camera.

"Are you ready?" I asked him excitedly.

"Sure. Where do you want to take the pictures?"

"I think here is fine." I stood near the edge of the pool.

I did several poses and made a funny face each time. Shenzy was trying to hide his amusement. He was such a professional. I decided to up the excitement by untying my bikini from around my back. Shenzy stopped taking pictures and gave me an odd look.

"What are you doing?"

"I want to be like the Mediterranean women. They go topless here, right?"

"Don't do that. Someone's going to see you." He looked over his shoulder into the house. "Don is sitting right in there on the chair."

"It will only take a moment. Can you get a couple quick pictures?"

I untied the top of my bikini and watched it fall to the ground. Shenzy put the camera down on the ground and started towards me. I wrapped my arms around him and pulled him into the swimming pool. We both fell in with a loud splash.

When I came up for air, I started laughing hysterically. Shenzy looked at me with disbelief but he couldn't help from laughing too.

"You planned this didn't you?" He asked playfully.

"Don bet me that I couldn't get you in the pool." I was still laughing.
"Is that so?"

He swam over to me and grabbed me around my waist. I put my
arms around his neck and kissed his cheek. He looked down at my
breasts and I couldn't help but feel warmed by his stare. He leaned
down to kiss my waiting lips. The water around us was warm and it
felt good against my skin. I delighted in being close to him this way.
It was as if the last few days hadn't happened and we'd never been
apart. The only thing that could ruin this moment was a visit from
the king of impropriety.

"Now if I'd known you would be using the twins, I would never have
made that bet." Don spoke from behind us.
"We need a little privacy Don." Shenzy replied quickly.
"No problem. I'm leaving." Don said as he put his hands up and
walked back into the house.
"Can you reach my top?" I spoke into his shoulder.
"Now you're shy?"

He got out of the pool and handed me my bathing suit top. I turned
away from the house and put it on. When I walked out of the pool,
Shenzy was waiting for me with a towel. He helped me dry off and
then wrapped the towel around my body. We walked inside the house
and headed for the stairs. Don was pretending to read his newspaper
again wearing the silliest grin on his face. I wondered if he saw me
without my top on.

When we got up to the bedroom, Shenzy closed the door behind us
and locked it. He walked over to me and pulled the towel from
around my body. I waited for him to say something but he didn't. He
pulled me into his arms and kissed me lightly on my forehead. I
couldn't help but smile. Then he just let me go.

"I need to take a shower," he said lightly and walked into the
bathroom.
"Ok. I'll just wait here." I picked up the towel and wrapped it around
me again.

While I was waiting for Shenzy to finish his shower, I turned on the television and sat down on the bed. I was instantly shaken by the images of the Athens airport explosions. The authorities claimed to have the perpetrator in custody and they insisted he worked alone.

According to the news report, he was a disgruntled former airport employee. I just couldn't understand why he would want to hurt innocent people. I turned off the television and lay across the bed. I tried to get the images of the airport destruction out of my head. I shouldn't have been surprised when an uncomfortable slumber descended on me.

When I woke up, it was quiet in the room. I looked around but Shenzy was nowhere to be found. He must have gone downstairs to talk with Don. He'd showered and left the room without waking me up.

I decided to get a shower myself but I couldn't help thinking about when Shenzy and I came upstairs earlier. I thought we were going to reconnect after that whole Garland situation. Maybe he just needed a little encouragement. I put on the black halter dress that Shelby had given me. She bought it on her trip to Atlanta without trying it on. When she got it home, she didn't like it anymore. We thought it looked great on me.

As I walked downstairs, my attention was taken off my outfit. Rafael had prepared Fasolada and it smelled wonderful. When we sat down to dinner, the food was really good but the conversation was lousy. Don and Shenzy spent most of dinner talking about sailing to Crete. So I just sat there finishing my dessert and smiling.

I'd never been on a boat before and I didn't find the idea of getting on one particularly interesting. I caught Shenzy looking in my direction a few times though. I loved when he watched me. I was completely lost in my thoughts when Don announced that he was going out.

"I'm meeting a friend for a drink." Don said matter-of-factly. "Her name is Sasha."

"Do you really think that's a good idea Don?" Shenzy seemed a little uneasy.

"Of course; she's a nice girl."

"So why is she hanging out with you?" I chimed in.

"I do have some friends Ronnie. Everybody doesn't think I'm a jerk."

"Well, they just don't know you like I do."

"I'll be back later." He looked directly at Shenzy. "Don't wait up."

He walked out the door and left Shenzy and I at the dining room table. Shenzy suddenly stood up and held his hand out to me.

"Come on. Let's go outside for a minute." He had a playful grin on his face.

"Why are we going out there?" I asked as I gave him my hand.

"It's really pretty at night. I want to show you the view."

We walked outside and Shenzy flipped a switch on the wall. Several lanterns came alive and the dim light illuminated the deck just enough to make it cozy. He held onto my hand and led me over to the gigantic lounge chair that could have easily accommodated ten people. He sat down before I did and stared at me from head to toe.

"You look so beautiful in that dress." He said.

"Thank you. I'm glad you noticed."

"I notice everything about you. Like right now there's something on your mind."

"Actually, there is." I sat down next to him. "I just saw the news story about the airport explosions."

"And it bothered you?"

"Yes, of course. Doesn't it bother you? That psycho killed twenty-seven innocent people and injured hundreds more!"

"The things men sometimes do in the name of righteousness are deplorable. That is why we enjoy life in Seulmonde." He seemed as if he wanted to say more but he didn't.

"So what's on your mind? And don't say it's nothing." I insisted.

"Well, I've been thinking a lot about what's going to happen between us."

"We already know what happens. We spend what time we have together and then we both go home."

"You see, that's the problem. I don't want things to end that way."

"Neither do I." I didn't want to look at him.

"Come on, let's go." He stood up and reached his hand out to me.

"Where are we going?"

"We're going upstairs. I want to hold you."

"Can't you hold me right here?"

"Are you coming?"

He walked into the house and held the patio door open for me. I followed him in and we went up to the bedroom. He turned off the lights and joined me next to the bed.

He reached under my hair to unfasten my dress from around my neck. The silky material slid down and rested at my waist. He stared down at me with those dark eyes and I thought I would melt right there. I had a feeling that the holding he mentioned would come much later and that was fine with me.

Chapter 22

When I opened my eyes the next morning, the first thing I saw was his handsome face. He was still asleep so I had time to study every inch of him. His body was a work of art. What I wouldn't give to wake up next to him every single day. He started to move around a little and unexpectedly opened his eyes. I tried to turn away but it was too late. He'd caught me staring at him.

"Don't look away." He said softly. "Why do you do that?"
"Because I didn't want you to think that I was staring at you."
"But you were," he said and laughed.
"You're too good to be true. You'll look this adorable forever."
"You're the beautiful one."
"I might look pretty now. But I'll be dead in fifty years."
"Don't talk like that." He pulled me closer to him. "I'm ready to hold you now."

We lay in bed for a while. I snuggled up to him feeling relaxed and happy. There was something so comfortable about us together. I felt it so deeply and I know he felt it too. I wanted to say something else but I didn't want to ruin the moment. I could always depend on Don for that.

"Are you going to stay in bed all day?" Don spoke through the door.
"Of course not." Shenzy replied sounding irritated.
"Breakfast is in five minutes." Don said and walked back downstairs.
"Do we really have to go?" I said slowly.
"Yes, we should get a good breakfast. I have a fun day planned for us."

I pulled the blanket up over my head as a form of resistance

"Ronnie, we only have a few days left and if you don't actually see Greece you'll regret it." He sounded so sincere.

"All I need to see is you." I pulled the blanket down so he could see my face.

"You say that now. Come on, get dressed. I'll get ready in the other bathroom."

"Why can't we both use this one?"

"Because it would take too long." He smiled at me and jumped off the bed.

I reluctantly got up and went into the bathroom. I showered quickly hoping that Don wouldn't come back for us. I'd just finished getting dressed when Shenzy came back into the room.

"Ready for breakfast?" He asked sweetly.

"Ready as I'll ever be."

I followed him downstairs to where Don was waiting. As soon as we sat down, Don started talking about Crete again. I figured it might be a good idea to change the subject.

"So what are we doing today?" I asked Shenzy.

"We're going to do some shopping this morning. Then I thought we'd go for a walk. There's a spot at the edge of the island that I really must show you."

"That sounds like fun."

"And I thought we would go somewhere really fun later tonight." Don chimed in.

"Where might that be?" I replied cautiously.

"It's called the Hoxton Bar and it's probably the best place to go dancing in all of Athens."

"I'm up for that." I was excited about going out tonight.

"Oh great, we're going dancing." Shenzy was less enthused.

When we finished our breakfast, Don arranged for his car to take us downtown. It didn't take long to get there and I was enjoying watching the people. Shenzy was right, I was really glad we were out seeing Athens. I had no idea when I'd have the chance to come back.

Once we reached the shops, we were forced to continue on foot which was fine with me. We spent most of our time on Aeolu and

Ermou streets. I'm not usually big on shopping, but there was so much to see. The vendors offered clothing, shoes and jewelry of all kinds. I even found a pretty dress to wear tonight. It was a silk, mini dress with a tear drop opening in the back. The fuchsia color complemented my skin tone well. The dress cost more than I wanted to pay but Shenzy insisted on buying it for me.

The shopping trip was really paying off. I picked out a few souvenirs that were easy to carry. Shenzy even picked out gifts for Shelby and Chaunce. Don was doing more flirting than shopping which really didn't surprise me. He thought he was God's gift to the women of the world.

After a couple hours though, it started getting really crowded on the narrow streets.

"I think it's time to get going." Shenzy said flatly. He wasn't one for crowds. I was surprised he lasted as long as he did. "Are you done shopping?"
"Yes, thank you. I have everything I need." I replied.
"Alright, let's go."

"Is anyone going to ask me if I'm ready?" Don asked sarcastically.
"If you aren't, we can just send the car back for you," Shenzy added.
"That won't be necessary." Don shot back.
"Good then. Let's go." Shenzy spoke over his shoulder as he led me through the crowd.

It was hard to believe that so many people could fit into a few small alley ways. I was actually relieved to get back to the car when we did. It had become uncomfortably warm and we were all sweating.

When we arrived back at the villa, I excused myself and went upstairs to take a shower. Shenzy mentioned that we would be walking so I figured that dressing for the heat was best. I put on my white bikini and pulled a white, cotton romper over it.

When I got downstairs, Don and Shenzy were at the dining room table. They were engaged in an intense conversation, so I joined them at the table and tried to appear uninterested. My entrance into the room seemed to bring the discussion to a close. This didn't really surprise me though.

Rafael started serving lunch and I was glad that he did. It gave us something to focus on besides the uncomfortable silence that had crept into the room. I hoped that whatever they were discussing wasn't going to leave Shenzy in a bad mood. I wanted us to enjoy the rest of our time together.

"So Shenzy, what's next for today?" I asked excitedly.
"Well, we're going to drive out to the coast. There's a scenic area that not many tourists know about. Most of the surrounding area is private property."
"It sounds like fun."
"Hey, how about I go get Sasha and we join you two?" Don said matter-of-factly.

I couldn't tell if Don was being serious or not. Either way, Shenzy wasn't amused.

"I don't think so." Shenzy replied flatly.

I was glad Shenzy responded the way that he did. I was ready to be alone with him. We had the bag of fruit and bread Rafael prepared for us so we were ready to go. I stood up to leave when Don called to me.

"Ronnie, there's one more thing before you leave. Take two of these." Don slid a pill bottle across the table. "I can't have you getting sick on the yacht."
"What yacht?" I asked nervously.
"We're chartering a yacht tomorrow to take us to the island of Crete. I have some business there." Don replied.
"That's very thoughtful of you Don."
"Well, I do have my moments."

As I walked outside, I felt my excitement building. I knew wherever Shenzy would take me, I'd enjoy myself. As we drove down to the coast, I stole several glances at him.

The drive only lasted about twenty minutes but the view was unbelievable. I stared out the window at the unbelievably blue sky. Was the sky this blue at home? The sea blended in with it to create a picture of serenity.

When Shenzy pulled off the road, I could barely contain myself. I got out of the car and ran over to the beach. I pulled off my shoe for a moment to feel the warm sand on my toes. Shenzy came up behind me and put his arm around my neck. He was carrying the snack bag and a beach towel under his other arm. We stood there for a few minutes and stared out at the water.

"If you think this is nice, wait until we get to our secret place." Shenzy whispered in my ear.
"We have a secret place? Where is it?"
"If I told you, it wouldn't be a secret anymore. I have to show you. Come on."

He strode off towards a group of rocks that jetted out from the sandy shore. It looked like a man made pier. But instead of the rocks cutting off, they connected to a tiny island beyond the beach. I followed Shenzy out onto the rocks which were more slippery than they looked. I was glad that I wore my track shoes.

When we reached the other side of the rocks, we got a closer look at the little island. There was a large group of trees in the middle of an area the size of a football field. I thought that Shenzy would stop somewhere nearby but he kept walking. We moved around the edge until we reached the far end of the islet. We came upon a narrow piece of land that extended to another little island.

We walked across the little sand bridge to find a slightly larger isle than the one before. It had fewer trees in the center but the surrounding water was just as blue. This was the perfect beach.

"Wow, this is amazing. How many of these little islands are there?" I asked eagerly.

"I don't know. I found twelve of them in this area. I came here about ten years ago. But this is the first time I've been back. I thought it was beautiful; the kind of place you share with someone special."

"It is beautiful."

"And so are you." He smiled at me.

He put the blanket and the bag down in the sand and reached for my hand. I walked into his arms and he kissed me on my forehead. I smiled up at him and he kissed me again.

"I don't think that's quite the reaction I was going for," he said jokingly.

"So what were you expecting?"

"Well, women usually swoon when Don does that."

"That's because they're hoping to win some kind of competition."

"And what are you getting?"

"I get to be here with you." I replied lovingly.

I kissed him on his cheek and then walked over to the shore. I couldn't get over how amazing the view was from here. I turned back to see Shenzy unfolding the beach blanket. I stepped out of my romper and kicked off my track shoes. It was the perfect time for a swim but I didn't think he agreed. Shenzy sat down on the blanket and motioned for me to come and sit next to him.

"Hey, can I ask you something?" I asked carefully.

"Sure. What is it?"

"Why didn't you tell me that you saw me before that day at the lake?"

"Oh, I wasn't expecting that question." He looked a little uncomfortable. "I didn't think to bring it up. Why do you ask?"

"I was curious after Don mentioned it. So you just brought me to the house that day and never thought twice about me."

"I thought about you a lot. I wondered who you were and I was curious about what happened in Greece. I thought you were very pretty."

"Really?"

"Yes really."

"What else?"

"Well, what else would you expect? You know how my life is and I would never have thought that someone like you wouldn't have a boyfriend or a husband."

"I didn't."

"Let's not have that conversation." He stared at me warily. "Now, I have a question for you."

"Ok. What is it?"

"When am I going to see you again?"

"I don't know." I looked away from him. "When are you coming to Columbia?"

"I was thinking you could come to visit me."

"I already did, remember?"

Shenzy almost smiled but I could tell the conversation wasn't going the way he hoped. He suddenly got up off the blanket and began taking off his clothes. He was actually wearing swim trunks. Every time I saw him at the lake, he just had on a pair of shorts.

He started walking towards the water. I watched him for a minute before I got up. It felt a little like we were at the lake. Maybe that's why Shenzy liked it here. He felt comfortable. He got into the water and started swimming around. After a few moments he stopped to see where I was.

"Ronnie, come on in. The water feels great."

"Are you sure it's safe? There aren't any sharks in these waters?"

"Only me, now come and get in."

"Ok. I'm coming."

I waded over to where he was standing in the water but it was hard to keep from staring at him. Even though he was in the water up to his waist, I could still see his entire body clearly. He followed my eyes as I watched him and it made him smile. I tried to turn my attention to the water around us so I started swimming on my back.

I tried to find something to take my mind off his wet skin. I was so attracted to him. I wondered if he felt as strongly for me. I stared up at the sky watching the sun overhead. I felt so relaxed this way. I looked over and saw that Shenzy was swimming on his back too. I started flopping my arms and legs like I did as a child swimming in Ocean City. The sky was so big to me then and it still was. The thought made me smile.

"What's so funny?" He'd stood up so he was looking down at me. "Nothing's funny. I'm just happy. Is that alright with you?" I was still floating on my back.
"Of course it is." He said as he moved towards the shore. "I'm getting out. Are you coming?"
"I'm right behind you."

He walked over to the blanket and lay down on his stomach. I lay down next to him on my back. We started drying off pretty quickly from the heat of the sun. It had to be at least ninety degrees on that beach. We weren't really talking then. I thought it was so romantic until I realized that Shenzy had fallen asleep.

"I can't believe you're sleeping."
"I'm awake," he said groggily. "I just don't get a lot of time to relax and enjoy myself."
"I understand." I felt like an idiot. "Go ahead and finish your nap."
"That's ok. I'm awake."
"Can I ask you something?"
"Sure. What is it?"
"Who watches the fountain when you're not there?"
"Chaunce, of course." He glanced at me quickly. "Don't worry. Chaunce is very capable of protecting the fountain. You'd be surprised."
"Can I ask you something else?"
"I had a feeling you'd say that. Sure, go ahead."
"If you could choose your life, what would you be doing right now?"
"Let me think." He sat up and looked down at me. "I'd be a bank teller in Columbia, Maryland. What's the name of your bank again?"
"I'm being serious."
"So am I."

I sat up and kissed him gently. That was one of the sweetest sentiments I'd ever heard. I tried to think of something to say in response but nothing came to mind.

We spent the next few hours laying out on the beach and feeding each other fruit. Shenzy was also throwing grapes into the air and catching them in his mouth. I wondered if there was anything he couldn't do. I tried to catch a few but the grapes were going everywhere. He was trying not to laugh in my face but I could tell he was amused.

He was putting the empty fruit containers back in the bag when I noticed his mood had changed.

"We'd better get back to the house. I don't want to hear Don's mouth if we're late."
"Can I help you fold the blanket?"
"Sure."

Once we cleaned up, we headed back across the little islands. It didn't take long since I knew where we were going this time. Then we drove back to the house along the coast. It was a pleasant enough ride but I had the feeling that Shenzy had something on his mind. I didn't know if he would tell me but as usual I couldn't keep my mouth shut.

"Are you going to tell me what's wrong?" I asked.
"We're going to Crete so Don can meet a friend of his."
"So what's the problem with that?'
"This friend has been doing some research for him over the past few years but it's a waste of time." I could tell that Shenzy was uncomfortable with the conversation.
"We don't have to talk about this if you don't want to."
"You need to know before we get to Chania." He was staring straight ahead. "He's been looking for Maggie."
"Your mother, Maggie?" I couldn't believe my ears.
"I know it sounds crazy. But this guy Benito has Don convinced that Maggie's still out there somewhere. He owns a few vessels that sail the clipper route and a few of his men claim to have seen her."
"Is that possible?"

"No. Maggie is dead. But Don still follows up on these so-called leads that always ends up a dead end. I just wish I could change his mind about meeting up with Benito though."
"Is that what you two were arguing about before?"

He just nodded his head. I suppose the words wouldn't come to him.
"Do Chaunce or Shelby know about this?"
"No one else knows except for you." He glanced at me warily.

I knew that he was worried about Don. But Shenzy also seemed relieved to have someone to talk to about it. I was glad that he confided in me.

When we arrived back at the house, Don was in his room getting dressed. He didn't have a chance to hassle us about getting back from the beach late.

When we sat down for dinner, I was preoccupied with thoughts of Maggie. How could Don let someone manipulate him into believing his mother was still alive? I felt sorry for him.

I don't know if it was the talk about Maggie or my nerves about tonight but I barely had an appetite. I just sat there watching Shenzy. He probably ate five times the amount of food that I did.

I never realized how much he enjoyed eating. I guess that was one good thing about being away from Seulmonde. He could be himself. I loved Shenzy the rocket scientist but I also loved meeting Shenzy the man.

After we finished eating, we got ready to go out. I made sure to spend a few extra minutes putting on make-up. I wanted tonight to be special. When I came downstairs, Shenzy and Don were sitting in the main room waiting for me.

I didn't have to wonder what Shenzy thought of my outfit. The look on his face spoke volumes. Don looked mildly amused but insisted that we get going. When we stepped outside, I saw that Don had rented another obnoxious car. It was large enough to fit twelve people comfortably. When Shenzy and I got inside, we sat on the back row. Don sat directly across from us and started on his first drink of the night.

The Hoxton Bar was on Voutadon Street. It was about thirty minutes drive from our villa but I could tell when we started getting close. There were groups of well dressed people walking in the direction we were driving. I wasn't sure if they were going dancing or about to walk onto a runway. I must have looked anxious because Shenzy gave my hand a quick squeeze.

"You look beautiful. We're going to have a lot of fun tonight," he said smiling at me.
"Yes, we will." I replied.
"We're here. Let's go." Don chimed in.

Our limousine pulled up in front of the club and we stepped out. There was a line of people waiting to get in but Don just walked up to the door. He motioned for us to follow him so we did. The doorman shook Don's hand and waived us inside.

I was surprised by how nice the club was inside. There were paintings along the walls that had spot lights shining on them. And underneath the paintings were fancy lounge chairs with beautiful people draped over them. There was a long bar area that had stools lined up in front of it.

Every stool was occupied by enthusiastic club goers. Towards the back of the room was a spiral staircase that led up to a huge dance floor. Don headed for the stairs and we followed. The DJ was playing some sort of techno music and the dance floor was packed.

We maneuvered through the crowd to the back of the upper level. There were a few tables and another bar area. Don directed us to one of the reserved tables in the back by the bar. Moments later, a waitress walked over and asked what we wanted to drink. Don ordered champagne and the woman returned with a bottle and four glasses.

"So Don, how did you meet this friend of yours?" I asked casually.
"Sasha is actually a friend of mine and Shenzy's."
"Is that right?" I said as I glanced in Shenzy's direction.
"I wouldn't call her a friend," Shenzy said defensively.
"Shenzy, let's have a drink. You need to relax." Don said sardonically.
"I'm not thirsty." He replied quickly.
"I'll have one." I had a feeling I'd need it.

Something about this Sasha person was rubbing me the wrong way. I didn't know why I was so jealous but I was. My one drink turned into four. I saw Shenzy staring at me out of the corner of my eye but I tried to ignore him. It really wasn't that hard to do because I was feeling pretty good by this time. Well to be honest, I wasn't feeling anything which is probably why I said yes when Don asked me to dance.

I don't know if it was just the drinks but I was really enjoying myself. Don was a pretty good dancer but I still noticed Shenzy sitting at the table. He had one glass of champagne that he sipped on for about an hour. Don saw me staring in the direction of our table and somehow felt the need to disturb my thoughts.

"He's not a big dancer. The only reason he agreed to come is because you're here."
"Don, cut the crap. Who is this Sasha person?"
"She's a girl I met here earlier this year." He smiled at me before continuing. "Ok. She likes Shenzy but I thought if she saw the two of you together she would get jealous. Then I could get her to sleep with me."
"You brought us here tonight so you could get laid?"
"That's part of it."
"And what's the other part?"
"I wanted to talk to you but it's hard with you and Shenzy attached at the hip all of the time."
"What is it Don? This better be good or else I'm walking out of here and getting a taxi back to the villa."
"Have you and Shenzy talked about what's going to happen at the end of the week?"

"We both go home. Why? Has he said anything to you?"
"No, he hasn't. But I have a feeling he's said something to you."
"Don, I know you care about your brother but this is not something
I can discuss with you."
"Alright, whatever you say."

There was an awkward silence between us. I didn't want to talk about
Shenzy and me anymore. I just wanted to focus on having fun.

The music suddenly changed. The DJ put on a slow song and
everybody started dancing close together. I stopped dancing and
turned in the direction of our table. I wasn't going to slow dance with
Don. I was relieved to see Shenzy approaching us.

"May I cut in?" Shenzy said as he took my hand.
"Of course." I replied.

He moved in close to me and I put my arms around his neck. I didn't
understand the words to the song playing but I loved the music. I
loved anything that gave me an excuse to be close to Shenzy. I was
glad that he was holding me because I lost my balance just then. He
smiled down at me and shook his head.

"You know you don't have anything to worry about." Shenzy was
trying to talk over the music.
"What do you mean?"
"I mean Sasha. I don't like her; I never did."
"Oh, I'm not worried about her." I lied.
"Good because she's here."

I turned around to see Don slow dancing with a tall brunette. She
was wearing a black dress that was too short and heels that were too
high. She was exotic looking with shapely thighs and a small chest. I
didn't think she was Shenzy's type. But then I didn't really know what
his type was. I hated her instantly. The moment I saw the look she
was giving me, I realized that she hated me too. We had an
understanding.

The music changed as the DJ tried to get everybody dancing again. I figured this was a good time to get another drink. Shenzy and I headed back to our table. We were soon joined by Don and Sasha. Oh joy.

"Sasha, let me introduce you to Ronnie." Don said politely. "And you remember my little brother Shenzy."
"Of course I do. How are you Shenzy?" She ignored me and focused all of her attention on Shenzy.
"I'm fine Sasha; just showing my girlfriend around Athens." Shenzy said with a smile. "I take it you've been well?"
"I'm wonderful." Sasha replied. "So this is your girlfriend? I guess I expected something... well different."
"Who the hell cares what you think, anyway?" I picked up my glass and took a big gulp of champagne.
"I think we should get the check." Don said quickly. No one argued with his assessment.

Don paid for our drinks while the rest of us waited by the table. Then we headed down the spiral staircase and out the front door. As soon as we got outside, Sasha pulled Don over by the curb. I could tell she wasn't happy. It all made sense now. Sasha didn't know anything about me and Don's plan was working.

After a few minutes, our car pulled up in front of the club. Shenzy opened the door for me and we stepped in. I was surprised to see that Don got in with Sasha right behind him.

"Where is she going?" I might have spoken a little too loudly.
"I'm going with you. Maybe we can all have a drink together back at your villa." Sasha replied wearing a crafty smile.
"I don't think so." I replied quickly.
"Why not?"
"We're going straight to bed. We're really tired, right Shenzy?" I never took my eyes off her.
"Yes, we're exhausted." Shenzy promptly responded.
"That's too bad." Sasha replied wearing a fake smile.

I was done talking to her and I hated the fact that she and Don were sitting directly across from us. There was no way to avoid her stare. It wasn't that she was staring at me that was the problem. I decided that the only way to get her eyes off Shenzy was to show her something she didn't want to see. I leaned over to him and kissed his lips. When I leaned back in my seat, Sasha had looked away.

Shenzy surprised me by leaning over to kiss me. But he didn't give me a light peck. He covered my mouth with his and gently held my face to make sure I didn't move away. I thought we were just putting on a show to piss off Sasha. At least that's what I was doing.

But we actually started making out in front of them. All I could think about was how much I wanted him and I could tell he wanted me too. I'd almost forgotten where we were until I heard Don's voice.

"Excuse us. Sorry to interrupt." Don said sarcastically.
"What is it?" I asked breathlessly.
"We'll be at the house in ten minutes. Do you think you can hold it together until then?"
"Of course," I replied gingerly.

Shenzy didn't say anything. He was leaning on my shoulder and most likely trying to compose himself. In one instant, he'd shown me that he had no interest in Sasha and I was sure she was aware of that fact as well. He only had eyes – and lips for me.

When we reached the house, Shenzy and I got out first. We said goodnight as Shenzy practically carried me into the house and up the stairs.

We made love on the floor by the bedroom door. It was such a passionate experience. I actually wasn't upset about meeting Sasha anymore.

At some point in the night, Shenzy grabbed some blankets off the bed and wrapped them around us. I worked my way back into his arms and felt myself falling asleep. He whispered those familiar words in my ear.

"I love you."
"I love you too Shenzy." I whispered the words almost to myself.

He turned to face me and kissed me gently on my lips. Then he smiled at me and pulled me into his arms once again.

Chapter 23

I opened my eyes very slowly as the sun came through the patio doors. Shenzy lay next to me with his eyes closed but I was sure he was awake. We just lay there wrapped in our blankets on the floor.

Unfortunately my stomach didn't understand how beautiful the moment was. It started at a low rumble and I knew it would only get louder. Even Shenzy heard it.

"Are you ready for breakfast?" He spoke into my hair.
"I guess so. But I don't want to move."
"Neither do I but we need to eat and I'm sure Don will come upstairs to get us in a few minutes. Remember, we're going to Crete today."
"So when will he meet with Benito?"
"I'm not sure," he said cautiously. "Come on. Let's go take a shower."

Shenzy seemed to be going down a checklist to make sure we were ready to take our trip. He even suggested I wear one of my swim suits to make sure I was comfortable. I pulled a romper on over it and Shenzy and I headed downstairs.

When we reached the bottom of the stairs, I noticed that the furniture near the entry way was out of place. It looked like a small tornado had come through the area. Even the painting next to the front door had fallen.

"What the hell happened in here?" I said.
"Your guess is as good as mine." Shenzy replied slowly.
"Where's Fedor? Maybe he knows what happened."

Before Shenzy could respond, the door to Don's bedroom opened and Sasha came strutting out. She was wearing a pair of thong underwear and nothing else. She walked right by Shenzy and I. Then she reached down to pick up her dress. It was crumpled on the floor by the front door. Shenzy looked away quickly but I could tell he'd seen her. It took everything inside me not to scream at her right there.

"Good morning," she murmured and walked back into Don's bedroom.
"Is that the Mediterranean thing you were talking about?" Shenzy asked playfully.
"You do not want to joke with me right now," I said sternly.

A few minutes later Rafael and Fedor walked in the front door. By the looks on their faces, I could tell they had no idea what happened to the house. They explained that Don had given them the night off and they were instructed to return this morning. Looking at the house, I didn't have to wonder why Don wanted some privacy.

Rafael excused himself so that he could start breakfast and Fedor started cleaning the entry way. I went to sit out by the pool and relax. Maybe they could get Sasha out of the house without my having to look at her face again. As soon as I focused my attention on the Aegean, I started to relax. Minutes later, Shenzy came out and sat next to me.

"Are you alright?" he asked kindly.
"What was Don thinking bringing that woman here?"
"You know exactly what Don was thinking."
"He acts like an oversexed teenager."
"He's been that way for as long as I can remember." He stood up and faced me wearing a rather peculiar expression. "I wonder if he'll ever settle down. I wonder if I will, for that matter. I don't know if Shelby told you but Chaunce once guarded the fountain too."
"No, she didn't mention it." I tried to mask my shock as I stood up next to him. I wondered how much more he would say. "So he had an older brother?"
"Yes, he did."
"Why are you telling me this now?"

"When Garland showed up, I thought I'd lost you. And then you turned up here..." He suddenly turned towards me and stared into my eyes. "Ronnie, I don't want to lose you."

"I don't want to lose you either Shenzy." I had a huge lump in my throat.

"You know, my brother might be a lot of things, but at least he's not afraid to ask for what he wants. I know our life together would be complicated for a while but I want you with me. When we come back from Crete, I'm asking you to return to Seulmonde with me... for good."

I just stood there holding onto myself. I felt like my heart was about to explode. Shenzy wanted me; he wanted me as much as I wanted him. I was sure of that now.

"Shenzy, I have to admit... I really didn't know how I was going to go back to Columbia alone. I want to be with you too." I had tears in my eyes and my hands were trembling.

"Are you saying what I think you're saying?" Shenzy pulled me into his arms.

"Yes, I'm going back to Seulmonde with you."

He picked me up off the ground and twirled me around. Then he held me close to him. There was no other place in the world that I felt more at home than in his arms.

"I love you so much," Shenzy whispered to me.

"I love you, too."

Don walked through the patio doors with a confused look on his face. "What's going on?"

"Ronnie has agreed to go back to Seulmonde with us. Isn't that wonderful?" Shenzy said excitedly.

"That's great news. Let's eat." Don just turned around and walked back into the house.

"He really is excited for us." I said to Shenzy jokingly. He just smiled at me and led me into the house.

We all sat down to eat breakfast but I didn't have much of an appetite. I was pretty anxious about getting on the yacht. I was trying to calm myself when Fedor announced that the yacht was docked at the pier.

He carried our bags and we followed him out the front door. Around the right side of the house, was a brick path that led down to the pier. My legs felt a little wobbly as I watched the crew members hop off the yacht with ease.

There were four crew members including the Captain. Don introduced us to Captain Maximus and the Captain introduced the rest of the crew. Within minutes, we were getting a tour of the yacht. I'd never seen one up close before. It looked really fast.

I was a little nervous about walking around the exterior of the yacht. But after a few minutes, I was enjoying the view. Shenzy held onto me the entire time.

The interior was finely decorated. The furniture in the saloon was made of cherry wood with seating for eight. The adjoining lounge had comfortable seating that lined the walls and delicate flower accents.

The sleeping cabins were on the lower deck. They were massive in size; each with a large walk-in bathroom. I knew right away which cabin I wanted for Shenzy and I. Don didn't seem to care.

Nico continued our tour of the saloon and galley areas right up until we departed. I really was impressed by all of the high end furnishings and state-of-the-art appliances. This yacht was so much nicer than my apartment and much larger too.

Right this way, ma'am." Nico said kindly. "If you'll follow me, we're preparing to depart."
"Ok. Where should we sit?" I asked nervously.
"Why don't you relax here in the saloon? Would anyone like any refreshments?"
"We're fine, thank you Nico." Shenzy replied.

"My pleasure sir; I'll be right by the bar if you need anything."
Don sat on the short end of the sofa and appeared to be settling in
for a nap. Shenzy and I sat down on the opposite end. I was just
getting comfortable when Shenzy pulled a small rectangular box from
his pocket and handed it to me.

"What's this?" I asked nervously.
"It's a little something I picked up for you. Open it."
"If you insist."

I opened the box to find a round opal set on a platinum band.
Shenzy pulled it out of the box and placed it on my finger.

"It's my birthstone." I replied shyly. "It's so pretty."
"It's a promise ring. I promise to love you always." He was holding
my hand and staring into my eyes.
"I don't know what to say." I touched my hand to his face and kissed
his lips. I lingered there for a few moments not wanting to let him go.

Nico announced that we'd reached our cruising speed and were free
to move around. Don had fallen asleep and we didn't bother waking
him.

"Nico, can you bring some ginger ale and crackers down to our cabin
please?" Shenzy asked.
"Yes sir."

Shenzy stood up and reached for my hand. I got up slowly and
followed him. When we reached the lower deck, Shenzy led me into
the forward master cabin. It had a king size bed in it that looked very
comfortable. I couldn't resist the urge to lie down and test it out.

Shenzy locked the door and came over to lie next to me. I rested my
head on his chest and just listened to his heart beating. I suppose the
pills were working because the only thing on my mind was Shenzy.
Just when I was getting too comfortable to move, there was a knock
at the door.

"Who is it?" Shenzy asked.

"It's Nico sir. I have your refreshments."
"One second." Shenzy unlocked the door and motioned for Nico to come in.

Nico sat the tray on the table and quickly exited the room. When Shenzy closed the door behind him, I couldn't help laughing.

"I'm confused about something. Nico never looks directly at me. Fedor is the same way."
"It's considered disrespectful to stare at a lady." Shenzy replied playfully. "You should take it as a compliment."
"Oh, well when you put it that way."

He sat down on the bed next to me. "I think we should take one more pill. And by 'we' I mean you."
"I feel fine. What if it makes me drowsy?"
"That's fine too. Then you'll be well rested when we get to Crete."
"Alright. I'll take the stupid pill. Can you get them out of my bag?"
"Yes ma'am."

He opened the pill bottle and placed one in my hand. I drank it down with some ginger ale and started feeling drowsy almost immediately. I didn't even have enough energy to complain about Shenzy turning on the television. I lay on the bed in his arms without a care in the world. Within minutes, I was asleep.

I was awakened by a knock on the door. I couldn't move because Shenzy's arm and leg were draped over my body. My only option was to shout at the door.

"Who is it?" I said startling Shenzy from his sleep.
"It's Nico, ma'am. Lunch will be served shortly. Mr. Don is already in the saloon."
"Ok, thank you. We'll be right there."

Shenzy was fully awake now but he hadn't released me from his bear hug. I couldn't move a muscle until he did.

"Are you hungry?" I asked quietly.

"Yes but I'm too comfortable to move." He replied calmly. "Can't we stay like this a little longer?"

"We could but Don is waiting."

"He'll survive."

He sighed deeply and rolled onto his back. I got up off the bed and stared in the mirror at my rumpled clothes and hair.

"You're beautiful," he said softly.

"I think you're biased." I smiled shyly. "I need to clean up a bit."

I picked up my accessory bag and pointed at my hair. I started walking towards the bathroom and I could feel his eyes watching me. He made me blush so easily. I really needed to get that under control. I pulled my hair brush out of my bag and ran it through my hair a few times. Then I dug into my bag to find my toothbrush.

Shenzy came into the bathroom and started brushing his teeth too. I tried not to stare at him. How could somebody make brushing their teeth look sexy? I turned my attention to my own dental care when I realized he caught me staring again. He just smiled.

We made our way up to the saloon. Don was sitting at the table drumming his fingers against it as if Shenzy and I were children. I was truly gifted at ignoring him now.

"So Ronnie, you're going home with us?" Don's question was filled with disappointment.

"Yes, I am." I replied energetically.

"And this is what you want?" he quipped.

"Yes, it is." I stared at Shenzy and he just smiled back at me.

Nico brought us our lunch which was nothing short of a masterpiece. Chef Alexander was a true artist. Our salad was not merely sitting on our plates but it was staged. The shrimp were tied together by the stems and the lettuce and cucumber were sprinkled on top.

We made light conversation as we ate but I couldn't help feeling nervous about visiting Crete. I'd listened to Don and Shenzy talk about other times they'd visited the island but I knew this time was different. Benito would be there.

Don talked about all of the places he wanted to visit on Crete but he never mentioned his contact. I wonder what he'd say if he knew that Shenzy told me about his obsession with Maggie. Or maybe he was planning to tell me himself; I couldn't be sure.

I was disturbed from my thoughts when the engineer suddenly asked us to come up on deck. We were approaching Crete and we were invited to take a look.

"It's so pretty. I can't believe we're actually here." I was shaking a little when we reached the main deck.
"It's not the prettiest thing I've seen but it's a close second." Shenzy said as he smiled at me. He came up behind me and wrapped his arms around my waist. I covered his arms with mine.

"How long until we reach the port?" Don asked ignoring us both. "We'll reach the port in about twenty minutes Mr. Don." Captain Maximus replied.

We were advised to take our seats as Captain Maximus maneuvered the yacht into Souda bay. I felt like a five year old who couldn't sit still. When we were cleared to leave the yacht, Shenzy and I left first. He could see how impatient I was getting. Don spoke to the captain and then he joined us on the side of the yacht.

I was relieved to be on solid ground and eager to see the sights. We grabbed a map from the port office and started discussing our options.

We boarded bus number twenty one headed for the square. I really enjoyed the ride. The bus was full of tourists who looked like they were ready to shop. Don was irritated because he wasn't able to get a seat. He had to stand up and he cringed every time someone accidently bumped into him. I never realized he was such a snob.

As we road along, I stared out the bus window at the real Chania. It was where the locals lived. Their homes were modest but considering the back drop of the sky and the sea, I'd say it was a decent trade off.

I caught Shenzy's reflection in the glass. He was watching my excited expression. I really couldn't help myself though. There was so much to see. As we rode out of the residential areas, we moved into the more historic section of Chania. Only minutes later, we'd reached our destination. The bus came to an abrupt stop.

"We've reached the square." Shenzy whispered in my ear. "Come on, let's stand up."
"Alright. I'm right behind you." I replied.

We approached the door as Shenzy motioned for Don to follow us. When the doors opened, we walked off the bus and directly into the market building. Among other things, there were fresh fruits, spices and cheeses for sale. But the most interesting thing about the market was the shape of the building. The two main hallways formed a giant cross.

I wasn't hungry but I wanted the experience of walking through the entire market at least once. Don put up a little resistance but soon realized he was outnumbered. He would have to be patient before he tiptoed down delusion alley. Benito would have to wait.

After we negotiated the market floor, we exited the structure on the harbor side. There were tourists walking in every direction. I felt Shenzy gently take my hand as we strolled down the cobblestone pavement. We crossed Halidon Street adjacent to the lighthouse with the harbor stretching out in front of us.

I was immediately reminded of the summer trips I'd taken with my dad. I would stare out at the Atlantic Ocean for hours. Lee would tell me that my life was as vast as that ocean. I would imagine all of the possibilities that the world had to offer.

And I stood there realizing that I was about to embark on a wonderful adventure with Shenzy. We were from two different worlds but our worlds converged on Chania that day. I was excited but a little nervous too.

He came up behind me and put his arms around me. Instinctively, I turned towards him and buried my face in his chest. I felt so at home in his arms.

After a few minutes, I turned my face to peer over his arm. I'd forgotten about Don who must have been hovering around somewhere. He finally glanced down at my face and kissed my cheek.

"Are you ready to see more of Chania?" Shenzy asked softly.
"Yes, I am. You're the expert. What do you recommend next?"
"Alright, let's go to the museum. You'll really like it."
"Ok. Let's do it."

We walked towards the museum which we could see from where we'd been standing. Shenzy explained the history of the structure to me as we approached. I enjoyed listening to him tell the story. We reached the front door and Don appeared behind us. I had no idea where he'd been the last few minutes and I decided not to ask.

When we walked inside, I felt like I'd stepped back in time. The walls and ceiling were exactly as they had been for over four hundred years. Even though Shenzy had been here before, he had the same look of wonder on his face that I did. I glanced over at Don who was walking around with his eyes closed. I knew that at any moment, he was going to knock over one of the priceless artifacts. I couldn't watch.

When I turned to find Shenzy, he was standing at the far end of the museum in front of the statue of St. Francis. I went to join him but made sure to observe the statues I passed on my way there. We were enjoying a moment of silence when Don came barreling down toward us.

"Ronnie, Shenzy, don't move a muscle." He came to stand in front of us blocking my view of St. Francis.

"Don, what are you doing? And please keep your voice down," I said quietly.

"No wait, this is good. Take his hands." He motioned towards Shenzy.

I had no idea what Don was trying to do but I went along with it. Shenzy seemed mildly amused so I decided not to ruin the moment. He took my hands into his and stared down at me.

"Ok. Repeat after me." Don said with a nasally tone. "I, Ronnie, take you Shenzy, to be my love slave for all eternity."

I couldn't help laughing but I didn't say anything. I just stared back at Shenzy.

"Ok, the little lady is too shocked to speak." He turned to Shenzy before continuing. "And you sir, repeat after me. I, Shenzy, take you Ronnie, to be my love slave for all eternity."

"I do." Shenzy said and smiled at me.

"Ok, by the power vested in me by St. Francis here and myself, I now pronounce you truly pathetic. Now go ahead and kiss her before we get thrown out."

Shenzy leaned over and kissed me gently on my lips. A few people were staring at us and smiling. It was more attention than I was comfortable with. We also attracted the museum attendant's interest which let us know it was definitely time to leave.

We left out of the rear door and walked back towards the cobblestone pavement. Once we were outside, I figured it was a good time to get a bite to eat. But Don had other ideas.

He just couldn't wait to get to the beach. He told me that the women there could benefit from his method of applying suntan oil. I won't repeat what I said but let's just say I didn't agree with him.

Finally Shenzy stepped in and offered a solution. "Why don't we head up to Zambeliou Street and cut across to Theotokopouli? We can get food there and then we can walk straight up to the beach." He smiled and glanced from me to Don waiting for a response.

"Well, if she needs to eat again that's fine. If I had her thighs though, I would be careful." Don said the last part under his breath.
"There is nothing wrong with my thighs thank you very much." I replied angrily.
"What? I'm only kidding. I think Shenzy's plan is a great one." Don replied gingerly.
"It is a great plan. You know, maybe Shenzy should be the next leader of Seulmonde. He's the one with the brains and everything else that goes along with it." I spoke flatly and walked toward Zambeliou Street.

Even though I was walking briskly, it didn't take long for Don and Shenzy to catch up with me. I also noticed that our little group had become quiet. Maybe I'd gone too far with my comment about Seulmonde. It had to bug Don that everyone thought so highly of Shenzy; well everyone that mattered. I decided that when we sat down to eat, I would apologize to him. He was a royal pain but it didn't help if I acted the same way he did.

Theotokopouli was a Venetian style street that had little shops and restaurants running along both sides. I had no idea what to eat because there was so much to choose from. We settled on a small café that served gyros. I'd taken a few bites when I realized it was a good time for some humble pie.

"Don, I wanted to apologize for what I said before. I don't want things to get weird between us because I can't control my temper." I just stared down at my sandwich waiting for him to respond.

"You're joking right? That's the only thing I like about you. You're not afraid to stand up to me." He moved closer to the table as he continued talking. "Do you know how many people just do what I say without even thinking about it? And don't even get me started on the women. I don't know one woman that I actually respect."

"Well, when you compare every woman to the memory of your mother, it puts us all at a slight disadvantage." I replied sharply.

Don glanced suspiciously at Shenzy. "There's nothing wrong with having high standards. Looking at your last two suitors, I'd say you have some high standards of your own Ms. Ronnie."
"Let's not make this about me Don." I shot back.
"Ok, then it's decided. People do what I want and I like it that way. In the end, that's all that really matters to me." He replied.
"Your exactly right Don." I decided to just be quiet and finish eating. There was no point in trying to reason with him.

We finished our authentic gyros and washed them down with Coke soda. I felt so much better after we ate. I was glad that Don wasn't concerned about what I said earlier; especially since I meant every word of it.

Chania Beach was only a twenty minute walk from the little café. When we got there, it was packed with tourists and locals alike. We looked around until we found an empty spot on the beach. But by the time we'd set up our umbrella and put our towels down, Don had vanished.

I stared up the beach about twenty yards and that's when I spotted him. Don was speaking to a man who looked completely out of place. The man was wearing a dark suit and sunglasses. That must have been Benito. He handed Don an envelope and then walked away. I can't believe he came all this way for that brief exchange. I guess I was worried over nothing.

"What are you thinking about?" Shenzy asked with a smile on his face.
"I was thinking about how nice this is."
"And I was thinking about when we get back to the yacht." He flashed a sexy grin.
"Really? So when are we leaving then?"
"Let's give Don a little more time?"
"I can be patient."

When I looked back to where Don was a few minutes ago, he wasn't there. I didn't see the man in the suit either. I was getting worried again but I didn't say anything to Shenzy. I didn't want to worry him too.

A couple hours later, Don walked up the beach toward us. He seemed to come out of nowhere.

"Are you two ready to go?" Don asked playfully.
"We were just waiting for you." Shenzy had a concerned look on his face but he didn't say anything else.

When we arrived back at the yacht, Don climbed on board first. He went directly to his cabin which was odd. I actually started feeling a little tired myself. It had been a long day.

When we reached our cabin, I fell back on the bed. Shenzy helped me take off my shoes. Then he started massaging my feet one by one. I felt so relaxed and comfortable that I'd fallen asleep.

Chapter 24

When I woke up, Shenzy was on the bed next to me. He must have fallen asleep while watching television. I had no idea what time it was and I was hungry. There had to be something in the galley that I could grab at this hour. My first order of business was getting up without waking Shenzy. But that was easier said than done.

"Are you going somewhere?" Shenzy asked behind me.
"Yes. I'm hungry. I'd like to go up to the galley."
"Do you mind if I come? I could use a little something myself."
"No, not at all. Let's go."

When we reached the galley, Chef Alexander was there to greet us.

"Good evening. Can I get you both something?"
"Can you make grilled cheese sandwiches?" Shenzy asked.
"Of course sir." The chef then turned his attention to me. "What would you like to eat Ms. Ronnie?"
"I'll have the same. Thank you."
"Wonderful. You're welcome to relax in the saloon and your sandwiches will be brought to you shortly. Would you like something to drink?"
"Two ginger ales please." I blurted out before Shenzy could say anything. He just looked at me and smiled.

We went into the saloon and I stretched out across the behemoth sofa while we waited for our late night snack. We started talking about my father. I don't really know how we got on the subject. But Shenzy wanted to know what I would tell Lee about my plans when I spoke to him.

I knew I would have to tell him something. But I couldn't worry about that now.

Nico brought in our sandwiches and soda and placed them on the table. Shenzy thanked him and he disappeared from the room. We approached the dining table together and Shenzy pulled out my chair for me. I was about to thank him when I heard Don's voice behind me.

"Eating again Ronnie? Is there something you need to tell me?" Don said with his normal sarcastic tone.
"There are a lot of things I could tell you Don but I know it wouldn't make a difference." I replied calmly.

He moved closer to the table so he could see what we were eating.
"Grilled cheese sandwiches… Are you secretly twelve years old?"
"Shenzy is the one who ordered for us. Are you going to criticize him too?"
"I think my brother would eat quick sand if you were sitting there eating it with him. I have questioned his judgment on a few things lately."
"Sheldon, if you want to get something to eat, then go ahead." Shenzy finally spoke up from eating his sandwich. "Otherwise, you can just go back to your cabin."

I picked up my sandwich and took a bite as Don promptly left the room. I'd never seen Shenzy really angry but it was obvious that Don had pushed him too far on this trip.

"You're brother really doesn't like me." I spoke without looking up from my plate.
"It's not you Ronnie. I knew when we came here he would get this way. He just won't accept that Maggie is gone. And it prevents him from moving forward in his life or being happy for anyone else."
I touched Shenzy's hand. "I feel so badly for him."
"So do I. But no one can help him until he decides to let go of the past."

We finished eating our sandwiches and drank our ginger ale. I don't know how he knew we were done, but Nico came breezing into the room and carried away our dishes.

I held onto my soda so that I could take one more pill. I pulled my phone out of my purse to find the pill bottle when I noticed I had two missed calls. They were both from Garland. I didn't know if I should mention it but I didn't want to seem like I was hiding anything either.

"That's weird. Garland called me."
"Is that so?" Shenzy's jaw tightened. I knew that Garland was a sore subject for him. "Did he leave a message?"
"No, he didn't. Maybe he just wanted me to know that he made it back home."
"Wouldn't he have arrived a couple days ago?"
"Yes. But he might have just thought to call today."

I was a little bothered by Garland's calls. So much so that I forgot to take my motion sickness pill. We left the saloon and headed back down to our cabin. I just collapsed on the bed when we got there. Shenzy kicked off his shoes and lay down next to me.

"Are you sleepy?" I whispered to him.
"No, are you?" Shenzy whispered back.
"Why are we whispering?"
"I don't know." He laughed at me.
"I'm going to freshen up a little." I got up and headed for the bathroom.
"Take your time. I'll be right here." He said with a sly smile.

I washed my face and brushed my teeth. Then I changed into my nightgown. It was powder blue with spaghetti straps and it was really short; it fit exactly the way I wanted it to.

When I came out, it didn't take Shenzy long to notice what I was wearing. He got off the bed and walked over to me.

"Is this for me?" He asked.
"Of course it is."
"Thank you. I love it."
"You do?"
"Yeah, and I'll love it even more when it's on the floor."

He reached out for me and I let him pull me in. Being this close to him excited me so much. He started kissing me so passionately that it threatened to overwhelm all of my senses.

Then he leaned down and whispered in my ear. "Hold up your arms." He pulled my nightgown up over my head and I stood there naked before him. "You are the most beautiful woman I've ever seen."
"I feel beautiful when I'm with you." I kissed him gently on his lips and then I led him over to the bed.

As usual, our attraction for each other was palpable and it overpowered us. But there was something unique about this experience. I don't know if it was the feeling of being on the water or feeling like our relationship was reaching a higher plateau but I felt a closeness to Shenzy that I'd never felt with anyone before. Shenzy was the man of my dreams and I felt so lucky to be with him.

As we lay there, I started thinking about what would happen when we returned to Seulmonde. I couldn't wait to see Chaunce and Shelby again; they would be so surprised to see me.

I would get to spend my life with the man I loved. I would go to bed with him every night and wake up with him every morning. Just the thought of him made me smile.

I mean who am I kidding? There are people who go their entire lives and never experience what Shenzy and I have. My father found it with my mother. I knew Lee would understand if I told him how I felt now.

Shenzy started moving around a little. I knew he wasn't asleep yet. Maybe he was getting more comfortable. He leaned over and kissed the top of my head. I already knew what was coming next.

"I love you." He spoke softly into my hair.

I think I responded to him but I wasn't sure. My mind started quieting down and I felt myself drift off to sleep.

I woke up slowly. I could feel the yacht changing direction. We were approaching the mainland. When I turned towards Shenzy, he was already awake and staring at me. I just stared back into his dark eyes and smiled.

We eventually got dressed and packed up the few items we'd brought with us. Then we headed up to the saloon to enjoy our last meal on the yacht. Chef Alexander prepared omelets and in the spirit of celebration, we each had a glass of mimosa. It was a really nice send off for our trip.

Don wasn't talking a lot over breakfast and I think we were all glad about that. I wondered if he felt bad about yesterday; probably not. But I wouldn't let his issue become mine. Since I would be staying in Seulmonde now, I would become a master at ignoring him.

Once we finished eating, Shenzy and I went up to the upper deck to take in the view one last time. He wrapped his arms around me and we just stood there for a while. The sun was shining bright against an incredibly blue sky. And the gentle breeze coming off the water felt warm against my skin.

When we pulled in to dock at the villa, I felt relieved but also a little sad. Our trip to Crete was over. Nico helped us with our bags and we said our goodbyes to the captain and crew. Within minutes, they were disembarking and heading back to Piraeus.

Fedor was waiting for us when we reached the front door of the villa.

"Hello Fedor. How are you?" I said excitedly.
"I am well ma'am. I trust you enjoyed your trip." He replied.
"It was wonderful. Thanks."

We brought our bags into the house and Fedor put them in our rooms. Don surprised both Shenzy and I when he asked us to join him in the dining room. I couldn't imagine what he wanted to talk to us about.

"I have a new lead and I plan to investigate it." Don said coolly. "Once we get back to Seulmonde and you kids get settled, I'll head out."

"Don, why can't you just let go of this search?" Shenzy spoke so softly then. "Just let her go."

"I can't." Don looked away from us.

"Alright, fine. Do what you need to do." Shenzy replied.

Don suddenly had a wounded look on his face. "I know that you think I'm crazy but I'm not."

"Don, I never said that." Shenzy spoke defensively.

"Benito is sure this time. He thinks that someone is helping her."

"Why does he think that?"

"Because she has resources. She was last spotted in Paris a couple weeks ago. You can come with me; both of you."

"Don, we can't do that." Shenzy spoke so kindly to him.

"Well, suit yourselves." He got up from his chair and headed out of the room. "I'm going for a swim."

Shenzy and I just sat there at the table. I didn't know what to make of Don's announcement. Shenzy seemed to be just as confused as I was.

"Ronnie, I think I'll go for a swim too. Do you mind?" Shenzy asked calmly.

"No, not at all. I think your brother needs you right now."

We left the dining room and Shenzy headed toward the patio. I started climbing the stairs, when he called back to me.

"You know, you've made me the happiest man in the world."

"I'll remind you that you said that a year from now." I laughed as I continued up the stairs.

When I got to our room, I fell on the bed and rolled onto my side. I couldn't believe everything I'd experienced in the last few days. I couldn't wait to tell my dad all the fun I'd had. But more than anything, I needed to talk to him about the decision I'd made to stay with Shenzy.

I couldn't remember the last time I'd spoken to Lee. This was as good a time as any to try and reach him on the phone.

I got up off the bed and went to get my cell phone. I wondered if he'd tried to call me and I missed his call. But when I checked my messages, the only voice mail I had was from Garland. I didn't really want to hear from him but I decided to listen to his message anyway.

"Ronnie, I hope that you're getting your messages because I really need to talk to you. I've been trying to reach you since yesterday. I don't care when you get this message, just please call me back. I know things got really weird when I was there but please don't use that as a reason not to call. It's important. Good bye."

Garland really sounded worried. I started pacing back and forth trying to decide if I should call him. Or maybe this was just some kind of game. He might have been trying to find out if I was back in the states. I decided to just call him and get it over with. If he was calling to get on my nerves, I could always end the call. I dialed his number and he answered on the first ring. That was a first.

"Ronnie, thank goodness. Are you ok? I've been trying to reach you." He sounded almost frantic.
"Garland, I'm fine. What's the matter?"
"Ronnie, yesterday afternoon I received a call from Columbia General. They were trying to track you down and the satellite phone number was the only number they could get from your father."
"Garland, why is my father in the hospital? What's wrong with him?"
"I don't know how to tell you this but he's had a stroke. They're trying to stabilize him now."
"Oh my Goodness. Is he going to…?" I couldn't finish my thought.
"Garland, hold on."

I stumbled over to the patio door in the bedroom. I was struggling to stay on my feet. I opened the patio door and yelled down to Shenzy. Seconds later, he and Don were in the room with me. I was sobbing so badly that I couldn't say what I needed to.

I handed the phone to Shenzy as I felt myself losing my balance. Don helped me over to the bed and then he sat down next to me. I saw Shenzy tense up as he realized who I'd been talking to.

"Who did you speak with last?" Shenzy asked. "What's the prognosis?"

I didn't like the fact that I couldn't hear what Garland was saying on the other end of the phone. I just sat there crying and thinking the worst possible thoughts. A few minutes later, Shenzy hung up with Garland and called the hospital directly.

I don't know who he claimed to be but they gave him all of the information on my father's condition. He paused for a few moments and then came over to sit next to me on the bed. Don stood up and walked quietly out of the room.

"Your father has been stabilized but he's still in serious condition. We need to get you on the first flight home." Shenzy spoke kindly to me. He kept watching my face.
"I see." I tried to stand up without wobbling too badly. "I'll call the airline and change my ticket. I should be by his side right now. I'm all he has."
"Ronnie, please let me take care of it." Shenzy helped me back over to the bed. "Just sit down and relax."

Shenzy got on the phone and made several calls. As I sat there, I wasn't really paying attention to what he was saying. I just kept thinking about how selfish I was. I was planning to leave my father and my life behind to chase a man half way around the world. I felt awful.

If Lee made it through this ordeal, I would never think of leaving his side again. I would free my mind of all the fairytales it was filled with. My happily ever after was going to have to wait a little while longer and that was if it ever happened at all.

A few minutes later, Don came bounding into the room with a cup of water and two little blue pills. He told me to take both of them because they would help me relax. I glanced at Shenzy and he nodded his head in agreement. He was still on the phone but I had no idea who he was talking to. He looked pleased with the outcome of the call so that was at least something.

"Ok. We're in business." Shenzy hung up the phone and came over to me. "We're booked on a midnight flight so we need to get packing."
"Did you say we?" I replied cautiously.
"You don't think I'm going to let you go home alone, do you?"

I reached out for him as fresh tears flew from eyes. He held me to him as I sobbed uncontrollably. Somehow he must have known how afraid I was. I had no idea what I would be facing at the hospital but I knew I would be alright with him by my side. Out of the corner of my eye, I noticed a little of Don's reaction to this new development.

"Shenzy, I know you're worried about Ronnie but this wasn't part of the plan." Don said flatly.
"Don, I'm not having this conversation with you right now." Shenzy replied as he started packing our clothes.
"What do you think Chaunce is going to say about this?"
"I don't know. Why don't you let me know when you tell him?"
"Shenzy, I beg you to be reasonable."
"Don, would you let the woman you love fly thousands of miles alone not knowing what she'll face? Could you send her off knowing that her only blood relative was in the hospital fighting for his life?"
"Shenzy, I do feel bad for Ronnie. But you don't have a choice in the matter."
"Life is full of choices Sheldon. I'm making an important one right now. Why don't you go home and let Chaunce know what's happened. I'll return as soon as I can."
"How will we contact you?"
"Don't worry. I've already taken care of that."

I could tell that Don was upset when he left the room. He knew that Shenzy wasn't going to change his mind. Our clothes were packed and our suitcases were by the bedroom door. Shenzy glanced at me every so often to see if I was still sobbing. The valium had pretty much squashed my ability to do anything but lay down. I wasn't quite sleepy but I didn't have my normal level of awareness either.

Shenzy went downstairs but only for a few minutes. He was sending Fedor to pick up something he'd bought over the phone. When he came back upstairs, he was carrying two cups of soup. I wasn't really in the mood to eat but I didn't want him to worry. I took a few spoonfuls and lay back down.

He started eating his soup and trying to make small talk with me. I can't say it was a real conversation. I was pretty much just answering yes or no. When I finally said something, I'm sure it wasn't what he expected.

"Shenzy, what if we don't get there in time?" I spoke almost in a whisper.
"Don't talk like that." He put his soup bowl down on the nightstand and lay down on the bed facing me. "He'll be fine. You'll see."
"I feel so helpless."
"I know you do and that's normal." He touched my cheek.
"Is that how you felt when your mom went away?"
"Not exactly. When she left, I knew it was what she needed to do. I just tell myself that she's happy somewhere."
"I wish I had your optimism."

He smiled at me and touched my cheek again. I'm sure he was disappointed about our little detour, but he didn't show it. Things don't always work out the way we think they will. But I was still so grateful to him.

"Shenzy, I don't know what I'd do if you weren't going with me. I've never been more afraid of anything in my life." I said quietly.
"I would do anything I could to take away your pain. You must know that."

He took my hand and stroked it gently. After a few minutes, I started to relax. I was finding it hard to keep my eyes open.

When I woke up, I was in the bedroom alone. Shenzy must have taken our bags downstairs because they were gone too. I went in the bathroom to wash my face. My toothbrush was packed away so I decided to pop a piece of gum in my mouth. I headed downstairs to find Shenzy.

When he saw me coming down the stairs, he immediately started towards me. I felt a little like a psychiatric patient.

"Ronnie, what are you doing down here?" He asked cautiously.
"I wanted to find you."
"Well, we've packed up the car and I was just showing Don the new satellite phones I bought. They're similar to the one you had."
"You've thought of everything, haven't you?" I sat down on the chair closest to the entry way.
"I don't want my father to worry too much." Shenzy sat down next to me. He looked worried even if he wasn't admitting it.
"He's so proud of you Shenzy."
"Well, let's hope that lasts through the night." He laughed nervously. "We'd better get going. We need to get to the airport in good time to make our flight."
"I've got my purse. I suppose I'm ready."
"Don, we're leaving." Shenzy shouted down the hall.

Don came out to say goodbye to us. I was still surprised when he hugged me though.

"Ronnie, I hope that your father recovers quickly. Take care of yourself." Don spoke with sincerity.
"Thank you Don. That's kind of you. I promise that your brother will be back in Seulmonde very soon."

Don gave Shenzy a quick hug and then followed us outside. When we got in the car, Shenzy gave my hand a gentle squeeze. I'd never be able to thank him enough for going with me.

We pulled off from the villa and I turned to see Don standing in the driveway. I knew that I'd be seeing him again. I just didn't realize how soon it would be.

Made in the USA
Charleston, SC
25 October 2013